Her Pretentious Marquess

The Worthington Legacy
Book Nine

Marie Higgins

ARE YOU SIGNED UP FOR DRAGONBLADE'S BLOG?

You'll get the latest news and information on exclusive giveaways, exclusive excerpts, coming releases, sales, free books, cover reveals and more.

Check out our complete list of authors, too!

No spam, no junk. That's a promise!

Sign Up Here

www.dragonbladepublishing.com

Dearest Reader;

Thank you for your support of a small press. At Dragonblade Publishing, we strive to bring you the highest quality Historical Romance from some of the best authors in the business. Without your support, there is no 'us', so we sincerely hope you adore these stories and find some new favorite authors along the way.

Happy Reading!

CEO, Dragonblade Publishing

Additional Dragonblade books by Author Marie Higgins

The Worthington Legacy
Her Perfect Scoundrel (Book 1)
Her Dreamy Deceiver (Book 2)
Her Adorable Cad (Book 3)
Her Irresistible Charmer (Book 4)
Her Captain Enchanter (Book 5)
Her Sweetest Rogue (Book 6)
Her Brooding Duke (Book 7)
Her Scandalous Rake (Book 8)
Her Pretentious Marquess (Book 9)

Love's Addiction Series
A Wallflower to Love (Book 1)
A Governess to Protect (Book 2)
A Maiden to Remember (Book 3)

Chapter One

England, 1824

TODAY BEGAN LIKE any other day in Dominic Lawrence's life since his arrival in North Devon five months ago. But this morning, as he rose and dressed, something was markedly different—he was no longer himself. For the next several weeks, he would cease to be Lord Hawthorne and take on the role of his cousin, the local clergyman.

Dominic ran his hand over the rough, month-old growth of beard covering his chin and mouth. "By Jove, I believe I might just pull this off," he said, his voice tinged with amusement as he glanced at his cousin, who stood across the room. The man in the mirror hardly resembled the marquess he once knew. The transformation was, quite frankly, startling. But beneath the bravado, a flicker of doubt lingered.

Sighing, Dominic shook his head and scratched his chin. "Though I must admit," he added with a frown, "I have my reservations about the facial hair."

"What's wrong with the beard?" Frederick Woodland asked as he moved to stand behind Nic, glancing in the mirror. "I started to grow mine these last couple of weeks so that when we switched identities, you would look like me."

"This I know, cousin, but you have always been clean-shaven."

Frederick chuckled and peered closer into the mirror at his

own reflection. "Indeed, I have, but we needed this so you could take over my role. By now, my parishioners believe I've been afflicted with some kind of skin malady that makes it impossible to shave." Turning his head from side to side, he studied his profile. "And I must say I was inspired to create such a story. God has indeed assisted us in our plan to find the thief in our midst. I wouldn't have been able to do this without His help." Frederick's gaze met Nic's. "And yours, of course."

Nic chuckled softly, a sound that echoed with the memories of their boyhood. The two cousins had always been mistaken for brothers, so much so that family members often commented on their uncanny resemblance. From their dark hair to their broad shoulders and oval faces, they shared more than just a familial bond. As children, Nic and Frederick used to swap places for fun, fooling their relatives with brief but harmless trickery. The ruses never lasted long—Frederick was five years older, after all—but the resemblance was still striking.

Nic turned his gaze back to the mirror, studying his reflection with a critical eye. Despite the month-old beard and his altered appearance, there was one thing the disguise would never conceal—his eyes. He had been told countless times, mostly by women, that his eyes twinkled when he laughed, a mischievous gleam that betrayed his true identity. Even now, as he tried to assume Frederick's serious demeanor, the self-assured smile that played on his lips was unmistakably that of the Marquess of Hawthorne, not a humble clergyman.

Some things just couldn't be hidden.

Five months ago, Nic had eagerly arrived in North Devon to visit his cousin Frederick, excited to explore a part of the country he'd never seen before. The tranquil visit, however, had taken a dark turn about a month ago when a string of church robberies began to plague the area. At first it was small, insignificant items being taken, but as the thefts escalated, more valuable church possessions started to disappear. That was when Frederick had devised a daring plan—one that involved the two cousins swapping roles.

Frederick's logic was simple: while Nic posed as the clergyman during the day, Frederick could move about under the cover of night, spying on the townspeople and hoping to catch the thief in the act. Frederick knew the village well, and he believed that his intimate knowledge of the area and its residents would give him an edge in identifying who was being dishonest.

However, with his daily responsibilities as a clergyman, he couldn't risk staying up all night to investigate without raising suspicion. The townspeople were observant, and a fatigued and distracted vicar would quickly arouse curiosity—something Frederick couldn't afford.

At the time, the plan had seemed feasible, even clever. But now, standing in front of the mirror and reflecting on the complexities of the deception, Nic felt his confidence waver. What had once sounded plausible now felt perilous. He couldn't shake the feeling that they might be in over their heads. Would they really be able to pull this off, or were they setting themselves up for failure?

"I just pray that we can find this thief soon. I fear I won't be able to handle this bush on my face." Nic scrubbed his chin, realizing that although the hair was soft against his palms, it would become bothersome in due time.

"We may be five years apart, Hawthorne," Frederick said, patting his slightly rounder belly, "but as long as you powder your hair to make it look as if you're aging gracefully, I think you shall make my perfect double."

Inwardly, Nic grimaced, questioning his own judgment. What had possessed him to volunteer for this elaborate charade? It had all seemed so straightforward when they first discussed the plan—disguising himself as his cousin had sounded like a clever, even amusing, solution. But now, as he stared at his reflection, doubt crept in.

Did he really want to parade around as a slightly older version of himself, pretending to be something he was not? Still, a promise was a promise, and he had vowed to help catch the thief responsible for stealing church funds and framing Frederick for the crime.

At least, Nic mused with a wry smile, they were far enough removed from his usual circle of acquaintances. If anyone from his own social sphere saw him in this ridiculous role, they would likely never let him live it down. The idea of playing a clergyman was laughable enough as it was.

He should never accept the role of *man of God*, and in doing so, he might be struck down. The thought made him inwardly chuckle. He hoped the heavens wouldn't punish him for this deception—posing as a man of virtue when his own life was anything but holy.

A sudden thought struck Nic, causing a knot to form in his stomach. Frederick had spent a great deal of time with parishioners, meeting them in private to offer guidance and spiritual counsel. How was Nic supposed to handle those situations when he wasn't even remotely qualified to offer the wisdom of an ordained clergyman? He could hardly fake the knowledge or presence that Frederick naturally exuded in such delicate matters.

His mind raced for a solution. Then an idea hit him—he could play up his cousin's skin condition. If people believed he had a contagious rash, they might not want to get too close or request lengthy private conversations. It wasn't foolproof, but it could buy him some space and prevent any awkward interactions that could expose the ruse.

Relief swept over him. That idea actually might work. It wasn't ideal, but it would have to do.

Frederick moved away from the full-length mirror and approached a chair where his jacket lay draped over the back. When he picked it up, Nic's resolve hardened. There was no turning back now. The plan was already in motion, and he needed to play his part convincingly, no matter the risks.

Frederick carried the jacket to him and assisted Nic. "Now, let's complete your clergy attire so you can go out into the community and present yourself. It has been a few weeks since my friends have seen me out of the house. I'm certain they will be delighted that I have recovered from my sickness."

Nic continued to study his reflection, noting with some frustration how awkwardly his cousin's clothes fit him. While Frederick and he were both broad through the shoulders, Frederick was clearly wider through the middle, and the difference was obvious. The jacket and trousers practically hung off Nic's leaner frame, making him feel like a child playing dress-up. Surely the townspeople would notice the ill fit.

Still, he reasoned, it might actually work in their favor. Their story about Frederick being sick for a couple of weeks would now seem more credible—explaining away his gaunt appearance and poorly fitting clothes. With any luck, people would attribute it to an illness rather than suspect anything else.

Nic tugged at the loose jacket, adjusting it as best as he could. At least there was some comfort in knowing that his cousin's physical condition, real or not, might cover for the many ways he wasn't cut out for this deception.

"And don't forget," Frederick added, "this evening is Mrs. Burls' eightieth birthday party, and you must make an appearance. You recall who she is, don't you?"

Nic turned away from the mirror and met his cousin's stare. "Of course I know Mrs. Burls. She's the oldest woman in town." He shook his head. "I've been here a good four months already, so I do know most of your friends."

"Good, good." Frederick grinned and moved to the window. He carefully pulled back the curtains and peered out. "It's a fine day, is it not? Such perfect weather for a walk." He swung his head and looked back at Nic. "I almost envy you now. I shall have to resign myself to staying in the house and only leaving at night."

Nic shrugged. "This was your plan. Are you thinking of backing out?"

"No, I won't back out. The thief must be caught, and this is the only way." Sighing heavily, Frederick frowned. "I haven't lived in this area for a year yet, and already people are starting to believe I took the items from the church. It breaks my heart when even the local constable doesn't believe in my innocence. I must build the trust back with the community quickly." He motioned toward the door. "So go out, greet the people, and make me proud. I wish you good luck. I shall be praying that you turn out a splendid performance."

"Oh, trust me, I'll try my hardest to make them believe I'm you." Nic smiled wide. "One might even think that I playacted for a living."

"Well, we certainly did as boys."

Nic nodded. "That we did."

After settling Frederick's hat snugly on his head, Nic reached for the walking stick leaning by the door and stepped outside. The sunlight greeted him with an intensity that made him squint, his eyes unaccustomed to the brightness after spending weeks in the dim interior of his cousin's home. The adjustment was slow, but gradually the brilliance of the day came into focus.

The weather was nearly perfect for a stroll, though the crisp wind blowing in from the ocean carried a sharper chill than he had anticipated. As he walked, Nic found himself wishing for the company of a lovely lady to share the picturesque moment with. North Devon, with its lush green landscape and blooming flowers, seemed to be in full celebration of spring. The trees, newly budded, swayed gently in the breeze, painting the town in vibrant colors.

At a certain point, Nic knew he could climb the hill that overlooked the coastline, offering an unmatched view of the bluish-green waters stretching toward the horizon. The thought of it brought a sense of peace—a kind of serenity he rarely felt. The calmness of the scene always stilled his mind, filling him with gratitude for the beauty around him. As much as he hated to admit it, North Devon had a charm he found deeply soothing, more so than any place he had ever been.

He reluctantly tore his gaze away from the breathtaking

scenery and turned his attention to another of God's creations—the friendly, familiar faces of the village. As Lord Hawthorne, he had already met many of Frederick's acquaintances and, over time, had come to think of them as his own friends as well. Both he and his cousin had allowed the townspeople to believe that Nic had returned home weeks ago, which made his current guise all the more convincing.

The first couple he greeted on his walk were the newlyweds, Mr. and Mrs. Lambert. Nic had witnessed his cousin perform their wedding ceremony just three months earlier, and they still radiated the happiness of newlywed bliss.

Mrs. Lambert clung to her husband's arm, gazing at him with an expression of pure adoration as he spoke. It was a small but touching scene that stirred something in Nic's chest.

He paused for a moment, reflecting on the sight. It reminded him of his good friends, the Worthington brothers, who shared the same look of contentment with their wives. For just a fleeting moment, a pang of loneliness settled in Nic's heart, and he wondered if he would ever find that special woman meant for him. The thought of companionship tugged at him unexpectedly.

As quickly as the feeling arose, he brushed it aside, chuckling quietly to himself. What was he thinking? He wasn't ready to find that kind of happiness—not for several more years. The idea of settling down seemed distant, almost absurd. There were too many adventures yet to be had, and marriage, for now, could wait.

"Mr. Woodland. Good morning," Mrs. Lambert called out to him. She raised her hand and smiled.

The new bride was a lovely woman, and immediately, Nic wanted to make her smile. "Greetings," he said, quickening his step until he reached them. He must remember he was the clergyman, not a rogue. *No charming the women!* Instead, he should think *holier.* "What a pleasure to see you both this fine morning."

"Indeed, it's a very lovely day, Mr. Woodland," Mrs. Lambert said. "How happy I am to see you out. I trust you're feeling better?"

"Yes, I do feel better." He stroked his palm over his furry chin. "However, this beard is my only irritation now. I will be relieved when the tenderness in my face disappears and I'm able to shave once again."

"I do understand your frustration." Mr. Lambert nodded. "Two years ago I also had some kind of rash and I couldn't shave for a whole week. I don't know if I could have gone as long as you have, though."

Nic shrugged. "It is quite uncomfortable. But at least I'm out of that stuffy house and able to see your happy faces. Tell me, how are you faring since we last talked?"

As the young couple shared the joys of their new life together, Nic found himself laughing along with their stories, his smile so forced it made his cheeks ache. It wasn't that he was uninterested in their happiness—he was genuinely pleased for them—but he simply couldn't relate. Marriage, to him, was a distant and foreign concept.

At least Frederick had experienced it once, though tragically, his wife had died in childbirth six years ago. Nic had never understood why his cousin hadn't remarried, but then again, perhaps he never would.

Nic's relationships were fleeting by design, and he liked it that way. He cherished his freedom too much to let anyone tie him down. Women often adored him, and he made it a point to make them feel special, right up until it was time to move on. Nic had always been a charmer, and when it came time to end the affair, most women accepted that he wasn't the type to marry. Rarely did they harbor any lasting bitterness toward him.

But then his thoughts came to a screeching halt as a familiar face flashed in his memory—Tabitha Paget. An angelic figure he had once wrongfully suspected of murder. It had been six months since they crossed paths, but the image of her lingered as vividly as ever. Her mesmerizing blue eyes, framed by a heart-shaped face, and those lips—remarkably exciting and utterly unforgetta-ble.

In an instant, the carefree laughter of the moment faded, replaced by the haunting memory of a woman he hadn't been able to forget, no matter how hard he tried.

"Is that not right, Mr. Woodland?" Mrs. Lambert asked.

Inwardly, Nic kicked himself for not paying better attention to the Lamberts. He couldn't even recall what they had been saying. He chuckled and shook his head. "Ah, Mrs. Lambert, of course it is right, since it came from you."

The young lady nodded and looked at her husband, giving him a grin of victory. "Did I not tell you? Mr. Woodland is a very intelligent man."

Mr. Lambert held up his hands in surrender. "I'm not arguing with a clergyman."

Nic laughed and clapped his hand on the other man's thin shoulder. "And might I suggest not arguing with your wife, either." He glanced at Mrs. Lambert and winked. Her cheeks flared the color of rose petals. The shade clashed greatly with her bright orange-red hair. He tipped his hat and bowed. "I must be on my way. I pray you both will have a pleasant day."

"We will," Mr. Lambert said. "Will we be seeing you later tonight at Mrs. Burls' birthday celebration?"

"Indeed you will." Waving at them, Nic continued his walk.

Another minute later, his name was being called by a woman across the street. The widow, Mrs. Smythe, and her maiden sister, Miss Talbot, were the gossipmongers of the parish. If there was a story to be told, these ladies were the first to spread the news. Apparently, they knew everything...or they wanted to let everyone *think* they did.

Perhaps, if Nic became really close with those two, he might discover if one of them knew who the real thief was. Although he enjoyed charming women, he'd never had to work his wiles on women of their age. He supposed there was a first time for everything.

Mrs. Smythe was a short, round woman with a head full of brownish-gray hair that seemed perpetually in disarray, constantly slipping free from the coil she attempted to tame at the back of her head. Her plump figure and lively, bustling nature made her a familiar presence in the village. Standing beside her was her sister, Miss Talbot, who shared the same roundness but towered over her older sibling, thanks to her tall, big-boned frame. Miss Talbot's stringy brown hair, always looking as though it had never seen a comb, added to her disheveled appearance.

From the moment Nic had met her, she'd given the impression of someone perpetually caught in a windstorm. Her most distinctive feature, however, was the large, prominent nose that seemed to dominate her face, making it difficult not to fixate on it during the conversation, no matter how hard Nic tried to look elsewhere.

"Mr. Woodland," Mrs. Smythe called again from across the street. She hustled as fast as her round little body could carry her until she stood in front of Nic. Out of breath, she smiled, holding her hand to her chest. "Oh, Mr. Woodland. It's so refreshing to see you today. Why, I was just telling my sister, Mildred, earlier that we should drop in to see how you are faring." Slowly, her gaze slid over Nic, and her eyes widened. "Oh, heavens. It appears you have lost some weight. I didn't think you had been that sick."

He patted his midsection. "I didn't think I was that sick either, until I dressed fully this morning and realized my clothes didn't quite fit. Perhaps I should get sick like this more often." He ran his hands up and down his middle. "I believe I can feel my ribs."

"Oh, Mr. Woodland." Miss Talbot blushed. "You are just horrible! Feeling your ribs is not a good thing. You need to come to the house soon so that I can fatten you up with some of my food."

"I thank you, Miss Talbot. Mrs. Smythe. Taking in a meal with you does sound welcoming. Now, don't let me keep you from your walk. I was just heading to the church."

"Have a pleasant time." Miss Talbot's blush deepened as her gaze skipped around him, not meeting his eyes.

Nic suppressed a chuckle as he observed Miss Talbot, recalling how it had been clear from the beginning that she harbored deep feelings for Frederick. It baffled him that his cousin had never noticed—or perhaps Frederick simply hadn't recognized the subtle signals Miss Talbot sent his way. Then again, women were notoriously difficult to read, their emotions shifting like the wind. One moment they were reserved, and the next they were wild with passion.

Nic had seen it all. As a self-proclaimed rogue, he had encountered every type of woman imaginable. Some would glare at him with eyes blazing like fire, only to melt in his arms moments later, willingly sharing a heated kiss. But just as quickly as they'd surrendered to their desires, they would transform, spouting venomous words as if none of it had ever happened. Their unpredictability was enough to drive any man to madness.

Perhaps Frederick was wise to keep his distance. It certainly explained why Nic had steered clear of marriage—he had no desire to be ensnared by the fickle nature of a woman's heart.

Yet, even as he mentally reaffirmed his disdain for commitment, a familiar face crept back into his thoughts. A face that, despite his best efforts, refused to disappear entirely from his memory. Tabitha Paget. She lingered in his mind, resurfacing at the most unexpected moments, like now.

From the moment Nic first laid eyes on her, Tabitha Paget had captivated him. Her enchanting blue eyes seemed to pull him in like a siren's call, luring him closer with every glance. There was a mysterious air about her, something elusive that he couldn't quite grasp, and it drove him to dig deeper into her life, desperate to understand why she intrigued him so. He had spent far too much time unraveling that mystery, and now he was paying the price for it.

He cursed himself for the way she lingered in his thoughts. No matter how hard he tried, he couldn't forget her. She haunted his dreams, appearing unbidden during the still of the night, her face vivid and unforgettable.

Although their association had ended disastrously, with accusations and misunderstandings that left them both scarred, he could never shake the regret that gnawed at him. It bothered him deeply that he had never been able to apologize for accusing her of murder.

He inhaled deeply, trying to clear his head as he made his way toward the church. The familiar stone pathway stretched out before him, each step a reminder of the charade he was about to continue. As he drew closer, his pace slowed, and his gaze lifted toward the heavens.

Surely God wouldn't strike him down for walking into His house dressed as a clergyman. Or would He?

Gulping, Nic reached for the front door. The steel from the knob was cold against his palm, but the energy running rapidly through his body would turn the handle warm very quickly, he was sure.

God forgive me, for I have sinned… Yet, in this case of switching identities, he needed to help his cousin. God would forgive him. He hoped.

Chapter Two

TABITHA PAGET PRESSED herself against the side of the coach, her heart racing as she peered out of the window, watching the small township of North Devon come into view. The countryside rolled past in a blur, but all her focus was on the village she had longed to return to. She had arrived earlier than expected, and the surge of excitement within her was almost unbearable. Her chest felt tight, filled with anticipation for the reunion she had been waiting for.

After all these years, she was finally going to see her great-aunt, Clara Burls. The last time Tabitha had seen her aunt, she had been just seven years old, a lifetime ago. She couldn't afford to let more time slip by without visiting the old woman. At eighty years old today, her aunt wasn't getting any younger, and Tabitha knew this might be her last chance to reconnect with the woman who had once been such an important part of her family's history.

Aunt Clara had married well and, after her husband's passing, been left with a considerable fortune. Despite her newfound wealth, Clara had always been cautious with her spending. She had hired a trusted companion—a widow she had befriended over the years, whose own husband had left her with little means—and employed a couple of servants to help manage the house. Yet, despite her financial security, Clara never flaunted her wealth. She preferred to live modestly, blending in with the rest of the township rather than behaving like one of its wealthiest residents.

Clara was expecting Tabitha today. However, she had no idea about the life-changing events Tabitha had recently gone through. Tabitha had reunited with her half-brothers and, in a moment of great courage, confessed to being their father's illegitimate daughter. It was one of the hardest things she had ever done, and she'd expected rejection and heartbreak. Yet, to her astonishment, her brothers had welcomed her with open arms, accepting her into the family without hesitation. The relief and joy from that reunion still lingered in her heart, but now she faced another important connection in her life—her beloved Aunt Clara.

Tabitha wasn't ready to fully embrace her new role in the family. She had spent most of her life as a servant, enduring hardships and a lack of security. The transition to being recognized as part of a wealthy, well-known family was a daunting prospect. After revealing the truth to her brothers, she had begged them to keep it a secret, and she was confident they had honored her request. Yet her frequent appearances with them and her growing friendship with their wives had sparked rumors among the gossips. It didn't help that she bore a striking resemblance to two of her brothers, Trevor and Trey—similarities that the keen-eyed members of the *ton* could easily notice.

Despite the whispers, the Worthington brothers had been nothing but kind to her. They insisted on giving her an allowance, enabling her to leave her life as a servant behind. For the first time, Tabitha had her own maid—a luxury she could hardly wrap her mind around. The adjustment to such a lifestyle was still difficult for her, but it was a necessity in her current position.

However, living among the *ton* in this new, elevated status brought its own concerns. Tabitha feared that if people became too curious or suspicious, they might uncover the truth she had worked so hard to conceal. The last thing she wanted was to become the subject of scandal, or worse, be cast out of her brothers' lives because of Society's judgment.

A few weeks ago, she'd realized she needed to get away from it all. She needed to be somewhere that nobody knew her, or her scandalous father. Thankfully, she and Aunt Clara had kept in touch over the years, so when Tabitha had received a letter from her aunt, she knew immediately that this was where she could relax and let the gossip die down.

The coach came to a halt, and Tabitha felt the jolt as the driver and guard moved quickly to open the door, ready to assist the passengers as they disembarked. With gloved hands, she gathered the hem of her traveling dress, stepping gingerly out of the carriage and onto the cobblestone street. The wind hit her face sharply, cold and brisk, as if it had blown straight from the ocean and carried the salty air with it, biting at her skin. She shivered, pulling her fur cloak tighter around her neck, seeking warmth as her eyes swept over the quaint nearby buildings.

Behind her, she heard the familiar voice of her maid, already in conversation with the driver, instructing him on which trunk to retrieve. Tabitha turned back toward the coach and watched as the two men carefully lowered the trunk from the roof of the carriage, the weight of it requiring both of them to handle it with care.

Despite the cold and the rush of activity around her, a small thrill of anticipation stirred within her. She was here, at last, in North Devon, ready for a reunion she had been waiting for years to experience.

Tabitha stepped beside the trunk, bent, and clutched a handle. Her maid grasped the other side. "Well, Sally? Are you ready to embark on our new adventure here in North Devon?"

Sally grinned and nodded. "I'm very excited to be here. I've never really traveled."

"Neither have I. Indeed, it will be enjoyable to be away from the busy social life that my brothers live."

"I agree." Sally stuffed a loose blonde curl back in her bonnet. "I just hope it's not windy like this every day."

Chuckling, Tabitha nodded. "I hope not, too. Although I'm certain it won't take us long to get used to this weather." She moved her gaze toward the rolling green hills, then across to the ocean. "It's so beautiful, don't you think?"

"It is. I would enjoy it very much if we walked every day down toward the beach."

"I was thinking the same thing." Tabitha smiled. "Well, let's be on our way. My great-aunt is expecting us, even if we did arrive earlier than expected."

Thankfully, the trunk wasn't too heavy. But then again, Tabitha had grown accustomed to hard labor over the years. Both she and Sally had endured their share of hardships as servants under one of the most abusive lords in the realm. It felt like a lifetime ago, though it hadn't been all that long since her dear friend, Diana Hollingsworth—now Diana Worthington—had rescued them from that nightmare. Diana was, without a doubt, the kindest woman Tabitha had ever known, with a heart larger than anyone in England.

As she took in her surroundings, the small size of the township surprised her. For some reason, she had imagined North Devon to be larger, more bustling. But perhaps she had yet to see all of it. There were a few modest dress shops, a general store, and some blacksmith barns scattered around.

She shifted her attention toward the hillside, where a beautiful church stood, its steeple crowned with a cross that gleamed against the sky. The peaceful, almost picturesque scene gave her a sense of calm as she continued her walk.

It wasn't long before she spotted her great-aunt's cottage on the outskirts of town, just as Aunt Clara had described in her last letter. The details were so precise—right down to the last tree and the rosebushes framing the small stone house—that it felt as though she had already been here in her mind. A wave of warmth and nostalgia washed over her as she made her way toward the cottage, eager for the long-awaited reunion with the woman who had once been such an important part of her life.

The two-story white house stood charmingly before her, its trim painted a rich, dark brown that contrasted beautifully against the crisp white exterior. In the front yard, two large trees stretched their branches overhead, casting a generous shade over the house. A white picket fence neatly bordered the green grass and lined the walkway leading to the front door. It was a modest home, especially knowing that her aunt could easily afford something much grander, yet the simplicity of it spoke of a quiet, contented life.

With growing excitement, Tabitha quickened her pace, and Sally followed suit, both of them hurrying up the path. As they reached the door, Tabitha's heart pounded with anticipation. She knocked, the sound echoing in her chest. Moments later, the door swung open to reveal a middle-aged woman with a warm, welcoming smile.

"Good day," Tabitha said. "I'm Miss Paget, Clara Burls' great-niece. She is expecting me."

The woman's face lit up with a bright smile, making the freckles pop out more on her thin face. "Oh, it's so good to meet you. I'm Mrs. Burls' companion, Mrs. Stiles. Please come in."

The older woman ushered Tabitha and Sally inside. She waved her hands excitedly as her eyes sparkled with gladness.

"Clara has been talking nonstop about her great-niece. She is going to be so relieved you are here. But she is resting, and I don't dare disturb her."

"Oh, no." Tabitha touched Mrs. Stiles' arm. "Let her rest. She'll have a grand evening tonight, and she needs her strength for that."

"Indeed, she does." Mrs. Stiles grasped one end of the trunk. "Let me help you with this."

"No, don't even think of it." Tabitha stopped her. "Sally and I can handle carrying it."

"Fine." Mrs. Stiles stood then blew the lock of black hair away from her face. "Then follow me and I'll show you to your room. I'm sure you'll be pleased with the party we have planned for tonight's event," the older woman chattered on as she led the way.

Slowly, a smile tugged on Tabitha's mouth and she couldn't help but chuckle to herself. Mrs. Stiles acted like she hadn't had anyone to talk with for ages. Tabitha sincerely hoped her great-aunt wasn't so old that she couldn't keep her companion entertained.

They entered a room, and she set the trunk on the floor.

Mrs. Stiles swept her hand around the spacious room. "I hope this suits you."

"It's perfect, thank you." Tabitha nodded.

Indeed, the room was perfect. As someone who had spent years as a maid, Tabitha had grown accustomed to cramped quarters and sparse furnishings. But ever since her brothers had moved her into a townhouse of her own, her surroundings had changed dramatically. While this room wasn't quite as large as the one in her townhouse, it was far more beautifully decorated. Soft pinks and lavender hues blended seamlessly with daffodil-yellow accents, creating a cheerful and inviting atmosphere.

The large window, framed by delicate white curtains pulled back to let the sunlight flood in, bathed the room in warmth and brightness. The space felt light, airy, and full of life—an instant remedy to lift her spirits. Tabitha smiled to herself, knowing that this room would indeed cheer her up, offering her a sense of comfort and tranquility she hadn't realized she needed.

"I pray you and your maid will stay here for a while," Mrs. Stiles continued. "Clara is very happy to talk to you again. She can't wait to introduce you to all of her friends at the party tonight." The older woman stepped closer to Tabitha and grinned as she waggled her eyebrows. "And don't be surprised if your aunt tries to find you a man. You know, that's what women do when we get older. We want to see you lovely young ladies find a good man to marry."

Immediately, Tabitha's excitement dimmed. She had truly hoped her aunt wouldn't go as far as trying to find her a husband.

A relationship was the last thing she wanted. Too much had happened recently, leaving her wary—fearful, even—of men. Trust didn't come easily anymore, and it had taken her a long time to even trust her brothers. But they were different, exceptional in their kindness and understanding. The thought of finding another man like them felt impossible.

Somehow, she needed to convince Aunt Clara to abandon the idea of matchmaking. Tabitha wasn't ready for romance, and she doubted any man could possess the qualities she needed to heal the wounds of her past. Yet, as she stood there, a troubling thought crept in: what if fate had already set a plan in motion—one she couldn't avoid, no matter how hard she tried to resist?

THE DAY COULDN'T have gone better.

Dominic carefully dusted a little more white powder onto his hair, adding the finishing touches to his disguise for Mrs. Burls' party that evening. Stepping back from the full-length mirror, he allowed himself a satisfied smile. His transformation into Frederick was seamless. Throughout the day, everyone he had encountered believed he was his cousin, their only surprise being Frederick's apparent weight loss after his recent *illness*. Not one person seemed suspicious, and that was exactly the result Frederick had hoped for.

Earlier in the day, while Nic was at the church, Frederick had discreetly joined him in the office to discuss the remaining church inventory. Nic had been secretly relieved when the heavens didn't smite him for entering the holy sanctuary in disguise, so he wasted no time getting to work. Together, they reviewed a detailed list of everything stored in the church's back room. According to Frederick's calculations, nothing had gone missing in the two weeks since the last robbery—the very night before they had swapped identities. That night, the thief had made off with a statue of the Mother Mary and several gold candlesticks.

Nic couldn't shake the feeling that tonight's party might offer a critical clue about the thief's next move. As he straightened his jacket and prepared to leave, he wondered if the real culprit was among the very people he was about to mingle with.

Frederick, a compassionate and forgiving man of God, couldn't bring himself to believe that anyone in his parish would be capable of stealing from the church. His faith in his congregation ran deep, even though he had only known most of them for about a year. But Nic was more skeptical. After spending weeks in hiding while growing his beard for the disguise, he had carefully observed the people of the parish and compiled a list of men he suspected might be involved in the thefts.

When he presented the list to his cousin, Frederick had chuckled, shaking his head at the notion. He patiently explained why each man couldn't possibly be the culprit, dismissing the idea as unnecessary suspicion. But Nic wasn't so quick to write them off. He knew human nature could be far more complicated than his cousin's forgiving heart allowed. Nic's instincts told him that something more sinister was at play, and until he could prove otherwise, those names would remain firmly on his list of suspects.

The truth, Nic suspected, was closer than anyone dared to admit.

A knock came upon the bedroom door. Nic pulled away from the full-length mirror and turned toward the door. "Enter."

Frederick walked in, holding a small box that had been wrapped. "Give this to Mrs. Burls. It's my gift to her."

Nic took the package and nodded. "What did you get her?"

"I purchased a musical jewelry box for her a few months past while we were visiting Devonshire. The song playing in the box is her favorite. I know she'll be very happy with this."

"I'm certain she will." Nic set the gift on the table next to the washbasin, picked up his coat, and shrugged into it. "Is there anything special I need to do at this party tonight?"

"Not really. Just mingle and mention how much God loves them." Frederick shrugged. "That's what I do, anyway."

Nic arched an eyebrow. "So I'm assuming there won't be any liquor at this party?"

Frederick rolled his eyes. "Hawthorne, my good man, you are a man of the cloth now. Please remember that. Also keep in mind that drinking is something I would never do."

"I know, I know." Nic set the hat on his head before grabbing his walking stick.

"And even *if* there is liquor at this party," Frederick added, "you will not take a drink. Is that clear?"

Chuckling, Nic walked past his cousin as he headed out of the room. "Very clear. I know my character, and I'll act accordingly."

Frederick followed Nic down the stairs toward the front door. "Well, you had better keep in the clergyman character. The last thing I need is for you to give an eighty-year-old woman heart palpitations because she sees a man of God becoming intoxicated."

"Little do you know, dear cousin"—Nic opened the door and stepped outside—"that I rarely drink enough to become foxed." He bowed. "Have a pleasant evening, as I shall try to have."

Although he couldn't see Frederick, he could practically feel his cousin's watchful eyes on him as he strolled down the street toward the edge of town. He imagined Frederick standing there with his arms crossed, a wary gleam in his eyes, no doubt concerned about where this latest plan would lead them both.

Nic, determined to shake off the tension, whistled a light-hearted tune, hoping it would lift his spirits before he reached the elderly woman's home. When he first arrived in North Devon, he had eagerly anticipated the peace and tranquility that country life promised. After all, the bustling social scene of Mayfair and York had kept him busy, though not quite as tangled up as his close friends, Trey, Trevor, and Tristan Worthington. Especially Tristan, who had been embroiled in chaos when he was wrongly suspected of murdering the man who had married the woman

Tristan once loved.

Nic shook his head at the memory. *What a fiasco.* Thankfully, all of that turmoil was behind them. Each of the Worthington brothers had found love, and now their lives were filled with the happiness they so richly deserved. Nic couldn't help but feel a sense of relief for his friends, even if his own life remained a tangle of secrets and deceptions.

As he approached Mrs. Burls' cottage, that flicker of unease lingered. He had left the whirlwind of Mayfair behind, but the quiet countryside of North Devon had its own secrets to reveal. Yet, despite the mystery of the church thefts and his role in uncovering the culprit, he couldn't help but feel that his life had become dreadfully dull. The excitement and energy of city life had evaporated, leaving him restless. Even the thrill of pretending to be his cousin had lost its novelty.

He silently hoped that they would catch the thief soon so he could return home to the bustling life he loved. He couldn't fathom how Frederick found contentment in the slow rhythm of country living. The charm of the countryside was pleasant enough for a brief visit, but Nic longed for the energy and unpredictability of home.

Within minutes, he arrived at Mrs. Burls' house. A few guests had already gathered, their polite chatter carrying through the garden. He recognized most of them from his morning walk—he had already exchanged pleasantries and didn't feel inclined to repeat the small talk. Now, as he approached the door, he wondered if tonight's gathering would be just another stretch of boredom or if perhaps, tucked away in this peaceful setting, there might be an unexpected turn that would break the monotony. After all, the peaceful countryside seemed to hold more than met the eye.

For a woman of eighty years, Mrs. Burls still carried herself with a striking elegance. Though her face was deeply etched with wrinkles and her hair was as white as freshly fallen snow, he couldn't deny that there was something captivating about her.

When they had first met four months ago, he had immediately recognized her generous spirit and kind heart. Her smile was infectious, lighting up the room, and her laughter—soft and musical—had a way of making everyone around her feel lighter, happier.

As their eyes met from across the room, Mrs. Burls raised her hand, beckoning him to come closer. He kept a warm smile on his face as he made his way toward her, weaving through the small gathering of guests. The others, sensing her wish, gracefully parted to let him pass. He reached her side, and as she extended her hand, he took it with a small bow, feeling the warmth and strength still present in her grip.

"Mr. Woodland," she greeted him, her voice lilting with that familiar melody. "It's been far too long since our last chat."

He grinned and leaned in slightly, lowering his voice. "Indeed, Mrs. Burls. I can only hope I'll leave here tonight just as enchanted as always."

Her laughter rang out, and Nic couldn't help but think that, even in this quiet countryside, perhaps there was more charm—and intrigue—to discover than he'd first imagined.

"Mrs. Burls, you don't look a day older than forty." He winked. "I confess that seeing you so lovely tonight makes my heart skip a beat."

The old woman giggled as if she were in her childhood years. "Oh, you wicked man, Mr. Woodland. It is I who has the fluttering heart because of your false flattery."

"False?" He placed a hand to his heart. "You wound me, Mrs. Burls. I tell only the truth, you know. If not, the good Lord would choose someone else to lead this parish."

She shook her head. "Then if you aren't lying, you are stretching the truth farther than you have stretched it before."

The others standing around her chuckled, and he smiled. "But forgive me for intruding on your conversation." He glanced at the three other women and two men.

"Nonsense," Mrs. Clarkston said. She was probably the next-oldest woman in this township. "We enjoy your company, Mr. Woodland."

He held up Mrs. Burls' gift as he met her stare again. "I have brought you a gift, but I shall wait for more of your guests to arrive so that everyone can see your surprise."

"Mrs. Stiles has a table set up in the other room, specifically for my gifts." The old woman pointed in the general direction, toward the small corridor. "Please put it in there. I shall open my gifts in a few hours."

"Certainly, Mrs. Burls. If you will all excuse me, then." He bowed, turned, and strolled toward the room. As he walked by the front door, more visitors arrived. He smiled and nodded, but didn't stop to talk.

As Nic entered the cozy sitting room, his eyes immediately fell on Mrs. Stiles. She stood by the window, engaged in conversation with two younger women. The ladies, with their backs turned to him, were unfamiliar faces. Nic, always quick to notice new arrivals—especially young women—was certain he hadn't met them during his time in the small town.

Without hesitation, he moved toward the table, where various gifts were neatly arranged, and placed his own among them. Just as he turned back, he caught sight of Mrs. Stiles breaking away from her group and making her way toward him, her smile warm but unmistakably purposeful.

Nic straightened, his usual charm at the ready as she approached, wondering what conversation awaited him now. The unknown women behind her still piqued his curiosity, but Mrs. Stiles clearly had something on her mind, and he would soon find out what it was.

"Mr. Woodland. What a surprise it is to see you tonight." Her gaze slid over his torso, and her eyes widened. "Oh my… You have lost a little weight, haven't you? I didn't know you had been that ill."

He'd heard this phrase many times today. "Indeed I have, Mrs. Stiles." He patted his stomach. "But I'm doing much better, thank you."

"While you are here, let me introduce you to Mrs. Burls' great-niece." She moved aside and pointed to the young woman who stood behind her. "This is Miss Tabitha Paget from York."

The name hit him like a fierce northern wind, nearly knocking the breath from his lungs. *Tabitha Paget?* What was she doing here, so far from home?

His mind went blank, and his tongue felt as heavy as lead. There were so many things he wanted—*needed*—to say to her, apologies that had long weighed on his conscience. But the words wouldn't come. They couldn't.

Because to her, he wasn't Dominic Lawrence, the Marquess of Hawthorne. Would she recognize him at all? The thought sent a brief wave of dread through him, his heart sinking at the possibility. If she saw through his disguise, everything would unravel. Frederick's plan, the investigation—all of it would be compromised. And worst of all, Frederick would never forgive him.

Chapter Three

SWALLOWING HARD, NIC steeled himself, forcing his emotions to stay hidden. No matter what, he had to keep up the charade. He couldn't afford to let his true identity slip—not now, not when so much was at stake.

Tabitha turned to face him, offering a polite smile and a graceful curtsy. His heart flipped wildly, and for a moment, he struggled to catch his breath. She was absolutely stunning—more beautiful than he remembered from their last encounter, when he had unjustly accused her of murder. The transformation was astonishing.

Gone was the simple maid's dresses she had always worn. Now, she stood before him in the elegant attire of a refined lady. Her gown, a rich yellow satin with a delicate white-laced overskirt, flowed gracefully down her figure. The short, slightly puffed sleeves framed her shoulders, lending her an air of effortless grace. A strand of small pearls rested at her throat, adding a touch of sophistication that took his breath away.

Her hair, once plain and pulled back, now cascaded in perfectly styled russet ringlets that rested on her shoulders. Nic couldn't help but wonder if they were as soft as they appeared. His fingers itched to touch one and find out.

Yet the one thing that hadn't changed was her eyes—those striking blue eyes that had once captivated him. He had called them amazing, and they still were, the most beautiful eyes he had ever seen. In that moment, the past seemed to fade away, leaving him with only the undeniable pull she had always had over him.

"It's nice to meet you, Mr. Woodland," she said.

Even the sound of her voice sent a wave of memories crashing over him, making his breath hitch in his throat. Their time together had been brief, but unforgettable. He dropped his gaze almost instinctively to her mouth—a mouth that had robbed him of all coherent thought in the past, especially when he remembered the softness of her lips against his.

But just as quickly, her demeanor shifted. Her eyes flickered nervously from Mrs. Stiles to the other woman near the window. His heart skipped a beat when he recognized her companion—Sally, the maid. Why was Sally with Tabitha?

A storm of questions brewed in his mind, but he forced himself to focus. His pulse quickened, and he cursed himself for standing there in stunned silence. *Say something, Hawthorne,* he inwardly shouted, but he couldn't be sure what kind of expression he was wearing—probably a mix of shock and confusion.

Whatever he did next, he needed to stay in character. He couldn't afford to let Tabitha catch even the slightest hint of his true identity. Taking a breath, he steadied himself, reminding his heart to stay composed even as it raced uncontrollably beneath the surface.

He cleared his throat and smiled. "Miss Paget, it is a pleasure to meet the grand-niece of such a wonderful woman." He bowed. "Mrs. Burls is one of God's greatest blessings in this township."

Tabitha nodded. "I thank you. I'm sure my aunt will be happy knowing you hold her in such high esteem."

"How long will you be staying with her?" he asked.

She shrugged. "It's undecided now. If my aunt will have me, I wouldn't mind staying for a few months."

He silently groaned, but at the same time, his heart sped with excitement. This confusing reaction from his body would not do! He could not—under no circumstance—let her know who he truly was. To be sure, her presence here would not be a good thing if he and Frederick planned to trap a thief.

"Well, I'm certain your aunt would love your company, and I can assure you, the community—as well as myself—will welcome you with open arms." He gritted his teeth. Why had he said it *that* way?

She gave a hesitant nod as her smile weakened. "Uh, I thank you again."

The silence stretched, thick and uncomfortable, leaving Nic in an unfamiliar and unsettling position. Never in his life had he felt so tongue-tied. As the Marquess of Hawthorne, his smooth words had always been his escape, capable of turning the tide in any awkward or messy situation. But now he wasn't the marquess—he was Mr. Woodland, a simple clergyman. And at this moment, he could summon none of the charm or wit he was so known for.

Tabitha seemed equally uneasy, her eyes darting nervously around them, searching for an anchor in the uncomfortable quiet. When her gaze finally landed on him again, it wasn't on his face—it was on his beard, as if she were trying to reconcile the man before her with the one she once knew.

The tension mounted with every passing second. He needed to say something—anything—to break the silence, but all he could manage was to stand there, wondering if she was beginning to see through his disguise, or if perhaps the mere sight of him brought back the same cascade of emotions that it did for him.

Chuckling, he ran his hand over his hairy face. "You're probably wondering why a clergyman sports a beard. Am I correct, Miss Tabitha?"

She shrugged. "I suppose that thought did cross my mind."

"My sickness made it impossible for me to shave. And until I'm fully healed, I must leave this on. I hope you don't mind seeing me so scruffy."

"Not at all, Mr. Woodland."

"Perhaps," Mrs. Stiles interrupted, "we should join the others now." She turned to the maid still by the window. "Sally, will you make sure there's enough food being served, and just help the other two servants tonight?"

"Yes, ma'am." Sally curtsied and hurried past him into the other room.

Mrs. Stiles smiled. "Well, shall we go now?"

"Splendid idea." Nic breathed a relieved sigh. He motioned with his hand. "After you ladies, of course."

As Mrs. Stiles and Tabitha walked by, Tabitha's curious stare stayed on him. Uncomfortable, he dropped his gaze as he followed behind.

Did she recognize him? She couldn't possibly...yet why did she look suspiciously at him with narrowed eyes?

TABITHA STEPPED INTO the large room where her aunt sat surrounded by guests, the lively hum of conversation filling the air. More people had arrived since she had first entered, and Mrs. Stiles had eagerly taken on the task of introducing her to each one, as Aunt Clara was deeply engaged in conversation. However, through all the introductions and polite exchanges, Tabitha found her gaze continually drifting toward one man—the clergyman.

There was something about him that unsettled her. She wasn't sure if it was the way his eyes seemed to follow her every move, or the fact that whenever she caught him looking, he quickly averted his gaze, as though trying to hide his interest. He thought she hadn't noticed, but she wasn't foolish. He had been watching her—constantly.

The strange part was, despite never having met him before, something about him felt oddly familiar. It gnawed at her, the sense that she should recognize him, though she couldn't quite place why. Was it his eyes? His voice? Or was it simply the unnerving way he looked at her, as if he could see through her outer façade, straight into the deepest parts of her soul?

Whatever it was, it left her feeling both curious and unsettled, and she couldn't shake the sense that there was more to this man than met the eye.

"Oh, Miss Tabitha." Mrs. Stiles leaned closer and whispered, "I do believe you have caught the eye of Mr. Woodland." She grinned. "He's a handsome man, is he not?"

Handsome? Tabitha rubbed her forehead. She hadn't really noticed. "I suppose for a man of his age, he's handsome."

"His age? Oh, Miss Tabitha, he isn't very old."

"What age is he? He looks like he's in his fortieth year."

"But that's not too old, is it? He probably looks a little older to you because of his recent illness. But he's well now." Mrs. Stiles bumped her elbow against Tabitha's. "And it seems to me that he fancies you quite a bit. He is unwed, you know."

Tabitha's stomach roiled with worry. "Mrs. Stiles, I appreciate your trying to play the matchmaker, but I'm not here to look for a husband. In fact, I don't believe I wish to marry at all."

"What?" Mrs. Stiles gasped. "Are you jesting? You are too lovely not to marry. Why would you not want a husband?"

"I'm just not ready to be married." Taking a deep breath, Tabitha calmed her raging mind.

Whenever she reflected on her past and the hardships she had endured, she was certain that marriage was not something she could ever consider. The idea of relying on a man—of opening herself up to vulnerability—seemed utterly foreign and unwelcome. She was convinced that she would be far happier and more content if she never had to deal with a man again.

Thankfully, time passed quickly this evening, and Tabitha kept herself getting to know her aunt's guests. They were kind and warm, just as the clergyman had predicted. They welcomed her with open arms, making her feel more at home than she had anticipated.

Inwardly, she chuckled as she recalled the way Mr. Woodland had said it. There had been something about his expression right after the words left his mouth—an almost startled look, as though he hadn't meant to reveal his thoughts so openly.

What an odd fellow. There was something about the clergyman that didn't quite fit with the small town's simplicity. Yet she couldn't quite place what it was that made him so difficult to ignore.

When the time came for Aunt Clara to open her gifts, she settled comfortably in the center of the room, surrounded by her guests. The giver of each present stepped forward, offering it to Aunt Clara, who received each with the delight and enthusiasm of a young girl, her eyes sparkling and her laughter light and girlish. Tabitha watched with a warm smile, charmed by her aunt's joyful spirit.

When Mr. Woodland stepped forward to present his gift, Aunt Clara's face lit up with eager anticipation. She tore at the wrapping with surprising energy, her fingers trembling with excitement. A gasp escaped her lips as she held up a beautifully painted box adorned with butterflies, hearts, and delicate flowers. The old woman's expression glowed with delight as she turned the box over in her hands, marveling at the intricate designs.

"Oh, it's simply lovely!" Aunt Clara exclaimed, her eyes shining as she looked at Mr. Woodland with deep appreciation.

The whole room shared in her joy, but Tabitha couldn't help but notice the subtle way Mr. Woodland shifted, as if the attention made him slightly uncomfortable. Still, there was something undeniably sincere in the way he smiled at her aunt—a warmth that made him seem, for a fleeting moment, more familiar than ever.

"It's a music box." He reached over and lifted the lid.

As the room quieted, the soft strains of music filled the air, weaving through the crowd like a gentle breeze. The melody was unmistakable to Tabitha—an old Irish song her mother used to sing to her when she was just a child. The familiar tune stirred something deep inside her, and in an instant, tears pricked at her eyes. A wave of homesickness washed over her, settling heavily in her chest. Those memories of her mother were among the happiest she had, filled with laughter and love. But the reminder that her mother was no longer alive made her heart ache, the bittersweet nostalgia clinging to her like a shadow.

"Mr. Woodland…" Aunt Clara brought a hand to her mouth. Tears filled her eyes as well. "You remembered my favorite song."

"Indeed, I did." He smiled brightly.

"Then if you remembered, I'm certain you also recall that I enjoy hearing you sing it to me." She waggled her thin eyebrows. "Would you do so now?"

Mr. Woodland's eyes widened, and for a fleeting moment, the color drained from his face. Tabitha noticed the brief, almost imperceptible shift in his demeanor—his usually composed expression had faltered, giving way to something that looked unmistakably like panic.

It was strange, almost unsettling, to see such a reaction from a man who should be well accustomed to public speaking. After all, as a clergyman, he regularly stood before his congregation, delivering sermons and leading them in hymns without hesitation.

Yet here he was, in a room filled with familiar faces, reacting as though the simple idea of joining in song terrified him. Tabitha couldn't shake the feeling that something was off. Why would a man so accustomed to the spotlight of spiritual leadership appear rattled by the mere thought of singing in front of a few guests?

The contrast between his role and his apparent fear intrigued her, deepening the sense of curiosity she already had about Mr. Woodland. There was something more to this man, something hidden beneath his calm, clerical exterior. She couldn't help but wonder what it was—what secret he was guarding so carefully that even a simple gathering like this seemed to threaten its exposure.

Very curious, indeed.

Chapter Four

I'M GOING TO *kill him!*

Nic struggled to maintain his composure as anger simmered beneath the surface. Frederick knew full well that Nic hadn't sung in public for years. Yet his foolish cousin had still allowed him to give the music box to Mrs. Burls, putting him in this precarious situation. Now, everyone in the room was watching him, their eyes filled with expectation. They could see it, too—the panic that had gripped him the moment the music began to play.

His mind raced as he tried to think of a way out, but nothing came. He had been caught completely off guard, thrust into a position he was unprepared for. His chest tightened as the reality of the moment sank in.

Keep calm, Hawthorne, he reminded himself sternly, using his title like a mantra. He needed to regain control, to not let his panic show any more than it already had. He couldn't afford to give his audience any reason to doubt him—or, worse, to see through his carefully crafted disguise.

With a slow breath, Nic forced himself to steady. He had faced worse situations before and emerged unscathed. This was just another challenge—one he had to handle with the smooth precision that had gotten him out of so many tight spots in the past.

He cleared his throat and smiled the best he could under these awkward circumstances. He aimed his attention at Mrs. Burls. "Oh, my dear friend, you catch me unawares. I haven't sung since I first became sick a few weeks ago. I daresay that if I sing now, all the mirrors in the house will crack and the dogs will howl."

Chuckles ripped through the air, setting Nic a little more at ease. Mrs. Burls' smile waned. His heart wrenched. Blast it all, why did she have to look at him like *that*? Of course she didn't know why he—Nic—had stopped singing in public, or why he'd vowed never to do so again. But Frederick did...and Nic would indeed kill him, tonight!

"I understand," Mrs. Burls said. "I didn't realize the illness had affected you so."

Another man in the room stepped forward—Mr. Jacobs, the town's blacksmith. Nic had observed him before and found him to be a decent, hardworking fellow, despite the hardships life had thrown his way. Jacobs' wife had passed away two years ago, leaving him to raise their seven-year-old daughter on his own. The whole town knew he was seeking a wife, but unfortunately, his search had been fruitless so far.

To make matters worse, Jacobs had recently suffered a serious injury in his shop, taking a hard fall and badly injuring his knee. Now he struggled to get around with crutches, and the injury had made it nearly impossible for him to keep up with the demanding work of a blacksmith. The once-strong and capable man was now a shadow of his former self, limping through life with quiet determination, but clearly weighed down by his circumstances.

As Jacobs stepped forward now, Nic could see the strain in his movements, the awkward shuffle of his crutches. There was a humility about the man that Nic admired, even in the face of such adversity. While he stood there battling his own panic, Jacobs' presence was a quiet reminder of how differently people handled their burdens.

"Mrs. Burls," Jacobs said, "please permit me to sing the song for you. I know my voice won't be as glorious as Mr. Woodland's, but it would be my honor."

Ice surged through Nic's veins, freezing him in place as bitter memories from his past clawed their way to the surface. His gut twisted painfully, and the acrid taste of bitterness coated his tongue, making him feel like he might gag. This was exactly what had happened all those years ago—the last time he had been asked to sing in public.

Back then, it had been the sting of Lady Anna's rejection that threw him off balance. Hurt and angry, he'd allowed another man to sing in his place at a dinner social. The disappointment in the room had been palpable, and people had looked down on him for shirking the task when they had asked specifically for him. The humiliation of that night had burned deeply, a wound that never fully healed. From that moment, he had vowed never to sing publicly again—never to let himself be so vulnerable, so exposed to judgment and failure.

But now, standing here, with all eyes on him, that familiar sense of panic surged. He would not let history repeat itself. This time, he would not be made a fool. The shame of that past incident had haunted him for too long, and he couldn't allow it to control him any longer.

Yet time was slipping away. He could feel the moment threatening to pass him by, the weight of expectation heavy in the air. If he didn't gather the courage to act, to sing as he'd been asked, he knew he would regret it forever. With every passing second, the window to reclaim his dignity and prove to himself that he could do this was closing.

Nic took a deep breath, forcing himself to stand taller. His heart pounded wildly, but he knew that if he didn't seize this moment now, he would never forgive himself.

"I thank you, Mr. Jacobs," Mrs. Burls said. "But perhaps another time. I just remembered another person who loves this song as much as I." Her gaze flew to Tabitha. "Her mother was my favorite niece and used to sing it to Miss Tabitha when she was young." She held out her hand toward Tabitha. "Would you sing it to me, my dear?"

As he observed Tabitha's face, his heart softened. She looked even more panicked than he had felt just moments ago. The seconds dragged on, and tears filled her eyes, her chest rising and falling with deep, anxious breaths. She seemed to brace herself, stepping closer to her great-aunt with an expression that made it clear she was struggling internally.

Nic remained silent, feeling the weight of her emotions. The flicker of doubt, the fear of failing in front of others—it was all too familiar. Her face was a canvas of shifting emotions: uncertainty, fear, and then, finally, resolve. The color had drained from her cheeks, but despite her obvious distress, there was something undeniable in her gaze. The determination shining through her watery eyes spoke volumes—she was going to do it, no matter how afraid she was.

He couldn't help but admire the strength it took for her to press forward, even as her emotions threatened to overwhelm her. In that moment, his panic was overshadowed by a deep empathy for Tabitha. He understood now, more than ever, what it meant to face one's fears.

"Yes, Aunt Clara." Tabitha's voice shook. "I shall sing the song for you as best as I can." She cleared her voice and began the old Irish song.

Her voice trembled, filling the room with her quiet, hesitant notes. Though her voice wasn't terrible, it was clear how uncomfortable she was with all eyes upon her. He could feel her distress, and it tugged at something deep inside him. A surge of protectiveness came over him. No one should have to endure that kind of torture.

She blinked back tears, her voice rasping with emotion, and that was all it took to spur Nic into action. He cleared his throat softly and stepped toward her, picking up the song where she faltered. His voice wavered at first, uncertain and rusty from years of neglect. But as he continued, something clicked. The more he sang, the more his confidence grew. His voice strengthened, deepened, returning to the rich, smooth timbre it had once been long ago.

Tabitha's eyes widened in surprise as a tear slid down her cheek. But within seconds, her expression shifted, relief washing over her like a wave. A small smile tugged at her lips, and she straightened, regaining her composure. When she opened her mouth to join him, the song flowed effortlessly. Her gaze never left his, and together, their voices intertwined in perfect harmony.

Nic's heart swelled with happiness. Tabitha's voice was angelic, sweet and pure, and it matched his so perfectly that it felt like magic. A few times, she even harmonized with him, her soft tones lifting the melody higher than he could have imagined. It was the most beautiful sound he had ever heard, and he found that he couldn't tear his gaze away from her—not even to glance at the old woman for whom the song was intended.

In that moment, there was nothing but the music and the connection between them, a shared joy that seemed to resonate in every note they sang together.

Nic's heart was so full by the time the music box fell silent that he feared he might lose all control and pull Tabitha into his arms right then and there. *What's wrong with me?* He felt foolishly sentimental, yet none of it seemed to matter. What mattered was the joy lighting up Tabitha's face, her smile growing as they sang the final note together. When she mouthed *thank you* to him, his heart melted completely.

Cheers and applause erupted in the room, snapping him back to reality. For a moment, he had been lost in the music, and especially in her presence. Now, as he turned his attention to the rest of the gathering, the scene unfolded before him. Mrs. Burls clapped the loudest, tears streaming down her face, clearly touched. Mrs. Stiles was wiping her eyes, as were several other guests. Even the stoic townspeople had been moved by the duet.

Yet, as Nic swept his gaze around the room, he noticed something odd. While Mr. Jacobs clapped along with the others, his smile seemed forced, strained at the edges. There was a flicker of something beneath the surface—perhaps jealousy, perhaps something more. It was a subtle reminder that despite the warmth of the moment, not everyone's intentions were as pure as they seemed.

But for now, the room was filled with warmth, and Nic allowed himself a brief moment of satisfaction. He had not only saved the performance but made Tabitha happy—and for reasons he couldn't quite grasp, that was enough.

"Oh, that was just beautiful," Mrs. Burls said. "Your voices are heavily together. My birthday is now complete."

He smiled at the older woman and nodded. "I must agree. Your niece has a very lovely voice."

Nic still wanted to wring Frederick's neck, but at least the initial surge of anger had subsided. His cousin couldn't have possibly known that Tabitha would be asked to sing that particular song. What luck, though, that she was musically inclined. Was she naturally gifted, or had she received singing lessons? It struck him as odd, since she was a maid, like her mother before her—and maids didn't typically have the luxury of formal music instruction. Yet there was something about her voice, so pure and practiced, that suggested otherwise.

As the gift-giving resumed, he stepped back, allowing the room to flow around him. He watched as Tabitha moved back to her quiet spot, standing by herself. For a moment, she seemed distracted, watching Sally move through the crowd with a tray of food. But then, slowly, Tabitha's gaze shifted toward him. This time, when their eyes met, the curiosity and suspicion that had lingered in her expression earlier were gone. In their place was something warmer—gratitude.

Nic let out a slow, pent-up sigh. The tension that had gripped him all evening began to melt away. He marveled at the simple fact that he had actually enjoyed singing with her—relished it, even.

Why had he allowed Lady Anna Rutledge to take this from him all those years ago? He had been young and foolish back then, and her rejection had left an indelible mark on his mind. The shame and humiliation had driven him to shut down that part of himself, to guard his heart so fiercely that he turned to the reckless life of a rogue. It had been easier to embrace the fleeting pleasures of life, never lingering long enough to risk that kind of pain again.

But now, for the first time in years, he felt something shift. The joy he had experienced with Tabitha during that brief duet tugged at the locked doors of his heart. The question arose, quietly but insistently: could it be possible to find a good woman to share his life with, to open himself to love and family, without the fear of rejection haunting him again?

For now he pushed the thought aside, but he couldn't deny the flicker of hope that had begun to grow.

After the gifts were opened, the crowd began mingling again. Refreshments were on the table in the corner of the room. He wanted to get a bite to eat, but more than anything he wanted a drink. Whiskey, in fact, and not the watered-down sort. Unfortunately, he wasn't going to find that here.

As Nic made his way toward the refreshment table, guests frequently stopped him, offering compliments on his singing. Many remarked how much stronger his voice had become, noting they couldn't recall him ever singing so well in church before. *What have I done?* A ripple of panic rose within him. Frederick had a decent singing voice, sure—but clearly not good enough, since most of the townspeople had noticed the difference.

His thoughts wandered as he scanned the room, searching for Tabitha. There she was, standing among a small group of guests. Her cheeks were flushed with color as she laughed at something someone said, her expression bright and warm. But when he saw Mr. Jacobs leaning on his crutch beside her, Nic narrowed his gaze. Even from across the room, he could tell Jacobs had set his sights on her—she was likely to be his next attempt at finding a wife.

A bitter taste settled on Nic's tongue. He wasn't sure if it was the thought of Jacobs wooing Tabitha or simply the sudden realization that he really needed a strong drink. Either way, the discomfort created a fire in his belly.

Finally reaching the table, he surveyed the array of refreshments. Everything looked delicious, though in truth, he wasn't picky when it came to food. Just as he reached for a plate, someone moved beside him, and his arm lightly bumped against another. He turned, startled by the unexpected contact.

"Oh, forgive me—" He paused, staring into the most amazing eyes he'd ever seen.

Tabitha gasped and withdrew her arm. "No, it was my fault, entirely. Please excuse me, Mr. Woodland."

He reached over and grabbed a plate, then handed it to her. "Here you are, Miss Tabitha. I'm assuming this was what you were after?"

"Yes."

"Do you mind if I chat with you while I fix my plate?"

She laughed. "Of course not. Why would I mind?"

"Splendid." He picked up a plate for himself. "I have noticed you are making friends quickly. These people are very kind, don't you agree?"

"Indeed, I do, Mr. Woodland."

Silence stretched between them as they placed food items on their plates. Tabitha kept glancing his way, but only briefly. Finally, she cleared her throat and faced him.

"Mr. Woodland, I really need to thank you for saving me earlier. I have never been placed in that kind of situation, and, well…I wasn't sure how to act."

"I could tell how uncomfortable you were. Believe it or not, I hadn't planned on singing the song, so when I belted out the words, it rather shocked me as well."

She shrugged. "I couldn't tell. You have a very lovely singing voice."

"As do you." He tilted his head, staring deeper into her eyes. "Tell me, where did you learn to sing? I assure you, I have not heard a more exquisite voice before—and being a clergyman, I have had the privilege to hear a lot of people sing." He winked.

She stared at him blankly for a few awkward seconds before her expression turned to suspicion. He sucked in a quick breath. What had he done? Did she finally recognize the man talking to her now?

Chapter Five

UNEASE SPREAD THROUGH Tabitha, a feeling she couldn't quite shake. Why did this man create such confusion in her mind? He seemed pleasant enough, and her aunt's guests clearly adored him. They laughed at his jokes, hung on his words, and treated him like a cherished friend. But despite all that, something about him felt…off. There was a certain falseness to him, a sense that he was hiding something beneath the surface.

She shouldn't judge him so harshly when she barely knew him. Perhaps she was being unfair. Yet it was his wink—so casual, so confident—that truly unsettled her.

A shiver ran down her spine at the memory, though she couldn't tell whether it was from discomfort or something else entirely. Disgust? Or was it, strangely enough, a flicker of delight?

Either way, she brushed the thought aside. It wouldn't do to dwell on it. Whatever strange feeling he stirred in her, she had no choice but to treat Mr. Woodland kindly and with respect. After all, everyone else seemed to approve of him, and for now, that was enough.

"You flatter me too much, Mr. Woodland. I've never had singing lessons. Well, not professionally, that is. My mother is the one who taught me how to sing."

He arched an eyebrow. "Indeed? Well, then you truly have a talent beyond compare."

Heat consumed her face. She really hated it when people made her blush. "Thank you, again. I do recall that my mother had the perfect singing voice."

The clergyman placed another sweetmeat on his plate. "I would enjoy hearing about your mother, Miss Tabitha. She sounds like a true angel."

Tabitha smiled. "She was indeed. She died when I was in my sixteenth year." She released a heavy sigh. "I miss her so much."

"Forgive me if I brought back bad memories for you. That was not my intention."

"I know." She shook her head. "I don't have any bad memories of my mother, only pleasant ones. I just wish she hadn't died so young."

"I do understand what you're feeling. Death is not something anybody wishes on people, yet it's a part of life. Unfortunately, we all must experience the pain of losing someone sooner or later."

"Yes, we must. How else would we know happiness if we have never felt sorrow?"

Suddenly, the color of his eyes softened—if that were at all possible—and he stroked his hand over his hairy chin. Another chill swept through her, and she wanted to scream with frustration. Why did she act this way?

"Such a profound thing to say, Miss Tabitha, but you are correct." He cocked his head. "Perhaps you would like to give a sermon one of these Sundays about that topic?"

She laughed loudly then quickly slapped a hand over her mouth. Shaking her head, she lowered her hand. "Oh, Mr. Woodland. You are very humorous. There's no way I'm qualified to give sermons. I'll leave that in your capable hands." She held up her palm. "As you can see, these hands are not saintly."

When he grasped her hand gently, her heart nearly stopped. Why had he touched her so personally? Yet his eyes lightened with a familiarity that she didn't understand, and when he brushed his thumb across her palm, her heartbeat quickened. The feeling was quite disturbing.

"Forgive me for saying, Miss Tabitha, but they look perfect to me."

Oh heavens! Why did he say that? And for goodness' sake, why did her heart continue to speed up? This was not good.

"Uh, thank you, Mr. Woodland." Slowly, she slid her hand away from his touch. "But I still don't think your parish would agree to having someone like *me* teach them about God."

"And why not? Are we not all God's children?"

She suppressed a growl of frustration. Quickly, she reasoned that he was just making small talk and that was the reason he kept pressing the issue. She gave him her best smile, even if it was forced. "Indeed we are, but some of us are more qualified for giving sermons than others."

His chest shook with a light chuckle and his eyes sparkled. As before, the feeling of familiarity came over her. Did she know him? She must. Yet she didn't have any opportunities in her life to mingle with ministers.

"Mr. Woodland, it has been very nice talking with you, but I should go see how my aunt is doing."

"Of course you should. Perhaps I shall see you again on Sunday?"

Tabitha hesitated, unsure how to respond. She didn't want to admit that she hadn't set foot in a church since shortly after her mother passed away. The grief had been too raw, the idea of sitting through a service unbearable. And besides, she feared that confessing this to Mr. Woodland might invite an impromptu sermon, one she wasn't prepared to hear.

Although she wanted to avoid the topic, she was certain that Aunt Clara and Mrs. Stiles would likely insist she accompany them to church soon enough. She could already imagine their gentle prodding and well-meaning insistence. It was only a matter of time before she found herself sitting in a pew, whether she liked it or not.

"I'm sure I'll be there."

"Marvelous. Then I bid you goodbye until Sunday. I'm already looking forward to hearing you sing." He winked.

He did it again! Why did he keep winking? And why did she feel as if she knew him?

Without another word, Tabitha turned and made her way toward Sally, who stood quietly in the corner of the room, watching the guests with the practiced attention of a servant ready to assist. As she walked, Tabitha's mind wandered, puzzling over the strange encounter with Mr. Woodland. She couldn't recall any other man ever winking at her—not in such a way, at least.

Well, except for the man she wished she could remove from her mind—Lord Hawthorne. The mere thought of his name sent a wave of anger coursing through her. That insufferable man! He had treated her like she was special, a princess, even—only to turn around and accuse her of something so vile, so unforgivable.

Murder.

The memory still burned, a festering wound that had never quite healed. She had no idea what had become of him, but part of her hoped he was rotting in hell for what he had done to her.

She clenched her fists as she neared Sally, determined to shake the memory of Lord Hawthorne from her mind. He was a part of her past—one she would never forgive—but she refused to let him poison her present.

Suddenly, unbidden images of Dominic's face filled her mind—his mischievous smile, his rich laugh, and, most vividly, that flirtatious wink that had always made her insides tremble. She had never been able to forget the way his eyes sparkled, a constant twinkle that had always betrayed his playful nature. That twinkle was unmistakable, as was the way he carried himself, with a confidence and charm that could hardly be hidden.

So much like…

Her heart pounded in confusion as she spun around, searching for the clergyman. There he was, standing with a small group of men near the far wall, listening intently to their conversation.

Just then, his smile broadened, and he threw his head back in laughter, the sound rich and familiar.

Shivers raced up her spine, her skin tingling as though it were on fire. There was no mistaking it now. Her confusion melted away, replaced by a startling realization that shook her to her core. *Lord Hawthorne in the flesh!*

But why on earth was he here, dressed as a man of God? What was Dominic Lawrence, Marquess of Hawthorne, doing in this small town, hiding behind a false identity?

TABITHA PACED THE length of her bedroom, her mind swirling with uncertainty. She clenched and unclenched her hands, trying to calm the storm of emotions brewing inside her. Aunt Clara had called last night's party a success, but to Tabitha, it had been anything but. What was supposed to be a pleasant evening had turned into a confusing puzzle she couldn't shake.

Was Mr. Woodland really Dominic Lawrence, the Marquess of Hawthorne? Or was her mind playing tricks on her? She replayed in her mind every interaction with the man. She had watched him closely throughout the evening, looking for the telltale signs—the familiar expressions, the subtle mannerisms. But within an hour, he'd made his polite excuses and left, leaving her no closer to confirmation.

She hadn't dared mention her suspicions to Sally. Her maid had been through enough, and Tabitha knew the mere idea of Lord Hawthorne being nearby would send Sally into a spiral of fear. Their shared history was too dark, too painful. After what had happened with Lord Elliot, the mere thought of another powerful man in their lives felt like a shadow creeping back in. Sally, always on edge, would not react well if she believed Dominic was the clergyman.

Tabitha's own past weighed heavily on her, memories of

Lord Elliot seeping in like poison she couldn't expel. Both she and Sally had suffered under his cruelty when they worked for him, enduring the worst kind of abuse. Tabitha had lost count of the times she had wished for his death, her hands shaking with the urge to end him herself. When the news of his demise had finally reached her, she had felt no sorrow—only a grim satisfaction that the world was rid of one more monster.

She hadn't killed Lord Elliot with her own hands, but in her heart, she had wished it every day. Now, standing in the silence of her room, the past felt like a dark cloud over her. And if Dominic Lawrence—Lord Hawthorne—truly was here disguised as Mr. Woodland, then she had to ask herself why. What was his purpose? And most importantly, could she trust him—or would he prove to be another dangerous man she would have to guard herself against?

Did that make her a sinner? If so, then she would certainly go straight to hell.

Tabitha moved to the window and flung open the curtains. The bright morning sunlight spilled into the room, beckoning her with the promise of a beautiful day. She longed to take Sally and escape for a peaceful walk through the parks, or even down by the beach, where the salty breeze might clear her troubled mind. But the thought of running into Lord Hawthorne kept her trapped. The turmoil within her was too great, and she feared what might spill from her lips if they crossed paths again. She needed answers, not another confusing confrontation.

If the clergyman was indeed Dominic, what could possibly drive him to disguise himself this way? She knew the man well enough to know he wasn't the type to suddenly devote himself to God and a quiet life of service. No, something was off. If Nic was hiding behind the mask of a clergyman, there had to be a reason—a dangerous reason. And blast it all, she needed to find out what it was.

Feeling the room closing in on her, Tabitha turned from the window, her restlessness growing. The walls seemed to inch closer, suffocating her with every second she remained. She needed to get out, needed air, needed to escape the confusion swirling inside her. If she stayed in this room any longer, she feared she might scream.

Without hesitation, she moved toward the door, desperate for space and clarity. Downstairs, in the sitting room, she found Aunt Clara and Mrs. Stiles quietly enjoying their tea. The peaceful scene was a stark contrast to the storm raging within her. As she stepped into the room, both women looked up and smiled warmly at her, their faces gentle and welcoming.

"Good morning, dear," Aunt Clara greeted her. "You're up early."

"How could I not be?" Tabitha moved to them and sat next to her aunt on the sofa. "Most of my life I've been a maid and had to get up before anyone in the household."

Aunt Clara tapped her hand on Tabitha's knee. "There's nothing wrong with that, and don't you let anyone tell you differently."

"I won't. But besides that, I needed a change of scenery," Tabitha replied, her tone light despite the weight pressing on her. Perhaps tea and a conversation with the women could offer some distraction, if not answers.

She smiled lovingly at her relative, suddenly wishing she could go back in time to when she was a little girl. There was some resemblance between her aunt and her mother. Tabitha supposed if her mother had lived to be as old as Clara, she would look the same.

"Do you have any plans with Sally today?" Aunt Clara sipped her tea.

"Nothing at all. What could we have planned when we don't know what North Devon holds for us to see?"

"Oh, my dear." Aunt Clara gasped and met her companion's stare. "We need to find someone to take our Tabitha and Sally on a sightseeing tour. Do you not agree?"

"Most assuredly." Mrs. Stiles nodded so fast, her cap bounced on her head.

"Oh, I think I know just the person." Aunt Clara placed her hand on her chest, sighed, and looked back at Tabitha. "I noticed last night that Mr. Jacobs was paying you extra attention. I'm sure he'd love to take you around town."

Tabitha opened her mouth to speak, but Mrs. Stiles cut in.

"Oh, but Clara, dear…did you not see he has injured his leg? He was leaning on a crutch last night. I don't think he would be the right man to escort our dear Tabitha around."

Tabitha shook her head. "Mr. Jacobs is a very nice man, but I must agree with Mrs. Stiles."

"Then that won't do at all." Aunt Clara huffed and folded her hands in her lap. "Bertha, dear? Who else do we know who could escort our girls around?"

Mrs. Stiles tapped a finger to her chin as she stared at the tea service on the table in front of them. Her forehead creased as her frown deepened.

Tabitha hurried and spoke before the companion could come up with another name. "Actually, I don't believe Sally and I need to have an escort. We both love to walk, and we could wander through the town—"

"I have it!" Mrs. Stiles interrupted. Her face beamed with excitement as a smile stretched across her face. "What about Mr. Woodland? He would be a splendid tour guide. He's only been here less than a year, but he walks everywhere, and he knows the town well."

Tabitha's thoughts came to a sudden halt. Mr. Woodland had lived in North Devon for less than a year? That couldn't be right, especially when she'd met Lord Hawthorne in York approximately six months ago. So when Bertha said *less than a year*, what were the exact months?

Aunt Clara nodded, her ringlets shaking. "Yes, Bertha. That's the perfect choice." She looked back at Tabitha. "He's such a wonderful man, and last night when he sang to me…" She placed her hand on her bosom and sighed. "What a lovely voice he has.

Indeed, I could have listened to the two of you all night."

"Actually"—Mrs. Stiles reached across the table and touched Aunt Clara's arm—"the way it looked to me was that he was singing to our Tabitha." She waggled her eyebrows.

Tabitha wanted to groan aloud, but refrained for now. "I must admit, Mr. Woodland is a very nice man, and yes, he does have a pleasant singing voice, but Sally and I don't need an escort. I assure you, we shall be fine by ourselves."

"Nonsense." Aunt Clara flipped her hand in the air. "You will need someone who can assist you up and down the rocky slopes near the beach. I wouldn't feel right if you tried to climb those hills without a man present. It's very easy to slip and fall."

"Oh, Aunt Clara…really." Tabitha shook her head. "Must I keep reminding you, I'm not a pampered, genteel lady who can't climb up and down? I'm used to hard labor, which means, I'm stronger than you think."

"Tabitha dear, that's not the point." Aunt Clara sighed as her smile slowly faded. "You're not a servant any longer, so why not allow a man to treat you like a lady? Now is a good time to start, you know."

Tabitha wanted to throw her hands up in surrender. Obviously, arguing with her aunt wasn't getting her anywhere. What a stubborn woman. And here Tabitha thought *she* was stubborn. Now she knew where she had inherited it.

"So, I do believe," Aunt Clara continued, "that Mr. Woodland would be the best choice."

Tabitha sat back on the sofa and folded her arms. "Tell me, Aunt Clara, what do you really know about Mr. Woodland?"

"I know quite a bit."

"Such as?"

"He's in his late twenties, or perhaps early thirties, and he was married, but his wife and child died during childbirth. He has a heart of gold, and he's truly a messenger of God. This whole town is his family, and he would give the shirt off his back just to help someone in need."

Tabitha frowned, her mind swirling with doubt. Perhaps this man wasn't Lord Hawthorne after all. The possibility flickered in her thoughts, but it didn't erase the lingering unease. If he wasn't Dominic, why did he resemble him so closely, and why did he behave in a way that stirred her memories and made her body shiver with the same awareness she had always felt around Lord Hawthorne?

Things simply didn't add up. His mannerisms, his laugh, the way his eyes twinkled in that all-too-familiar way—it was all unsettling, as if she were standing on the edge of discovering something profound, yet the truth remained just out of reach.

If it wasn't him, then who was he? And more importantly, what was the reason for this strange charade? Tabitha's heart twisted with uncertainty, and she knew she wouldn't find peace until she unraveled the mystery.

"Do you know if he has any relatives in York? He looks familiar to me, somehow."

Both Aunt Clara and Mrs. Stiles glanced at each other and grinned. "He does have relatives in York," Aunt Clara answered. "A few months ago, his cousin came for a visit."

"What a nice gentleman." Mrs. Stiles sighed. "And such a charmer, too. He was here for quite a few months, wasn't he, Clara?"

Aunt Clara nodded. "Five, I believe, but he left not too long ago."

"Who is his cousin?" Tabitha asked.

"He's a lord." Aunt Clara tapped her fingers on the table. "A marquess, I believe."

"That he was, my dear." Mrs. Stiles bobbed her head.

Tabitha's heart picked up rhythm. What were the odds… "His name wouldn't have been Lord Hawthorne, would it?"

Aunt Clara sighed. "Yes, that's his name. Nice man, just like his cousin."

"Oh, Clara dear, do you recall when Lord Hawthorne was the center of attention at Miss Julia's birthday party?" Mrs. Stiles chuckled. "The whole town celebrated her eighteenth birthday, and when Mr. Woodland arrived with his cousin, all the single women at the gathering were stuck to his side. I daresay the man is a bit of a charmer, and had all those women sighing. I'm quite sure they were all hoping he'd stay with his cousin for an indefinite amount of time, too."

Of course Hawthorne was a charmer. Tabitha gritted her teeth at the thought, the familiar frustration bubbling up. It was painfully clear the man hadn't changed one bit. As Aunt Clara and Mrs. Stiles gossiped about Dominic's various exploits, Tabitha had to resist the urge to roll her eyes. She didn't want to hear about which woman he'd seduced recently, or which poor soul in town was foolishly hoping for an offer of marriage from him.

While the two older women chatted away, Tabitha took a moment to reflect. Perhaps she was mistaken about Mr. Woodland. If he and Dominic were truly cousins, it would explain the similar features—the resemblance that had unsettled her so much. That could be why she had jumped to the conclusion that it was Nic. It was a little eerie, though, how his eyes sparkled the same way, how he winked and laughed just like his cousin. Perhaps that was why her mind had merged them into one man.

But what truly unsettled her wasn't the resemblance—it was her body's reaction to Mr. Woodland. Before now, only Nic had ever made her feel so aware, so alive, with just a glance or a laugh. Why was she feeling that same pull toward this man? That was the question she couldn't shake. As much as she wanted to believe Mr. Woodland was just a clergyman, the way her body responded to him left her more confused than ever.

Chapter Six

DOMINIC RESISTED THE urge to wallop his cousin on the head, but he was still very upset at the man when he had returned home. Frederick was sneaking around town to do some spying, which gave Nic time to think…and fall asleep.

This morning he awoke feeling slightly better, but still annoyed, nonetheless. Panic was another emotion swimming through him right now, which he didn't like at all. A few times during the evening, Tabitha had acted as if she knew his true identity. Yet she didn't say anything. The woman he knew from six months ago would have confronted him immediately.

Perhaps this was what confused him more than anything.

Nic waited at the breakfast table for Frederick to awaken. Their discussion could not be put off a moment longer. By the creaks from the ceiling, Nic guessed that Frederick was up.

Drumming his fingers on the table, he sipped his coffee as he silently grumbled for something stronger to drink. But even Lord Hawthorne didn't drink spirits this early in the morning. If only he was back home, he'd be doing so many things differently. This country life was definitely not doing anything for Nic's sanity.

He turned and peered out the window. The cliffs and seaside provided a lovely view. As he watched the gentle waves splashing against some large boulders, peace settled inside of him. He wouldn't mind this kind of relaxation every morning instead of the hustle and bustle of York and Mayfair, where two of his townhouses were located.

The longer he stared, the more his vision became distorted, and images popped into his head whether he wanted them there or not. Tabitha's lovely face became clearer, and her amazing blue eyes gleamed with happiness. He could still hear her light laughter and especially the angelic ring of her voice as she sang with him. Memories of their verbal swordplay from six months ago came to mind. She had such a quick wit that kept him on his toes. Not often did he meet servants like Tabitha, or even *ladies* like her. Surprisingly, he had looked forward to seeing her again just so he could hear what would come out of her mouth next.

And speaking of mouths…

Groaning, Nic tore his attention away from the window. He rested his elbow on the table and rubbed his forehead. The memory of her kiss was definitely powerful.

"Is this not a beautiful morning?"

Frederick's chipper voice brought Nic out of his thoughts. He snapped his head up and glared at his cousin. "Not really, no."

Frederick arched an eyebrow. "No? And why not? Look outside. The sun is shining, the gentle wind—"

"Frederick, please quit prattling on like a woman and sit down. There is a matter of great importance that we need to discuss."

Huffing, Frederick took a chair and plopped down. "All you had to do was ask. You didn't have to be uncouth about it."

"Then forgive me for being so short with you. I had a most disturbing evening, and this morning isn't any better."

Frederick sat forward, resting his arms on the edge of the table. "What happened at Mrs. Burls' birthday social?"

"Well, for now I won't yell at you for giving the old woman a music box with her favorite song that you *knew* she would want you to sing to her, so I'll save that until another time. However"—Nic folded his arms and leaned back in his chair—"there are bigger problems afoot here."

"Does someone suspect you are not the clergyman?"

"No one from the community. I did an excellent job acting like a preacher." He took a deep breath. "However, do you recall the fiasco I told you about with Tristan Worthington and Diana Hollingsworth?"

"Of course I do. The murders were the talk of England."

"Then you recall me telling you about Diana's maid, Tabitha?"

A grin stretched across Frederick's mouth. "How could I forget about her? She made you behave badly, if memory serves."

Nic grimaced. "Indeed, I did not act like a gentleman, and my accusations were out of line."

"Whatever happened to the woman?"

"I'll tell you what happened." Nic pushed away from the table and stood. "She's here visiting her great-aunt, Clara Burls!"

"Oh dear," Frederick whispered. "That cannot be good."

"It's not. Especially now when Lord Hawthorne *needs* to stay hidden." Nic waved his hands in the air as he talked. "And what's worse is that I suspect she knows."

"No." Frederick jumped to his feet. "How could she? You look like me."

"We might look alike, but I still have the qualities that make me the lovable, charming rogue I've always been."

Frederick rolled his eyes. "If you say so."

Grumbling, Nic marched to his cousin and stopped inches in front of him. Nic's chest heaved with the angry breaths he took, and he clenched his hands into fists. "Then if I don't have those qualities, how else did Tabitha become suspicious?"

"Are you certain she suspects you are Lord Hawthorne?"

Nic held his breath for a moment as his mind went back over what had happened last night. "I...don't know. At times she acted like she thought it was me, and other times she didn't."

"All right." Frederick raised his hands in surrender. "Let's think this over clearly, before we jump to conclusions. After all, *you* of all people know the folly of doing that. Especially with that particular woman."

Nic scowled and nodded. "You don't have to remind me."

"Because Tabitha didn't actually confront you about the disguise, there might be a possibility that she doubts her own thoughts." Frederick moved away from Nic and paced the floor. "And if she doubts her thoughts, then we need to make certain she continues to do so."

"Go on." Nic nodded, hoping his cousin would say something he didn't already know.

"What you need to do"—Frederick stopped near Nic, pointing to his chest—"is to reassure her that your cousin, Lord Hawthorne, has returned home. While you're doing this, you should try to repair the damages that your *lovable, charming, roguish* self has done to the poor girl."

Nic fisted his hands again. "Are you done insulting me?"

"I'm not insulting you, dear cousin. I'm just using your words." Frederick lifted his chin stubbornly.

Growling, Nic raked his fingers through his hair and moved away from his cousin before he followed his instincts and slugged him in the face. He mulled over what Frederick had suggested. If Nic could convince her that he was indeed the clergyman, there *might* be a chance that he could persuade her to forgive Lord Hawthorne. Perhaps he'd even try to soften her heart toward him...Lord Hawthorne, that was. If he could accomplish this, Tabitha would be more obliged to talk to him and mayhap even forgive him.

He took in a deep, cleansing breath, releasing his anger and doubt. His hopes that this may indeed be the very thing to do lifted. His future looked slightly brighter. At least he might have this heavy burden of guilt that had been resting on his shoulders lifted, and he'd finally feel good about the whole situation.

"Frederick, I believe you're right." Nic met his cousin's stare and nodded. "Now, let's plan a way that the good clergyman Mr. Woodland can soften Miss Tabitha's heart quickly."

NORTH DEVON CLIFFS were absolutely spectacular. Many paths weaved through the slopes toward the cliffs. Some were steeper than others and very rocky. Sweet William flowers assisted the grass in decorating the slopes. At certain points on the cliffs, small waterfalls streamed foamy water down their thick green sides.

This afternoon the ocean was clear and bluer than Tabitha had ever imagined. She stopped along one of the smaller cliffs and inhaled the fresh, salty air. Closing her eyes, she smiled and was content to hear the waves splashing against the rocks below, as birds squawked overhead in the cloudless sky. Since she was sixteen years old, she hadn't found a chance to take a leisurely stroll anywhere. She hadn't done *anything* leisurely, not until she met her half-brother, Tristan Worthington, and confessed the secret she'd been holding for several years—that she was his illegitimate sister.

She had worried that her half-brothers Trevor, Tristan, and Trey might hate her because their father had cheated on their mother. Any lord in the realm would have turned up his nose at such a scandalous situation. But not the Worthington brothers. They were unlike anyone she'd ever met. They were so kind and so forgiving, and they welcomed her into their family with open arms. Their mother was even pleasant to Tabitha—after getting over the initial shock of it all, of course.

Trevor, the eldest, had set her up a trust fund. She explained he didn't need to do that, but he pushed the issue until she relented. Her brothers told her that they didn't want her to ever be a servant again. Considering she'd been a maid all of her life, it was very hard to sit back and allow someone else to do the cooking and cleaning for her.

She glanced down at her day dress and plucked at the sides of her green floral-print skirt. The weather was a little chilly, so she'd worn her forest-green waist jacket with matching gloves.

Her bonnet was the same floral print as her dress. Dressing this way still seemed foreign to her. She felt as if she should be wearing the normal gray uniform with a white apron around her waist, as what was required while working for Lord Elliot.

A cold shiver passed through her and she folded her arms, hoping the chill would soon leave. Little by little, her nightmares over the last several years were slowly disappearing. Although Lord Elliot was dead, she knew there were still men out there who abused their servants or wives. Men like this should be horsewhipped, in her opinion. She couldn't tolerate men who had no respect for women.

Then there were men like Lord Hawthorne, who behaved exactly opposite, but were still snakes. They charmed their women and doted on them, merely for sport. It built their egos as they spouted words of kindness and love as if reading directly from a book of sonnets, and yet when it came down to devotion and commitment, they didn't have an ounce of courage in their distrustful bodies. She couldn't abide men like Lord Hawthorne, either.

After hearing her aunt and Mrs. Stiles chat about how wonderful Mr. Woodland was this morning, Tabitha wondered if she'd been mistaken. She finally convinced herself that the clergyman reminded her of Dominic so much that she saw similarities which couldn't have possibly been there in the first place. There was no way Mr. Woodland was Lord Hawthorne. Especially because she didn't think Nic would sink so low as to portray a man of God.

In coming to this decision, she was more comfortable about going out with Sally to walk along the beach and cliffs this afternoon, because she knew she wouldn't meet up with Lord Hawthorne.

Tabitha glanced at Sally. Her maid even appeared more relaxed here. They were far enough away from Society's gossipmongers not to be caught up in their dramatics. Out here Tabitha and Sally wouldn't have to cower if someone spoke to them. They wouldn't have to wonder if anyone would recognize them from working for Lord Elliot, and Tabitha definitely wouldn't have to be concerned that anyone in North Devon would have heard the whispers about her being the old Duke of Kenbridge's *bastard* daughter.

"Sally?"

The girl's head snapped up, and she looked at Tabitha. "Yes?"

"What would you think if I decided to live here?"

The blonde maid's eyes widened, and she smiled. "Are you jesting?"

"Not at all."

"Why would you want to live here? Don't you like York?"

Tabitha shrugged. "York is a nice town, but I haven't felt very comfortable there. Perhaps it'll grow on me soon enough, but North Devon seems so peaceful. Nobody is rushing around. So far from what I've seen, the people are pleasant and very welcoming. Things are just so…serene."

"Yes, they are. I have enjoyed myself so far. It is definitely a relaxing place—compared to York, anyway."

"I agree." Tabitha linked her hands together at her back as she stepped slowly along the grassy edge. "I have realized how nice it is to be close to my only living relative as well."

"What about your brothers? Are they not your family now?"

"They are." Tabitha gazed out across the sea. "But I have only just met them. With Aunt Clara, I have some memories of when I was a child and my mother was still alive." She sighed heavily. "I would like to stay out here at least until my aunt dies."

"That's understandable."

Tabitha glanced back at Sally. "Is that all right if we stay, then?"

The maid's smile broadened. "Absolutely."

"Splendid." Satisfaction spread over Tabitha as she continued her walk. It was so lovely out here. She was surprised that there weren't more people taking a late morning stroll. From the corner of her eye, she noticed one other person out walking.

She stopped and studied the man as he grew closer by the second. Her heartbeat sped up, and that familiar, uneasy feeling enveloped her. She recognized his swagger even if he used a walking stick, and she tried to convince herself that this was *not* Nic. This was the clergyman. But would Mr. Woodland walk like his cousin? Would the shape of his face have the same curves as Nic's? Something deep inside her told her that this was *not* Mr. Woodland, but Nic in disguise.

There was only one way to find out. She must force herself to talk to him. She must study him completely. Not only that, she must rely on her heart to convey to her who this man really was.

"Good day," he called out, lifting his hand in greeting.

She smiled, mainly for show. "Good day, Mr. Woodland. It's nice to see you out walking."

He stopped beside her and nodded. "On days like this, how could I stay inside when the Lord has offered such beauty for me to observe and enjoy?"

The flip of her heart reminded her that Nic would say something like this, especially because he stared right at her instead of looking across the ocean or at the breathtaking cliffs.

"That's why Sally and I had to take a stroll. Would you like to join us?"

"Indeed, I would."

He kept in step beside her as Sally walked a few steps back. Although Tabitha shouldn't make a spectacle of herself by staring at him, how else could she study him to see if he was really the cocksure marquess she remembered? This man's hair was shorter than what Nic's had looked like the last time they were together, but the areas of white in his dark locks made her pause. Then again, men powdered their hair all the time. Maybe he had done the same. However, that beard was throwing her off. Nic had a dimple in the middle of his chin, but because this man had hair covering that spot, she wouldn't be able to see if it were there.

Another thing that was evident was the size of his clothes. They were very large on him. She recalled Mrs. Stiles mentioning how much weight he'd lost. Yet, from what Tabitha had heard, Mr. Woodland was only ill for a few weeks. She had been by her mother's side when sickness had taken her parent's life, and her mother hadn't lost that much weight in such a small amount of time.

She moved her focus back to his eyes…eyes that looked so much like Nic's that it was disturbing. That wink and twinkle could only belong to one man.

"Miss Tabitha," he began with a grin, "I must wonder why you are looking at me so strangely."

She hitched a breath and quickly pulled out of her serious thoughts. "Forgive me, Mr. Woodland. You just remind me of someone I met a few months ago."

"I do?" He arched an eyebrow. "I hope this man is a ruggedly handsome fellow. I wouldn't like it very much if I reminded you of an old man with no teeth."

A laugh sprang from her mouth. That was the kind of arrogant thing Nic would say. She didn't know the clergyman well enough to know if he could be so vain. Then again, from what she'd heard about him from her aunt and Mrs. Stiles, Mr. Woodland was an angel sent from heaven. In that case, the preacher would *not* be so vain.

"Rest assured, Mr. Woodland, the man I speak of is young and vibrant, and too handsome for his own good." She tried to keep her voice even instead of clipped with sarcasm. "And I assure you, he has all of his teeth."

He chuckled. "That's good to know. So tell me, who is this man?"

"Funny you should ask. I was informed this morning that he's a relative of yours."

His steps faltered until he stopped completely. "My relative?"

"Yes. His name is Dominic Lawrence, the Marquess of Hawthorne."

"Then you have heard correctly. Hawthorne is my cousin. In fact"—he scratched his chin—"he was here for a little while, but he had business back home, so he left."

"Then no wonder I see him when I look at you." She forced herself to smile even though she loathed every second of it. "I was beginning to wonder if the man I'd briefly known had taken on a different title." She tilted her head. "The man I knew would *not* have made a good clergyman."

He threw back his head and belted out a laugh. "Oh, Miss Tabitha, you are correct to assume such a thing. My wicked cousin couldn't do what I do." He rested his hand gently on her arm. "But if you see him, don't tell him I said that. After all, he's still my favorite cousin."

Warmth spread through her limb from just his light touch. There was only one man who could elicit this kind of reaction from her body. At this moment, her heart told her this was indeed Dominic Lawrence.

She gritted her teeth, keeping herself from spouting angry words. If Nic was playing a game, she would play along just to see why he was impersonating a minister. She didn't doubt he had a cousin whom her aunt and the rest of the town knew as Mr. Woodland, but the man standing next to her now was most assuredly Lord Hawthorne.

"Oh, no." She shook her head. "I wouldn't think of telling him that, Mr. Woodland. In fact, I wouldn't want to tell him anything at all. You see, we aren't on speaking terms right now."

He had the nerve to look surprised. What a great performer he was. She resisted rolling her eyes, but it was hard.

"You're not? But why would such a charming, lovely woman not want to speak to my roguish cousin?"

Another chuckle slipped through her lips. Funny that he would think of himself as charming. The roguish part was right, however. "Mr. Woodland, I'm not like the kind of women your cousin sweeps off their feet. I was able to see through his trickery and call him out on it. He didn't like the fact that he couldn't woo me as he was used to doing with other ladies."

He nodded. "And I assume that only served to injure his pride."

"I believe it did. It also made him think he could keep trying to win me over."

He sucked in a quick breath. "Oh, what a pompous man to believe such a thing."

"Yes…pompous is exactly what he is. His attitude is what turned me away."

Frowning, he shook his head as he turned and resumed walking. "I just don't understand my cousin sometimes."

"Me neither." She kept beside him, continuing to study his expressions. "But I really don't wish to."

"You don't?"

"Not now. Several months ago he accused me of something so vile that I cannot forgive him."

"Never? Oh, Miss Tabitha, you must forgive him. Have you not read the Good Book? God wants us to forgive—"

"Yes, I've read the Good Book, and although I might be sinning for refusing to forgive Lord Hawthorne, I just cannot. Not yet."

"But it's been six months."

Her mind came to a halt. Had she told him how long it'd been? No, she specifically remembered telling him *several* instead of an actual number. Only Nic would know it had been that long ago. She highly doubted the clergyman would know.

She shrugged. "It doesn't matter. My heart is not allowing me to forgive him."

He stopped again and leaned on his walking stick. "Is there anything I can do to change your mind?"

"Nothing."

"Well, I shall pray for you that your heart may be softened soon."

She fisted her hands and quickly folded her arms to keep him from seeing. "I thank you for your concern, Mr. Woodland."

"You know," he continued, stepping closer, "my cousin really is a good man, and he does have a kind heart."

"So his only flaws are that he's judgmental and speaks without thinking first?" She shook her head. "Oh, that can't be *all* of his flaws. He is arrogant beyond belief, which is probably his worst imperfection."

His jaw hardened and she noticed a muscle in his cheek jump. She tried not to laugh. Obviously, he didn't like hearing the truth. Well, if he was playing the clergyman and trying to fool her and the rest of the town, she would make his life difficult. One way or another, she'd make him confess and come out of hiding.

A FEW AWKWARD seconds passed as Nic boiled inside. He fought a constant battle, both with his mind and his heart. Honestly, he didn't think Tabitha should hate him this much, yet now he knew her true feelings.

How could he convince her he wasn't such a bad man? How could he make her see he indeed had a heart and was kind? No matter what Frederick said, Nic knew his cousin's plan wasn't going to work. But he didn't dare confess to her right now. Perhaps another day.

"As I'm sure you are aware," he said slowly, trying to think of something a minister would say, "we are all imperfect people. Only God is perfect."

"Yes, I'm aware." She started walking.

Her expression was hard, and her eyes were sad. He wished he knew what to do so she would think differently about him. He'd do anything he could. True, his ego couldn't stand knowing that a woman didn't hold him in *high* regard, but mainly he couldn't stand knowing that she wouldn't forgive him. He'd been human six months ago when he thought she'd killed those two lords for abusing their servants. What else was Nic supposed to think when he'd overheard her telling Sally one time that she had wished for Lord Elliot's death—and then another time when he heard Tabitha tell Diana that she had thought about killing Lord

Elliot and Lord Hollingsworth with her bare hands? How could he not assume the worst?

A few more minutes passed in silence, and guilt weighed heavily on his chest. Taking a deep breath, he released it slowly. Perhaps he needed to change the subject. Talking about the past was disturbing her greatly. He needed to make her happy again.

"So, Miss Tabitha, when will you allow me to hear your beautiful singing voice again?"

She stumbled and gazed at him with wide eyes. "Are you jesting?"

"Not at all. I have thought of nothing else since hearing you last evening. I would like it very much if you'd grace my congregation on Sunday and sing us a hymn."

A laugh burst from her mouth, sounding more like a snort. She shook her head, but a smile stretched across her face.

"Mr. Woodland, I think you're insane for wanting to hear me sing again. The only reason I tried to sing last night was because Aunt Clara requested it."

"Then perhaps I should have your aunt request you sing a hymn on Sunday?"

Rolling her eyes, she shook her head. "Not if you don't want to walk with a permanent limp."

It was his turn to let out a loud laugh. "Oh, Miss Tabitha, you are truly a spirited woman, and you say the most humorous things. I enjoy that."

"Then if you wish to keep enjoying my humor, I suggest you not ask me to sing again."

"If you insist. I would hate for you to hide the talent God has given you."

She didn't say anything more to him, turning her head to gaze across the sea. He wanted to say something that would make her happy—that would make *him* happy to see her smiling once again. But his mind drew a blank. Not very often did that happen.

"Oh look," she said, pointing down toward the beach, "there

is Mr. Jacobs."

Nic peered toward the beach. Mr. Jacobs looked to be enjoying the late morning with his daughter, Joanna. The seven-year-old girl dashed away, looking on the sand as if she searched for something. Her father limped along, leaning heavily on his crutch. Jacobs called for Joanna to come back, but she got farther away. He hobbled quickly to try and catch up to his daughter.

Immediately, Nic could see Joanna wasn't listening and not doing what her father had asked. As the girl ran closer to the water, Jacob's voice lifted in panic. The girl reached the damp sand and stumbled. Within seconds, she disappeared into what looked to be a hole. Jacobs tried to run, but because of his gimpy leg, he tripped and fell to his knees.

Nic peered across the water. The tide was coming in, and quickly. If they didn't get that girl out of the hole, the water would soon cover her—and drown her.

Chapter Seven

"OH, GOOD HEAVENS!" Tabitha gasped, before breaking into a run, and heading down the slope toward Joanna.

Urgency kicked Nic into action and he ran ahead of Tabitha, dashing down the cliff's trail toward the girl. Jacob screamed his daughter's name as he struggled to stand. Up ahead, Joanna's hair could be seen as she bobbed inside the hole. She sobbed for her father.

The tide crept closer. Nic didn't have time to stop and assist Mr. Jacobs. Instead, Nic sprinted toward the girl. Mere seconds before he reached her, the water rolled in, filling the hole.

Surprisingly, the hole was larger than Nic had expected—big enough for two. He slid down inside. When his hands brushed against a smaller body, he grasped her and pulled her up above the water level. Another wave came toward him quickly.

"Hold your breath again," he told the girl. Within seconds the water hit them, covering them once more. As the tide moved out, so did some of the water. He lifted Joanna higher so that her head was above water.

"Give me your hands, Joanna," Tabitha called.

Blinking the water out of his eyes, Nic tried to focus on Tabitha. She lay near the hole, her hands stretched out, as she latched on to Joanna's arms. The girl sobbed and flailed her arms, trying to get out as quickly as possible.

"Hold still, Joanna. I've got you," Nic reassured her as he lifted her toward Tabitha. As she pulled, Nic pushed the little girl until she was out of the hole. As soon as Joanna was on her feet, she broke into a run toward her father.

"Grab this limb," Tabitha instructed as she pushed the broken tree branch toward Nic, "and I'll help you out."

It took all of his strength to climb out of the sandy, slippery hole, but within minutes, he was out. Taking deep breaths, he inhaled the fresh air. He swiped his wet hair away from his face and nodded. "Thank you for thinking so quickly." He glanced at the tree branch.

"Thank heavens it was close by." She paused briefly, and then asked, "Are you all right."

"I'm fine." He motioned his head toward Mr. Jacobs and the little girl in his arms. "But we need to check on them."

"I agree." Tabitha hurried toward the blacksmith. The man was limping harder than before, but Sally was beside him, helping him walk.

When the three of them reached Nic, Mr. Jacobs' eyes were misty. "Thank you, Mr. Woodland. You saved my girl from drowning."

Nodding, Nic wiped away the mixture of water and sand still clinging to his face. "I'm just relieved I was here to help."

Mr. Jacobs looked at Tabitha and gave her a grateful smile. "I thank you for your assistance as well, Miss Tabitha." He switched his attention to Sally. "And yours, of course."

"Would you like us to help you back to your house?" Tabitha moved her attention to Joanna. Tabitha's expression softened as she stroked the girl's cheek. "We would be more than happy to help you both."

"That's very kind of you, Miss Tabitha." Jacobs beamed. "I'd greatly appreciate your help if you don't mind."

"Not at all, Mr. Jacobs. Sally and I would be very happy to." Tabitha looked at Nic, sweeping her gaze over him from head to toe. "Mr. Woodland, how are you faring? Since you have just recovered from being ill, I fear you are probably very weak right now."

His heart lightened to know she was worried about him—even if only a little. "I'm actually fine now. I thank you for your concern."

"Well, thank you for taking the time to talk with me earlier. I think you should return home and get changed before you catch your death with a chill, as well."

"Indeed, I will." He offered a small smile.

And with that, she and her maid walked Jacobs and his daughter back up the trail, toward the other man's home. Dripping wet, Nic stood and watched them until they disappeared from sight. She was right, and he should hurry home to get out of these wet clothes, but he wasn't sure he liked the way she had so easily dismissed him and then walked off with another man as if Nic had never been standing here at all.

Grumbling, he stomped back up the trail all the way home. When he opened the door and walked inside, he closed the door so hard the walls shook. Frederick scrambled from the kitchen, his eyes enlarged with surprise.

"What are you doing—" Frederick gasped. "Why are you wet?"

"Because I rescued a little girl from drowning." Nic raked his fingers through his hair, removing more of the wetness and sand.

"Oh, dear. Who was it?" Frederick hurried to Nic's side, helping him remove his overcoat.

"Jacobs' daughter, Joanna. She fell in a hole near the beach and the tide came in and filled the hole quickly."

Frederick wrinkled his forehead. "A hole? Are you sure?"

Nic rolled his eyes. "I'd think by now I'd know what a hole looks like. And since I was nearly trapped inside with her, I can assure you, it was a hole."

"But there aren't any holes that large near the beach."

"Nevertheless, she fell into one and I climbed in to help her out."

"Unbelievable." Frederick shook his head in amazement. "Is she all right?"

"Yes, she's a little shaken, but she's fine," Nic snapped.

"What has you so irritated?"

Once his overcoat was removed, he worked the knot loose on his cravat. "Before this all happened, I'd been visiting with Tabitha and hearing how much she loathes Lord Hawthorne." He met his cousin's gaze. "I really feel the need to tell her about our switch so I can at least defend myself and explain why I had accused her of murder."

"You can't." Frederick folded his arms and scowled. "If you say anything, she's going to mention it to her aunt. Not only that, but her resentment toward you will have the others in town wondering why she hates the clergyman so much. If that happens, then others will become suspicious. It's bad enough right now that someone in my parish is a thief and making it look like I'm the one taking these items." He shook his head, frowning. "Right now I need to do all I can to make myself look good. I cannot have people blaming me for something I didn't do. I cannot lose their trust. Not now. Not ever!"

Nic pulled off his shirt and wadded it into a ball. Fury raged inside him, but mainly because he couldn't do what he knew was right in his heart. Yet, Frederick made sense. They didn't need everyone in town being suspicious of Tabitha's actions.

Growling, he tightened his hold on his crumpled shirt, wringing out more water in the wash basin. "Fine, I won't say anything to her. I'm not happy about it, but I will keep my mouth shut."

"And look at it this way." Frederick moved closer and took the bunched up shirt from Nic. "During this time, you—as the clergyman—can be doing everything possible to make her like Lord Hawthorne once again."

"No, I don't think that's possible." Nic walked away from his cousin and to the window, peering out onto the street, now busy with the townspeople going from one shop to another. "I cannot think of anything that I could do. She simply doesn't like me, and discussing Lord Hawthorne only sets her on edge."

"Perhaps you can just become her friend."

Nic glanced over his shoulder at Frederick. "Friends?"

"Of course. Go on long walks with her and discuss any-thing—the weather, her life, her great aunt. Find out what she likes to do in her leisure time; what kind of flowers are her favorite, or what she likes to eat. In fact, invite her and Mrs. Burls over for dinner. Take Miss Tabitha some flowers or candy, whatever you can do to soften her heart. Gradually, she'll start to trust you and even like you."

"You are not thinking rationally." Nic turned away from the window and leaned back against the wall. "If I'm seen taking her flowers or candy, then the townspeople will think Mr. Woodland is trying to court Miss Tabitha."

Frederick laughed. "And what's wrong with that?"

"You haven't courted anyone since your wife died."

"No, I haven't, however that doesn't mean I won't eventually find a woman who interests me. It's been six years, my parishion-ers expect that I'll eventually emerge from grief enough to look for another wife."

Nic grinned out of the corner of his mouth. "Very true. There's always Miss Mildred Talbot. Perhaps I should start paying her extra attention while I'm playing you." He wagged his eyebrows.

Frederick scowled. "You will *not* do that with Miss Talbot, or anyone else for that matter! However, we aren't discussing my life. We are talking about yours and what *you* should do."

"Actually, we are discussing *your* life, because I'm the one playing you! Oh, this is so confusing." Waving his hands in a dismissive wave, Nic walked to the chair to collect his wet coat and shirt. "Nevertheless, I understand what you're saying. Let me think on it today. I honestly don't know what I'm going to do about Tabitha."

"You'll figure it out. I have confidence in you," Frederick said as he moved back into the kitchen.

Nic hurried upstairs to his room. Once inside, he closed the door and sat on the edge of his bed, pulling off his damp boots, which was no easy task. After a few minutes, he had his boots and socks pulled off and searched for a towel. As he passed the full-length mirror, he took a quick glimpse. Then stopped dead in his tracks. Staring at himself, worry washed over him like a bucket of cold water, making him colder than he already was. The powder in his hair had come completely out! His true hair color was on display.

Blast it all! Had Tabitha seen him like this? If she did, he prayed that she didn't suspect. Considering he didn't pray often, he really hoped God was answering his prayer now.

TABITHA WASN'T AN idiot, and if anyone called her one, she'd have plenty to say while stating her case.

The proof was quite plain—the man she'd spent the afternoon with and who rescued the child was *not* Mr. Woodland, but Dominic Lawrence. Once the water had splashed all over him, the powder in his hair had been removed, revealing his true colors. She now knew beyond a shadow of a doubt that the clergyman was indeed, Lord Hawthorne.

Whatever reason he had for playing the preacher, she didn't know, but at this point, she'd let him believe he had fooled her. Until, of course, she discovered what was really going on.

Tabitha and Sally had a nice little visit with Mr. Jacobs and his daughter earlier this afternoon. He really was a nice man, and eager to please. Then again, she had heard that he was searching for a wife. Tabitha didn't want to give him the impression that she would be open for an offer, but nonetheless, she did have a pleasant visit.

When she and Sally had arrived back at Aunt Clara's, Mrs. Stiles had plenty for them to do. They headed back into town to do some shopping while Aunt Clara rested. Mrs. Stiles was such a busybody, chatting with everyone who walked by. She was also very forgetful, Tabitha noticed, because the older woman insisted on introducing Tabitha to everyone she'd met last evening at her aunt's party. Thankfully, Tabitha didn't have to say anything because the others mentioned to Mrs. Stiles that they had previously met Tabitha.

By now the news of Joanna's rescue had spread through town. A lot of people were happy to hear that Mr. Woodland had saved the girl, and they oohed and ahhed over his heroics. Hearing how proud these people were of Nic grated on Tabitha's nerves a little. Mainly, because it surprised her that he would think of someone other than himself. A niggle of doubt crept into her head, and she was almost ashamed for disliking him so much.

Another part of the rescue that had the town buzzing with curiosity was when Tabitha had assisted Mr. Jacobs home and stayed in his house for three hours. It didn't matter to them that her maid was with her the whole time; these people couldn't stop chatting about it.

Tabitha couldn't believe how many people had something to say about the kind and lonely Mr. Jacobs and how he needed a good wife to help him raise his precious daughter. Although Tabitha agreed with them, she didn't want to be considered a candidate for the position like everyone seemed to believe she was already.

Their journey into town lasted longer than Tabitha wanted, and by the time they returned home, she was exhausted. While Sally helped Mrs. Stiles prepare dinner in the kitchen, Tabitha wandered into the music room. The pianoforte beckoned her to sit and run her fingers along the keys.

While she and her mother had worked for Lady Mathis, the old woman had taught Tabitha how to play. She hadn't touched the musical instrument since. Yet, memories resurfaced of those lovely, enjoyable years—before her life had been ruined by Lord Elliot—and she wanted nothing more than to see if she remembered how to play.

Sitting on a small table beside the pianoforte was a stack of music. She looked through the papers until she found one she remembered. It had been the first piece of music she'd memorized. She had played it all the time for Diana's grandmother.

Happiness lifted her heart as she opened the pages and set them in front of her on the pianoforte. She prepared her fingers to play, and slowly began. She stumbled with the tune at first, making mistakes as she progressed, but soon it all came back to her. Nobody could consider her a talented performer, but at least she could play to her own satisfaction.

She closed her eyes and was able to finish the piece from memory. Tears gathered in her eyes, but from joy, and she was grateful to have been able to play, and grateful that she had such cherished memories mixed in with those nightmarish years she'd rather soon forget. Perhaps in time, those good memories would override the bad.

From behind her, someone began clapping. Startled, she jumped and turned toward the doorway.

Lord Hawthorne, still dressed as the clergyman, walked toward her. His smile grew the closer he came.

"Miss Tabitha, you play as well as sing." He shook his head. "I definitely need your help every Sunday." He winked.

Her heart fluttered, and she cursed her weakness. Why couldn't she stop her body from reacting this way when he winked at her?

"Mr. Woodland, when will you give up?" She turned in the stool toward him. "I told you I don't perform in public."

"Such a shame that others won't be able to partake of your talent." He stopped near the pianoforte and ran his fingers across the edge. "You played that piece so beautifully. It's been a while since I've heard it. Thank you for making my heart glad."

"Thank you for the compliment." She really didn't know what to say. If she was rude to him, he'd realize that she knew his little secret. "Do you play?" She motioned her head toward the musical instrument.

"Indeed, I do."

"Then please," she stood and moved away, "play something and entertain me."

He stared into her eyes as if trying to read her mind. Uncomfortable, she shifted from one foot to the other, twisting her hands against her middle. She wished he wouldn't look at her like that. It was bad enough that his wink made her heart flip, but his exhilarating blue-gray eyes were her downfall. If she stared into them for too long, she'd melt. She must keep in mind what kind of a man he really was.

"I would love to play something for you." He moved away from her and sat behind the pianoforte.

Taking a relieved breath, she walked to the front of the musical instrument so she could watch his face as he played. He didn't need the sheets of paper, because once his fingers stroked the keys, music poured from the instrument. Through his serious expression, she could see the love he had for this song and the enjoyment it gave him while he played. A few times he had closed his eyes, but when they opened, he looked directly at her.

She found she couldn't stop watching his expressive face, and her heart pounded in rhythm with the music. He had literally entranced her. This particular piece didn't have words, but she could feel the emotion as he played. Heavens, he was good…just as his husky singing voice had nearly made her swoon last night.

Were all men like this? Some of his qualities were perfect. If only he wasn't such a judgmental rogue!

Once he ended that tune, he immediately started another one. This one she'd heard before, but she couldn't recall where. However, she did know the words, but hesitated to sing them. It didn't stop Nic. His voice caressed each word of the love song as if he meant what he sang about. Which of course, she knew he didn't.

When he started the second verse, he paused and said, "Are you going to join me this time? I can tell you know this song."

Curse him for reading me so well, and curse me for giving in so easily! She arched an eyebrow and started singing with him. Remarkably, the words came easily. It was as if she was meant to sing with him.

His smile stretched until the song ended. Clapping, he stared into her eyes. "Brava, my lovely Tabitha. Your voice melted my heart."

Pain twisted in her chest. He'd called her *my lovely*, which was the irritating nickname he'd given her six months ago. If she didn't dislike him so much, she'd….she'd… Quickly, she shook that thought out of her head. Plain and simple, she did dislike him, and she would *not* fall for his charm again!

Chapter Eight

NIC COULDN'T STOP staring into Tabitha's eyes. There for a moment, he truly believed he'd softened her heart. She enjoyed music just as he did, and he couldn't believe how much the thought thrilled him. But within seconds, the passion left her amazing blue eyes and they dulled with loathing. It would certainly take some time to convince her he wasn't the man she'd believed he was.

"That was just beautiful," Mrs. Burls proclaimed as she entered the room, clapping. "You two sing perfectly together."

He quickly stood and moved to her, taking her hand and helping her to the sofa. "You are most kind, Mrs. Burls, but I can tell you, Miss Tabitha's voice only makes mine sound better." He took a quick glance at Tabitha who rolled her eyes.

"Well, nonetheless, it was a joy to hear you two sing together." Mrs. Burls smiled. "Sit down with me, Mr. Woodland. Dinner is almost ready, and I would like us to chat awhile before we eat. I'm so very glad you accepted my invitation to dine with us tonight."

"I was very happy to accept."

Tabitha went to the chair farthest away from his and sat. No longer did she have a pleasant expression on her face, but instead, her smile looked forced. "I was just telling your niece," he added, "that she is very talented, not only on the pianoforte, but with her singing."

"That, she is." Mrs. Burls nodded.

"Did she have many lessons as a child?" he enquired, still curious to know how a mere maid could not only sing so well, but also learn to play. She'd mentioned Lady Mathis taught her, but it almost seemed impossible. Deep in his gut, he knew Tabitha was hiding something from him, and he was eager to learn the truth.

"Oh, yes." Mrs. Burls puffed her chest proudly. "I taught her a small amount, but the rest of her learning came from her mother and the lady they worked for, Lady Mathis."

He took another peek in Tabitha's direction. She'd arched her eyebrow and gave him a look that told him, *I told you so.* "Well, it doesn't matter," he said. "Your niece is one gifted woman."

Mrs. Stiles chose that moment to come in and announce, "Dinner is ready."

"Splendid," Mrs. Burls cheered. "I'm famished."

Nic stood and offered his arm to the older woman, helping her out of the sofa. Once she was standing, he turned to Tabitha and offered his other arm to her. Indecision played on her expression for a few moments, but finally she shrugged and hooked her hand around his elbow. Feeling like the luckiest man in the world, he escorted both ladies into the small dining room. Keeping in his role as a gentleman, he seated Mrs. Burls first, then turned and pulled out the chair for Tabitha. She mumbled *thank you* as she took the seat.

He sincerely hoped she was warming up to him. He couldn't understand why she would act this way around the clergyman, unless it was because he reminded her of Lord Hawthorne, the man she just loved to hate.

Dinner passed with idle chit-chat, mainly between him and Mrs. Burls and Mrs. Stiles. Once in a while Tabitha said something, but not enough in his opinion. He wanted nothing more than to stare into her eyes as the lamplight made the cobalt color shimmer like silk. Unfortunately, every time he glanced at her, she was either looking down at her plate or throwing him a glare.

It disturbed him that she would act this way, especially when he pretended to be a man of God. He also wondered if she truly knew his identity. But what hurt most was knowing that he had damaged her so much that she could not forgive him. One way or another, he had to soften her until she forgave. He couldn't live with himself if she didn't.

The meal had come to an end, but Mrs. Burls and her companion kept him at the table as they told stories of years gone by. He smiled politely, but inwardly, he wanted to return home. Frederick was having all the fun, sneaking out at night to spy on people. That's what Nic wanted to do.

Tabitha excused herself from the table. He stood and nodded to her. "Good night, Miss Tabitha."

"Good night, Mr. Woodland," she muttered before leaving.

As he sat, he noticed Mrs. Burls frowning and shaking her head. He felt like doing the same thing but refrained.

"I wish I knew what to do about her," Mrs. Burls said. "I thought she would be happy here, but today she has been so distant."

"Does she still live in York?" he asked.

"Yes, but I fear she is not happy there, either."

"Might I enquire to what she does in York? I mean, does she still work for Lady Diana Worthington?"

Mrs. Burls' eyes widened. "How do you know about Lady Worthington?"

He could have kicked himself for not thinking first. Quickly, he thought of an excuse. "My cousin, Lord Hawthorne, told me the story. After all, he was close with Lady Worthington."

The older woman nodded. "Yes, Tabitha did work for Lady Worthington, but she doesn't now. Tabitha no longer works for anyone."

Confusion clouded his mind. That didn't make any sense. How could a maid survive if she didn't work? "She doesn't?"

"Of course not, Mr. Woodland," Mrs. Stiles cut in. "She has been on her own since she discovered—"

"Mrs. Stiles." Mrs. Burls tapped her companion on the hand and shook her head. "Perhaps we should let Tabitha tell it. My niece's discovery is not our news to share."

Mrs. Stiles nodded. "That's correct." She met Nic's curious gaze. "Forgive me for speaking out of turn, but I should not say anymore."

Frustration grew inside him. What was going on? What had Tabitha discovered? Did it have something to do with what happened six months ago? Nic mentally berated himself for losing touch with Tristan and Trey after he'd come to North Devon. At least those two friends would have known what happened to Tabitha. First thing tomorrow, Nic would send a letter to Tristan and Trey, and ask about Tabitha.

"No need to apologize." He smiled at Mrs. Stiles. "I understand completely." He now couldn't wait to get home and get started writing that letter. He pushed away from the table and stood. "This has been a very lovely evening, but I must be returning home."

Mrs. Burls dabbed the linen napkin to her mouth. "I thank you again for coming to dinner. Have a good evening."

"And I hope you do as well." He bowed to her and Mrs. Stiles before leaving the room. Just before reaching the front door, he picked up his hat and cane that he'd left on the small table. He walked outside and closed the door behind him.

The night air was cool this evening as normal for the early spring weather. He bundled the collar of his coat around his neck and stepped away from the house. As he neared the largest tree in front of the yard, he noticed a movement. He slowed his gait and narrowed his gaze as he came closer. The image became clearer as the woman in a beige fur cloak moved from around the tree to face him.

"I know who you are, Lord Hawthorne."

TABITHA HAD WANTED to keep his identity to herself, but after what had happened in the music room and during dinner, she realized she couldn't carry on this farce any longer. She must let him know, and ask him to please leave her alone.

So maybe she wouldn't actually be as polite as she'd rehearsed it in her mind, but one way or another, he'd know her feelings tonight. Then perhaps she'd be able to sleep.

Even through the shadows, she could see the stunned look on his face. His mouth hung open, but no words were forthcoming. He would try to deny it. After all, he was a man who got caught and didn't want to accept his punishment for doing wrong.

Just like most every man she'd ever met. The only exception was her half-brothers.

Soon, he heaved a sigh and straightened his shoulders. "What gave away my secret?"

Her brain stopped functioning. He was actually going to confess? Where was the denial she'd been waiting for, and preparing to rebut?

Clearing her throat, she nodded. "There were many things that gave your true identity away. Unfortunately, I'm the only one who noticed since these people don't know you as I do."

"Enlighten me anyway. I tried hard to be my cousin, so I'd like to know where I went wrong."

She folded her arms, wishing she'd chosen a warmer night to confront him outside and in the shadows. "At first it was your famous wink and the twinkle in your eyes. Then this morning when you were all wet, I could tell you had powdered your hair because the white color was gone. This evening when you had called me *my lovely,* is when I knew for certain that you were Lord Hawthorne."

He smiled. "Ah, yes. I recall now how you used to scold me for calling you *my lovely.*"

"But it had somehow slipped your mind while playing a clergyman?"

"Perhaps." He shrugged. "Or maybe it was because deep

down inside my heart, I had wanted to tell you the truth but knew I couldn't."

"Why can't you?" Her heartbeat quickened. Apparently, there was a reason he pretended to be his cousin.

He glanced around the yard, then out into the street as if looking for someone. When his attention returned to her, he shook his head. "I cannot tell you out here. Who knows who else might be listening? We should talk, but somewhere private."

At first, she wanted to agree with him, until realizing that was exactly what he wanted her to do. She couldn't forget what kind of man he was and how he twisted everything around just to get his way. "No."

"No?" His eyebrows rose.

"I don't want to meet you in private. Tell me here. Now."

Sighing, he folded his arms. "Then I guess you will never know my deep, dark secret, will you?"

She gasped. "Are you telling me that you're not going to say anything?"

"Not unless you agree to meet me somewhere in private. Not only am I thinking of your safety, but my cousin's secret, as well."

"What does your cousin have to do with anything?"

"I'm playing him, am I not?" He took a step closer to her and lowered his voice. "My cousin has everything to do with this, since trading places was his idea." He came closer again. "Do you honestly believe I enjoy pretending to be a clergyman?"

She couldn't help but chuckle. "No, I don't think you would enjoy it at all."

"Exactly. So if I'm not doing it for my own entertainment, I'm doing it to help someone."

"All right, I understand now."

He came closer and leaned against the tree. She wished he would have stayed where he was when she'd first stopped him. Experience had taught her that being this close to him was dangerous. She could smell him, and the lemon tart he'd had for dessert was still on his breath. His cologne was still the same musky scent as what had been branded in her memory.

"Please meet me in private?" he whispered. "We have much to talk about."

"*If* I meet you in private, the only thing we'll be discussing is why you are in disguise."

"Are you sure?" He lifted his hand to her face and his fingers gently stroked her cold cheek. "If I remember correctly, our conversations always became a little…heated."

Warmth from his fingers melded into her skin. Suddenly, it became hard to breathe. Although she welcomed the temperature from his hand because she was cold, she didn't welcome the way it came. She pushed his hand aside. "Lord Hawthorne, please don't touch me like that."

"As you wish." He dropped his hand back to his side. "So, what do you say? Are you going to meet me or not? Or shall we stay out here shivering in the cold while we argue?"

She was relieved that he remembered about their arguments. "Fine, I'll meet you."

"Splendid. I know a small abandoned cottage up the street that overlooks the north-side cliffs. Meet me there at noon and we'll have lunch together. I'll have someone prepare our meal."

Frowning, she folded her arms again. "We are just meeting there to talk, remember?"

"What's wrong with eating while we're talking?"

She grumbled and shook her head. "Fine. I'll try to find where the cottage is located."

"It's easy, because the yard and house are in need of repairs. You cannot miss it."

She pulled the neck of the fur-lined cloak up around her ears. "Then I shall see you tomorrow at noon, my lord."

She turned, but he grasped her elbow, stopping her. He now stood straight and very close to her body. Tilting her head, she peered up into his shadowed eyes.

"Tabitha, I really wish you would call me Dominic…or Nic. While we're in North Devon, I'm not Lord Hawthorne."

"But you're not Mr. Woodland, either."

"Actually, I am, so please don't treat me as anyone else. At least in public. In private I would like you to call me by my given name." He stroked her cheek again. "Promise me you'll do that?"

Tingles shot through her because now the warmth was mixed with his cologne and sweet words. He was definitely getting harder to resist, but she must. "While we are in public, I promise to treat you like the clergyman," she whispered.

He didn't move for several moments, just content to stare into her eyes. Curse him, because his gaze penetrated deep inside her and entranced her, and she couldn't look away. She couldn't even pull away. All she could do was hold her breath and pray he didn't try to kiss her. For certain, she wouldn't be able to resist him now.

Slowly, the corners of his mouth lifted into a grin. "Have a pleasant evening, Tabitha."

He turned and walked away as if nothing happened. She grabbed the tree for support. What had happened to her knees? The cold must have numbed them somehow. She definitely needed to get inside, and she definitely needed to clear her head and put back the thoughts that should have been in there to begin with, but had somehow disappeared.

Tomorrow she would be on guard and prepare herself for his charming seduction. She vowed he would not win!

Chapter Nine

A SMILE STAYED on Dominic's face as he sat at the desk in Frederick's study, writing a letter to his friends Trey and Tristan. Six months ago when Nic had left Mayfair to come to North Devon, he'd let Trey and Tristan know he was leaving to help out family. They certainly wouldn't believe what Nic had to do in order to help his cousin.

He didn't say much in his letter, but asked how Tabitha was doing. He tried not to leave any hints that she was even here in North Devon. Hopefully, his friends would update him on her life since it was apparent she wasn't living the same way when he'd last seen her.

Last night's little meeting by the tree went well. She was the stubborn woman he remembered, but her vivid eyes gave away what emotion she struggled with whenever he was around. She still desired him, he could tell. That tidbit of information made him happier than he really should be right now. Nonetheless, he *was* overjoyed at seeing her eyes dance with uncertainty, and hearing her ragged breaths when he had moved close to her and touched her cheek.

Because of that, he was encouraged to continue his plan of softening her heart. Today for lunch he would do his best to show her the real Dominic Lawrence. Usually he was able to make women melt quickly, and although Tabitha resisted, he believed she was worth the effort. The end result would be most fulfilling.

He finished and folded up the pages, putting his seal on the outside. As he cleared up his writing utensils, Frederick walked in and sat across the desk. The expression on his face told Nic his cousin wanted a serious discussion. Nic would rather not participate since his mood was light and happy, but he'd oblige his cousin, anyway.

"I've been thinking," Frederick began.

"Yes, it does look like you have much on your mind." Nic leaned back in the chair, laced his fingers together and rested them on his chest.

"Something doesn't add up about Mr. Jacobs and his daughter's accident yesterday."

"What confuses you?"

Frederick scratched his chin. "The hole in the sand. Because of where the spot was so close to the tide, the hole should have been filled in quickly—within hours. That tells me the hole was freshly dug."

It took Nic a couple of seconds to toss this around in his mind, and by Jove, Frederick was right. "What do you think this means?"

"I'm not certain, but it's definitely unusual."

"Indeed, it is. Would you like me to check on it this afternoon?"

Frederick shook his head. "I don't think you'll find anything. Like I'd mentioned before, the hole would have been filled in by now because of the tides."

"Hmm…" Nic tapped his forefinger on his chin. "Perhaps the good clergyman should pay Mr. Jacobs a visit to see if the blacksmith or his daughter recalls seeing anyone that morning?"

"Now that's a very good idea." Frederick's eyes enlarged. "Maybe Mr. Jacobs had seen something, but isn't quite certain what he saw."

"Do you think this might have something to do with the thief we are after?"

"I can only suspect, but no matter, it's very odd and worth looking into. Do you not agree?"

"Very much." Nic nodded. "Did you find anything noteworthy last night while you were out spying on people?"

"Nothing. Thankfully, nothing was stolen from the church, either."

"You know, I was wondering about the last robbery you had. Was there anything suspicious or laying around after the thieves had left?"

"No. I've gone over that night in my mind several times, already." Frederick rubbed his forehead. "If I hadn't stumbled over the bench, I could have caught them."

"Yes, I remember you telling me. But everything happens for a reason, you know."

"Indeed, it does. However, it still bothers me to think I was so close to those men and I couldn't stop them."

"How many were there again?" Nic wondered.

"Two. Although," Frederick paused for a few seconds, "I recall one of the men falling down the back steps. Of course that was when I was detained by the bench, and by the time I reached the door, both of them were gone."

Nic arched an eyebrow. "One fell, you say?"

"Yes."

"By chance, do you recall anyone who came to church after that who was limping?"

Frederick's eyes grew large. "I don't know why I hadn't thought of that before. I'll certainly have to ponder harder about it today."

Nic shrugged. "At least it will give you some kind of clue to build on."

"I sincerely hope it will." He nodded. "You still need to ask around, especially ask Mr. Jacobs and his daughter about this morning."

"I plan on doing it today." Nic smiled. "However I'll have to do it after the noon meal. I have arranged a luncheon with a lovely lady."

"You have?" Slowly Frederick rose from the table and stood, but his stare remained on Nic.

"Yes. I shall be meeting with Miss Tabitha."

"Dominic," Frederick's voice had a warning tone to it. "You will be playing me, remember?"

"Of course I remember. However, she knows the truth now. She guessed it last night while I was dining with her aunt."

"Oh, dear. That cannot be good." Shaking his head, Frederick paced the floor, taking measured steps. "What if she tells her aunt or Mrs. Stiles? What if they notice how she treats you?" He pushed his fingers through his crop of dark brown hair that held streaks of gray.

"My dear cousin." Nic stepped around the desk and stopped Frederick by placing a hand on his cousin's shoulder. "That's the very reason I'm meeting her in private. I need to explain to her what we are doing and why. I believe that she will understand and will work with us."

"Can she be trusted?"

Nic rolled his eyes. "Of course she can."

"But you had mistakenly accused her of murder, so she must have had some qualities to make you suspicious."

"Please, Frederick, don't bring that up again. What happened in the past was my blunder entirely. Tabitha is an honest person and will not say or do anything to foil our plans, I assure you."

Frederick stared at Nic for the longest time, and he wondered what questions were passing through his cousin's head. Nic couldn't allow Frederick to question Tabitha. She was a trustworthy person, and he wished he'd realized this when they had first met. It would have saved him a lot of heartache.

Finally, Frederick nodded. "Fine, but if anything happens with her, I'm blaming you."

"I'll gladly take the blame, but nothing will go wrong." Nic ended the conversation with a nod, and then proceeded to walk out of the room and into the kitchen.

He stopped in the middle of the floor and glanced around at the cupboards. Almost two months ago, Frederick had sent his cook on holiday so that nobody would know about Nic and Frederick's switch. They still had a laundry maid do their washing once a week, but she never came into the house because Frederick took the clothes to her.

Because they'd been without servants, Frederick and Nic had struggled to learn how to cook by themselves. Thankfully, their friendly neighbors had invited them to dinner quite a bit.

Now Nic was determined to make lunch for him and Tabitha. He really wasn't very good at it, but it wasn't for a lack of trying. However, he figured he could put some meats, cheeses, bread, and fruit together. In the process, he hoped to impress her with his knowledge. Certainly she would be surprised to know he didn't need a servant for everything.

He stood in the kitchen, staring at the ice box. The bread, meat, and cheese were easy to find, but where would he get the fruit? If he remembered correctly, strawberries would be coming in season soon, if they weren't already. Frederick had a nice garden area that the neighbors helped keep growing for him, so Nic was certain there would be strawberries out back.

He hurried around the kitchen to collect the things he needed, and then stacked them in a basket. He was certain the abandoned cottage still had a table and chairs, so he wasn't worried about bringing a blanket for them to sit on.

Satisfied with what he'd accomplished so far—and by himself, no less—he grabbed a bowl and went outside in back to find some strawberries. A light wind blew from the east, making the temperature cooler than expected. He glanced up in the sky. Dark clouds formed slowly. Nic groaned. Soon, a storm would be coming. With any luck, it would arrive later in the day.

He found the strawberry plants, picked a bunch, and placed them in the bowl. Once he had enough, he rushed back inside to wash them and pat them dry. Then he placed them in the basket with the rest of the food.

A sense of achievement burst in his chest, and he smiled. This was his first time preparing a meal by himself, and he had to admit it wasn't as hard as he thought it would be. Still, he couldn't help but appreciate the servants.

Time crept by as he waited for the noon hour to approach. He tried to read a book from Frederick's library, but after checking the clock every ten minutes, Nic realized he wasn't reading at all, only skimming over the words, so he closed the book.

The more he checked out the window to see how the weather was progressing, the quicker the storm clouds formed, and the wind had picked up. It still didn't look as if it would rain on him, so everything was going forward as planned.

Nic dressed in his own clothes for this meeting with Tabitha. He not only wanted to look like himself, but he wanted to *feel* like Dominic Lawrence, the Marquess of Hawthorne. The weather would keep most people inside, and if he wore his raincoat and top hat, he was certain nobody would know it was him and not Frederick.

Ten minutes before the noon hour, he slipped on his raincoat and hat, grabbed the basket and stepped outside. A drizzle of rain fell on him, and he groaned. His first reaction was to become upset, but then he realized this would be perfect for his afternoon enjoyment. The light moisture would keep curious townsfolk from venturing outside and it would keep his lovely Tabitha inside the abandoned cottage, exactly where he wanted her to be. It would be difficult to convince her of his sincerity, to be sure, but the longer he could get her to stay in their secluded hideaway, the more he could work his charms on her.

At first he tried to act as if carrying a basket was a normal routine for him, and he casually made his way up the street toward the opposite side of town, but after a few minutes, the rain fell faster and he wished he'd brought along his umbrella. Soon, he was quickening his pace and hustling up the side street that was on an incline. The road became slick with water and his boots slipped a few times. He contemplated walking in the grass, but he realized that would only make his boots wetter and more slippery.

A disturbing thought struck him just as he neared the abandoned cottage…what if the rain kept Tabitha from venturing out, as well? It was possible. After all, what excuse could she give her aunt and Mrs. Stiles for taking a stroll on a rainy day?

As he reached the door, his hopes sank. She wouldn't be here. No woman, no matter how enamored she was with him, would go out in this weather to meet him in private. And because Tabitha was *not* smitten with him, she wouldn't be here.

He stopped on the porch and glanced down the hillside. Not one person was out and about. Apparently, he was the only fool outside at this time. Well, he'd go inside the cottage and wait out the storm, then return home. It would probably be best to eat the food he'd prepared in the basket. It would give him something to do while he waited for the perfect time to leave.

He jiggled the door handle, but it was locked. Frowning, he studied the door and the places around the porch, hoping there would be a key somewhere close by. But after a few minutes of not finding one, he shrugged. He'd try the back door and if that was locked, he'd trudge back through the rain and return home.

As he turned to step off the porch, the door handle rattled, followed by a squeak. Panicked of someone actually still living there, he whipped his head toward the opening door and held his breath. At first he didn't see anyone, but seconds later, a woman's head—still wearing a white bonnet—peeked through the shadows. Big, curious blue eyes met his gaze. Recognition must have struck her because she expelled a relieved sigh.

"Oh, it's you," Tabitha exclaimed. "I wondered if someone was trying to break in."

The sight of her calmed his nerves, and he grinned. "Break in? Like we are doing?"

"Yes, exactly." She opened the door wider for him to enter.

"How did you get in?" He walked in and she closed the door behind him.

"The back door was unlocked."

"I was about to go around when you opened the door for me." He placed the basket on the floor, and then shrugged out of his raincoat. That was when he noticed the bare room. Not a stitch of furniture. Even the grate from the fireplace had been removed. He glanced at Tabitha who was removing her bonnet. She still wore her gray rain-cloak. "How long have you been here?"

"Only a few minutes." She shook the moisture off her bonnet.

He glanced at the wall by the door. "There isn't even a place to hang my coat."

"There are a few nails in the wall right there." She pointed. "Shall we see if they are strong enough to hold our coats?"

"We can certainly try it." He adjusted his coat over the nail until it settled in place. Returning his gaze to her, he noticed her lovely long-sleeve lavender dress with a beige lace over-skirt. Once again, he was reminded what a beautiful woman she was, and her fancier clothes brightened her face more than the servant's dresses he'd seen her in before.

"Here," he said, taking her cloak, "let me hang that for you."

"Thank you." She handed him her bonnet to place on another nail. Thankfully, it stayed there.

He sighed. "Well, now. I wonder what the kitchen looks like."

"Just as bare, I'm afraid."

He headed to the other room with her following. Once he entered the kitchen, he stopped short. Only one chair was left in the room, and it looked almost too rickety to sit upon. He scanned the floor and cringed. Disgusting!

Shaking his head, he groaned. "I must apologize, Tabitha." He met her gaze as she stood next to him. "A little over a month ago, the place actually had furniture."

"Indeed?" She arched an eyebrow. "Am I to assume this isn't your first time meeting a woman here for a little privacy?"

He didn't enjoy the snicker of her voice or the accusation written on her face. Soon, he'd change her mind about him, he was certain. "If you must know, I was with my cousin, Frederick. We were visiting some people in the parish and he wanted to check this house out because he knew the man who'd lived here had moved out."

"Oh." Her cheeks stained with a pink color. "If that is the case, I wonder why the place is stripped bare now."

"I'm wondering the same." He glanced toward the stairs. "It makes me wonder if the rooms upstairs are also free of furniture."

She motioned her arm. "Shall we investigate, then?"

"Yes, we shall." He pointed ahead of him. "After you, my lovely."

Her gaze stayed on him long enough for him to see her roll her eyes. He held in the chuckle that wanted to escape his throat. He'd make sure she'd come to like that endearment.

Tabitha lifted her dress to her ankles as she climbed each stair. Behind her, Nic couldn't keep his focus off the way her dress clung to her calves and the top of her boots. Once again, it struck him odd to see such fancy footwear on her when she'd been a maid not more than six months ago. Perhaps he could convince her into sharing with him what had happened to bring her into some money.

They reached the top floor and he moved to walk beside her. As they passed each room, they peeked inside. Nothing but dirt coated the floors. The last room they stopped at had several footprints in the dust near the corner by the window.

"How very curious," Tabitha said.

"I agree. I'll be certain to inform my cousin of our findings. This definitely has me perplexed."

"Do you think the matter needs further investigation from the magistrate?" She tilted her head as she kept her eyes on him.

"Indeed, I do. If this house had furniture not more than six weeks ago, and the owner is not living here now, where has everything disappeared to?"

"It does look suspicious." She nodded.

"I agree."

"Well," she sighed heavily, "shall we return downstairs to see what we can eat for lunch?"

He gave a light chuckle. "I do have our meal prepared, but now I'm wondering where we can eat it." He led them back down the hall. "When I was here last, there was a table and chairs."

"That does present a problem." She started down the stairs first. "I suppose we could use the chair to be our table, and we'll have to sit on the floor while we eat."

Nic groaned under his breath. That option was out of the question. How could she ask a man of his status to sit on a dirty floor? As soon as the thought passed through his mind, he had the answer. Tabitha was a servant. She had sat on dirty floors before, so to her, this was a simple solution. If Nic tried to argue, would she think less of him than she did already? Of course, she would. So, in order to make peace with her, he must act as if the thought didn't disgust him.

"Or perhaps," he said, "we could keep the food in the basket and you could sit on the chair. I shall lay my coat on the ground as somewhat of a covering, and sit on it."

She laughed, and when she reached the bottom of the stairs, she faced him, folding her arms over her bosom. "You would have me sit on a chair that is broken? If I didn't know you any better, I would think you wanted me to sit on that rickety piece of furniture just to have it break underneath me." She paused for a moment, before adding, "But I do know you, so perhaps I assume wrongly."

Although she was still upset at him, he detected a glimmer of hope in her eyes. Maybe she was finally ready to hear him out and forgive him.

"If you think it will help, I shall sit on the chair first. If it doesn't break for me, then it won't break for you."

She released a tiny snort, which was most humorous.

"*You* are willing to take the fall?" Her laughter grew and she shook her head. "Oh, my lord, that is something I didn't expect from you."

"You think I jest?"

"Actually, I do."

"Then please watch carefully, my lovely, because I assure you, I'm quite serious." Keeping his shoulders straight, he strode into the kitchen and right to the chair. He held his breath as he turned and plopped his butt—as easy as he could—on the old seat. At first, the wood creaked, groaned, and even wobbled. He gritted his teeth, waiting for the moment the aged wood would break beneath him.

Waiting, he kept his eyes locked to hers. Anticipation nearly jumped out of her gaze, and the longer he sat, the more her mouth stretched wider.

Unbelievable, but nothing had happened. Sighing with relief, he raised his hands, palms up, and shrugged. "Apparently, this chair is sturdy enough—"

Suddenly, the chair shifted and the legs crumbled. In an instant, his bottom hit the ground with a loud *crash!*

Worry splayed on Tabitha's face, but within seconds, she threw back her head and laughed heartily. "Oh, Dominic." She stepped to him and offered her hand. "Forgive me for laughing, but your expression just now was priceless." Tears gathered in her eyes as she gripped his hand with her own. "I don't think I shall ever forget the look on your face when you fell."

His backside didn't sting as much as his pride, but hearing his name on her lips erased all the pain and made falling worthwhile. The warmth from her palm sliding against his, created havoc inside of him as desire weaved its way throughout his body. He couldn't understand why seeing her smile and laugh made him react so quickly.

He couldn't be feeling this way about her. Not when she had

accused him of having seduction on his mind all the time. He didn't think that way *all* the time.

Right now he needed to say or do something quickly to keep both of their moods light. He couldn't mess this up!

Chapter Ten

TABITHA COULDN'T RECALL the last time she'd laughed so hard. But it was impossible to stop now. Nic was trying—almost too much—to be gallant and heroic so far this afternoon. Although she questioned his motives, she kept the doubts to herself and allowed him to show her what he probably figured she'd wanted to see. Knowing that it nearly killed him to sit on a broken chair with the end result being on his backside on a dirty floor, was most humorous.

When he'd slipped his hand into hers, she didn't like the jolt of awareness that shot through her limbs. Hopefully, Nic couldn't feel it, or he would certainly act on her reaction. Whether or not he'd felt it, the spark in his eyes had changed. No longer were they laughing eyes, but the gray color had lightened and it appeared as if desire coated his gaze now.

Drat! She knew it! He couldn't even be with a woman without trying to turn it sensual. Just when she was feeling hopeful that Nic had actually changed since the last time she saw him in Mayfair, he went and proved her wrong.

Within a blink of an eye, the shade of his eyes changed and no longer appeared that desire was roaring through him. In fact, he looked light hearted and almost playful.

Before she knew it, his hand gripped hers tighter. Even his smile was different…almost mischievous.

"I'm delighted to have entertained you, Tabitha. But I have never enjoyed being the center of attention for very long."

In one quick jerk, he pulled her arm. She lost balance and fell on him. A surprised gasp released from between her lips once her body touched his. Before she had time to process the very improper position they were in, he made another quick move and wrapped his arms around her waist before rolling her onto her back with him looming over her.

"I figured it just wouldn't be fair for me to enjoy the dirty floor by myself." He shrugged as he rose to his knees and pulled her to a sitting position.

It took her a few moments to realize he was back to teasing again, so she hesitated in scolding him for trying to charm her. Yet, in a way, his playfulness was rather charming in itself.

She smiled, but not fully. "Unfortunately, we don't have a table for our lunch now." She grabbed the basket and pulled it toward them. "So I suppose we'll just have to use our laps as plates." Confusion creased his features, so she continued, "Allow me to demonstrate."

Tabitha opened the basket and proceeded to take out the food, placing it on her lap. Immediately, she detected a strange odor coming from within the wicker basket. Since she wasn't too certain where the smell was coming from, she decided not to say anything. It wasn't until she removed the wrapped-up meat that she knew. Silently, she groaned. The meat was spoiled. If they ate this, they would be sick. Whoever cooked for Nic and his cousin, needed to be relieved, and very soon, or the cook would have both men violently ill.

"I understand now," Nic said as he reached into the basket and pulled out the bowl of strawberries and loaf of bread, setting it on his lap. "Tabitha, I must say how nice our visit has been thus far. Thank you for being so polite and kind when I know you would rather not."

She arched an eyebrow. Funny, he should mention it, because she had literally forgotten. "It's only because you have shown me a different person so far this afternoon. Once you bring back the Lord Hawthorne I remember, then I'll return to the Tabitha you remember."

The corner of his mouth lifted. "Then I pray that man doesn't come back."

"I pray, as well." She picked up a slice of cheese and sniffed it before she dared to put it in her mouth. From what she could tell, the cheese was edible. "So tell me, why are you pretending to be your cousin, the clergyman?"

Nic took the loaf of bread and broke it in half, giving her one half. Then he handed her some strawberries. "Several months ago while I was still in Mayfair, I received a letter from my cousin. Frederick was worried about some recent items that had been stolen from the church. At first he thought he'd just misplaced them, but a few weeks later, he realized they were indeed, stolen." He lifted the bread and bit off a piece. Pausing, he chewed until it was swallowed before continuing. "A few people in his parish had discovered some of these missing items. The gossip circulating was putting the blame on Frederick. Worried that the thieves would never get caught, and eager for my help, my cousin invited me to come visit. He had a plan."

He paused again, popping a small strawberry in his mouth. Immediately, his mouth puckered and a distasteful expression came on his face. Tabitha glanced down at her strawberries. Their color didn't look very red and she doubted they were even ripe enough to pick, let alone eat. By the look on Nic's face, she had her answer. She couldn't eat the meat, and now the strawberries were too bitter. That left the bread and cheese. When she lifted the bread to her mouth, she detected another odor. Immediately, she could see why. A blue fuzzy spot had formed on the edge of the bread.

Tabitha really needed to say something to Nic who appeared not to notice anything was wrong with the food. Indeed, his cook needed to be dismissed!

"When I arrived in this township," Nic began after a few

awkward seconds, "Frederick told me of his plan. We look enough alike that we could switch roles—which we'd done many times as young boys. Anyhow, with me playing the clergyman, this gives Frederick the space to sneak around at night and spy on people in hopes of discovering who the thief is and catching him in the act." He shrugged. "That's why I look like my cousin. Everyone seems to believe I'm the clergyman, so I must be excellent at acting the part."

"I see."

"So please, don't say anything to your aunt or Mrs. Stiles. Nobody can know my true identity."

She nodded. "I won't say anything. Thankfully, you have the good fortune that nobody knows Lord Hawthorne as I do."

"Actually, Tabitha," he reached his hand and placed it on her arm, "you don't know me as well as you think."

"I beg to differ. I know a rogue when I meet one."

"The man you met in Mayfair was only after one thing from you, and it certainly wasn't what you had thought. I was desperately trying to help my friend. As you recall, he was accused of murder, and we all knew he didn't do it."

Anger rose inside of her, making her head throb. Working for Lord Elliot had been a nightmare, but this part of her life when Hawthorne had accused her of murder was a different kind of heartbreak. "And that gives you the right to accuse anyone just to ease your mind?"

He frowned. "Tabitha, it wasn't like that—"

"It was exactly like that, and you know it." Taking a deep breath, she placed her hand on her chest, hoping to calm herself before she said things she didn't really mean. "But we have gotten off the subject. If you remember correctly, the *only* thing we were going to discuss today was why you and your cousin switched places. And now that you have told me," she pushed the food off her lap and back into the basket, "it's time for me to leave."

"Tabitha, no." He grasped her wrist. His gaze begged for her to stay. "Please don't go. Not like this."

"Not like this?" She arched an eyebrow. "Pray tell, how do you want me to leave?"

"Not angry."

She tried to calm the rage building inside of her, but the more she stared into his face, the more upset she became. Not often did she loathe someone so much that she couldn't forgive him, but for some reason, Dominic Lawrence was a man who made her edgy. He always had, and she feared he always would.

"Fine." She took another deep breath. "Then I'm not angry, but I do know our conversation is over and I must leave."

She yanked her hand out of his grasp and stood. He, too, had scrambled to rise. The food on his lap spilled to the floor unnoticed by the man.

"Please, Tabitha. We really need to discuss what had happened between us in Mayfair. I haven't been the same since."

For the nerve of him! She wanted to scream, to slap his face, and maybe even kick him in the knee. *He* hadn't been the same? Yet, she was the one who had almost turned herself in to the magistrate for a murder she hadn't committed…just to save her friend, Lady Diana. Tabitha had been the one partially seduced by the rouge, Lord Hawthorne, and then had her heart trampled upon during a weak moment when she gave into passion—only to have him accuse her of killing not one, but two lords of the realm!

Was it any wonder why she couldn't trust men?

Closing her eyes, she rubbed the pain knocking against her forehead. For the past several months she'd tried to forget all that had happened. She tried to be a different person, tried to be the *lady* her half-brothers treated her as. Unfortunately, she could never feel at peace. Something was always there reminding her of everything, and building a wall around her heart.

She blinked her eyes open and looked at him. He still wore that pathetic expression, begging her to talk. "I'm sorry, my lord, but I'm not ready to discuss what happened."

Tabitha moved past him and to the front room to collect her

cloak and bonnet. He hurried after her, stopping by her side as she placed the bonnet on her head.

"Please, Tabitha, don't go. Stay just a little longer. If you're not ready to discuss what happened, then we won't. I'm confident we'll find other things to talk about. Besides," he pointed toward the kitchen, "we still have all that food. I'd hate to see my efforts wasted."

A part of her wanted to laugh, but she refrained. *His* efforts? "Lord Hawthorne, you have me confused. What efforts are you referring to?"

"Our luncheon, of course. I prepared our meal." A hesitant smile touched his face.

Now she did want to laugh, but she knew it would be rude, especially since he hadn't the slightest notion of what a shamble he'd made of the meal. "My lord, I do appreciate the fact that you took the time to fix the basket. However, I must advise you to let your cook prepare food from now on."

His eyes broadened, and immediately, she could see he was on the defensive. "Why would you say that?"

Sighing heavily, she shook her head. "Because the meat is spoiled, the bread is moldy, and the strawberries are not ripe enough to eat. However, the cheese tastes just fine."

Dejection was the emotion clouding his eyes now as his gaze dropped to the floor.

Something tugged at her heart. Perhaps she'd been too harsh. Considering here was a man who she never thought would stoop so low as to do servant's work, and yet he still prepared their meal. Obviously, he was trying to change…if only in a small way.

Placing her hand on his arm, she waited until he looked at her. "Forgive me, my lord. I'm very impressed that you did this for me." She forced herself to smile since her heart still wasn't in it. "I honestly thought your cook was trying to poison us. If I had known beforehand that you had done this, I wouldn't have said anything."

A chuckle escaped his mouth and he didn't appear as crushed

as he'd been a moment ago. "Frederick tried to teach me a few things, but it's clear that I haven't the slightest idea what I'm doing in a kitchen."

At first she wondered if he was acting. After all, she knew he had wanted to make her think he was changing. Then again, the sincere look in his eyes looked genuine. Nobody could act that well.

"I don't hold that against you," she said. "After all, you have never had to work inside a kitchen before. You probably don't know how to care for meat or bread, or when to pick strawberries."

"I don't."

"Well, for what it's worth, I'm impressed that you wanted to do this for me." She smiled, although it was still hard. She set the bonnet on her head and tied the ribbons underneath. "But I still must go. I fear if I stay any longer, the chance of us getting caught in a scandal grows by the second. That's not what a clergyman wants anyway. And since the rain has stopped," she glanced out the window, "I'm certain more people will be venturing outside."

He nodded. "You are correct." He took her cloak off the nail and held it out. "Will you allow me to assist you?"

"How very kind of you, my lord."

Standing in back of her, he helped her as she slipped her arms into the sleeves. With his hands still holding the shoulders of the garment, he moved closer to her. His breath breezed across her neck, making her shiver.

"Tabitha," he said in a low voice, "must I remind you not to refer to me as *my lord*. I'm the clergyman."

She turned her head and glanced at him over her shoulder. "But we're not in public. I promised not to call you that name when we are around other people, and I shall stick to our agreement."

It was rather difficult to move away from him, only because the warmth from his body brought a little comfort to her agitated state. Strange to think how much more relaxed she was.

She stepped to the door, placed her hand on the knob, and turned, but before she could open it, he moved behind her and stopped the door with his hand. She gazed up into his gray eyes.

"Thank you, Tabitha."

"For what?"

"For not leaving angry at me." He grinned.

His soft voice and kind eyes began to soften her heart. She couldn't have that! "Um, well...yes. You are welcome. And I thank you again for sharing your cousin's secret with me."

"Perhaps one of these days in the near future, you will share one of your secrets with me?" His brows lifted.

Clearing her throat, she shook her head slowly. "That, my lord, will *never* happen."

"Never say never." He winked.

LATER THAT DAY, Nic was back to looking like the clergyman. Although he'd ruined the afternoon meal for Tabitha and even made her upset, the day hadn't been a total wreck. He'd made her laugh, which he couldn't wait to do again. There for a little while, they carried on an amicable conversation. All in all, he had enjoyed the time spent with her and anticipated the next time he'd see her. Of course, he would be dressed as Frederick, which now Nic realized he really didn't like because of the baggy clothes and powder in his hair to make him appear older. It was rather nice to look like his young self again.

And this beard—he scratched his chin—needed to go! It would drive him insane if they couldn't catch the thief soon.

The temperatures had warmed up slightly since the rain had stopped. The first thing he'd do was to wander down by the beach and look for the hole in the sand...which of course probably wasn't there now. Frederick's worries had been on Nic's mind since his cousin had mentioned his concern.

He casually strolled down the middle of town toward the ocean. Just as he had predicted earlier, more people had ventured outside once the rain had stopped. Several ladies were shopping, and some men were gathered outside one of the local pubs. Nic only nodded a greeting to those who acknowledged him first. He didn't want to start a conversation he couldn't end quickly.

From one of the shops, a familiar face caught his eye. Miss Mildred Talbot—and without her widowed sister, Mrs. Smythe this time. When Miss Talbot noticed him, her eyes beamed and color brightened her cheeks. He chuckled to himself. Indeed, this woman had eyes only for Frederick. It was a shame Nic's cousin couldn't return the interest. Even if Miss Talbot wasn't as attractive as Frederick's late wife had been, Nic was certain the older woman had a kind and loving soul. It was obvious the woman was smitten with the clergyman.

"Good afternoon, Mr. Woodland." Miss Talbot's smile widened. "What a pleasure to see you in town."

He stopped in front of her and bowed slightly. "It's certainly a pleasure to see you." He took a quick glance around them. "Is your sister not here with you?"

"Not this time. She was feeling under the weather and so stayed inside."

"Under the weather, you say? Has she gotten terribly ill?"

"Nothing to worry about, Mr. Woodland. She just has the sniffles, and since it rained earlier, she didn't want to take a chance in getting worse."

"Oh, I see." He nodded. "Well, give her my best, and I pray you won't get sick, either."

"Why thank you, Mr. Woodland. I really appreciate that." Hesitantly, she laid her hand on his arm. "My sister and I need to have you over for dinner again. I have missed our visits."

"As have I." He smiled. "But let's wait until we know Mrs. Smythe is completely well."

"Oh yes, of course." Miss Talbot snapped her hand away and entwined her fingers against her middle in some sort of nervous gesture. "Good day, Mr. Woodland."

"And a good day to you."

He walked away, but could feel her staring after him. Daring not to turn around to see if she still watched—for fear she'd get the wrong impression—he continued moving up the road. If he kept going straight, he'd be on the beach very soon.

Thinking about Miss Talbot, he couldn't stop the chuckle bubbling up from his throat as a mischievous idea took root in his mind. Since he played his cousin, perhaps he should give her the impression that Frederick was interested in her. Then when his cousin stepped back into his role as clergyman, Miss Talbot would not be shy around him, and maybe the two of them could finally fall in love.

A loud laugh escaped him. Hard to believe that he'd gone from helping his friends solve mysteries, to becoming a matchmaker.

The closer he came to the ocean, the stronger the wind blew. The tide didn't seem to come as close to shore as it had when Mr. Jacobs and his daughter were here, thankfully. But Nic knew that finding any kind of clues as to why someone would dig a hole was probably buried deep in the sand and beyond reach. He was certain this was a mystery they would never discover by themselves. Indeed, if Mr. Jacobs and his daughter had seen anything, that would be the only assistance Nic and Frederick would get.

Even he had tried to recall that morning and if he'd seen anyone near the shore besides the blacksmith and his daughter. The only other two people out here were Tabitha and Sally. They, of course, looked as surprised to see Mr. Jacobs as Nic had been.

He reached the spot where he'd been standing when he first saw the blacksmith. Carefully, as not to slide, Nic made his way down the small hillside as he moved closer to where the hole had been that practically swallowed the little girl.

Another chill swept over him, but it had nothing to do with

the breeze coming off the ocean. In fact, he felt as if someone was watching him. Slowly, he glanced around the beach but couldn't see anyone.

Shrugging off the feeling, he tried to convince himself there was no reason for him to think this way. If anyone saw him right now, they would just believe he was out enjoying a nice walk, which was what a clergyman would do.

Now…where was that spot where the hole had been? Even if someone was watching him, he didn't want to look conspicuous that he was actually searching for something. So taking slower steps, he acted as if he was gazing across the water as he walked, and at the same time, scanned the area closely for anything that might have been left by the diggers.

So far, nothing looked out of place. Then again, he really didn't think he'd find anything. Clouds had covered the sun, even though they would move shortly, so it wasn't that easy to spot things lying around. Perhaps this was a wasted trip. After all, the wind and rain from earlier today, would have erased all signs of—

His foot caught on something and made him stumble. From the feel of it against his boot, he thought he had bumped against the root of a tree or very large bush since it was so heavy.

He stopped and turned to see what had made him trip. From out of the sand grew a strange kind of pale root. Yet, it didn't really look like a root.

Crouching closer, he narrowed his eyes, trying to see it more clearly. Just then, the clouds moved away from the sun and shone on the object. Realization struck him. Gasping, he jumped back and cursed.

There was a human hand coming from under the sand, and by the pale color of the skin and fingernails, Nic was sure the limb was attached to a dead body.

Chapter Eleven

"OH, FOR THE nerve of that man!" Sally exclaimed, shifting the basket in her arms as she and Tabitha walked toward the small, red-bricked house with white shutters. "Honestly, Miss Tabitha, I don't think that man will ever change. He'll always be so full of himself that there won't be any room for others inside his heart."

Tabitha really shouldn't have told Sally about Nic, but she desperately needed someone to talk with about it. She needed someone to listen to her frustrations. Of course, she swore Sally to secrecy. "He'd tried to show me that he'd changed, and at times, I thought he had." She shook her head. "But you are correct, Sally. Men like Lord Hawthorne never alter their lives no matter what."

Several hours ago, this was the very idea pushing Tabitha into her aunt's kitchen as she took out her frustrations on making pastries. She had needed something to slam against the cooking board, and since it was out of the question to use Nic's head, she chose to use dough instead.

It bothered her that even as much as she knew what kind of a man Lord Hawthorne was, she still kept him in her mind. Two hours of making pastries; Shrewsbury cake, bread and butter pudding with currants, and jam tartlets, she finally came to a decision. The only way to stop thinking about Nic was to replace him. Although she felt she wasn't ready to find a husband, she must. It was the only way.

She climbed the porch and stopped in front of the door. She rapped her knuckles on the hard wood, anticipating the moment the door would be answered. She glanced at the basket in Sally's arms. The aroma from the pastries they had made earlier still smelled heavenly. After all, the way to a man's heart was through his stomach…and what better way than to make such tasty morsels?

"Do you think he'll like these?" Tabitha asked her maid, nodding toward the house.

"Of course. *This* is what one would call a mouth-watering basket—not the pathetic excuse Lord Hawthorne had brought to your meeting."

"I agree." Although, Tabitha couldn't come down too hard on Nic. He really hadn't known any better.

When nobody answered the door, Tabitha frowned. "Perhaps he's not home."

Sally leaned closer to the door and pressed her ear against the wood. Suddenly, her eyes enlarged and she quickly pulled back. "I hear someone coming now."

Seconds later, the door opened, and when the man locked gazes with Tabitha, his smile grew. "Miss Tabitha. What a surprise to see you."

"Good day, Mr. Jacobs. I hope my maid and I aren't inconveniencing you, but we made some pastries earlier, and because we had so many left over, I just had to share them."

"Pastries?" His eyes moved to the basket and he licked his lips. "Miss Tabitha, you have a heart of gold. Please come inside." He opened the door wider, limping as he moved.

"Oh, think nothing of it, Mr. Jacobs." Tabitha went in first as Sally followed. "We are just happy that you'll eat them."

Chuckling, he shut the door. "If they taste half as good as they smell, I won't just eat them—I'll devour them." He motioned his hand toward the sofas. "Would you care to sit and visit for a little while?"

"Yes, we do have some time to visit." Tabitha sat on one of the sofas and Sally settled beside her.

Scanning the meager front room, she noticed it was cleaner today than when she and Sally had been here before. Then again, the man didn't have servants. It was just him and his daughter. Once more, she moved her gaze around the room, but this time, she listened for any sounds of Joanna. The little girl would be out of school by now. Tabitha didn't detect any other sounds.

"Mr. Jacobs? Where is your lovely daughter? I'd hoped to see her again as well."

His smile faltered. "Joanna has been working in the afternoons for Mr. and Mrs. Littleton as a way to help bring in extra money while I'm laid up. My leg hasn't allowed me to work for very long during the day in my barn." He shrugged. "The pay my daughter receives is not a lot, but it does help."

Tabitha's heart twisted. She knew very well how it was to help a parent earn money to put food on the table. Thankfully, though, her mother had a great employer—Lady Mathis, may she rest in peace.

"Mr. Jacobs, have you informed Mr. Woodland of your situation?"

His eyebrows arched in skepticism. "The clergyman? Why would I inform him?"

Sally glanced at Tabitha with a raised brow, looking at her as if she'd grown two heads. Obviously, Tabitha had spoken out of turn.

"To see if he knows of anyone who will be able to help you." She folded her hands in her lap. "Forgive me if it's none of my business, but I would think a man of God could assist you in some way. Also, he might know of others who could lend a helping hand until you're back on your feet."

Sighing deeply, he rubbed his forehead. "Miss Tabitha, I do appreciate your thoughtfulness, but I am a prideful man. It's extremely hard for me to tell people of my dire situation. I'm not certain at this time whether I want Mr. Woodland knowing about my circumstances."

"Please accept my apology then." She smiled. "I didn't mean to offend."

"Oh no, you didn't offend me at all, I assure you."

"Then I shan't say a thing to the clergyman, either. Unless you want me to."

He chuckled. "No, Miss Tabitha. My knee is gradually healing and I'm sure I'll be back to working all day in my barn very soon."

"That's very good to know."

Perhaps it was wrong of her to offer the clergyman's—Nic's—services, but the idea merely slipped from her mouth. Regardless, she wanted Mr. Jacobs to know she cared about him. He was a very nice man, after all. During Aunt Clara's birthday party, Tabitha had noticed him looking at her quite a bit. He had talked to her a few times, almost in a flirty way.

The man was perhaps ten years Nic's senior. Where the marquess had dark hair, Mr. Jacobs was nearly blond. His eyes were a deep brown, and granted, they didn't have that flirtatious twinkle in them like Nic's did, but Mr. Jacobs was still a fairly good-looking man. For being a blacksmith, she half expected his body to be more muscular, but unfortunately, Nic still had broader shoulders and more muscles in his arms and legs.

What am I thinking? It didn't matter if Mr. Jacobs wasn't built like Lord Hawthorne. Inside a person was what mattered. So far, Mr. Jacobs had shown her a kind and loving man. Nic...well, all he'd shown her was how seductive he could be.

"Would you like to try one of my pastries?" She pointed to the basket as Sally brought it toward him.

"I thought you would never ask." His grin broadened as he looked inside. "They all look so tasty."

He withdrew a jam tartlet and then bit into it. Satisfaction spread across his face. Tabitha smiled, relieved that he enjoyed them. The blacksmith sighed heavily. His gaze met hers and the look in his eyes told her she had gained his favor. At least with her pastries.

"Miss Tabitha, I've never tasted anything so wonderful. Indeed, you are a magnificent cook."

She laughed. "You may want to hold that thought until after you have eaten a meal I've prepared. I fear you may change your mind."

"Never."

"Well, your compliment is very kind, nonetheless, and I shall cherish it always." She stood quickly, and Sally rose as well. "I believe we have stayed too long," Tabitha continued. "I hope to see you again very soon."

Mr. Jacobs scrambled to his feet, using the crutch to lean on. "Indeed you shall." He limped toward the door and opened it. "It was lovely visiting with you, Miss Tabitha. And I thank you again for these delicious pastries."

"You are very welcome." Tabitha stepped outside and stopped. "I'll send Sally back later to collect the basket. But you had better save some of those treats for your daughter, Mr. Jacobs, or I shall be very vexed with you."

"Not to worry. I shall save her some."

"Good day," she said and turned to walk back toward the street.

Once they were far enough away from the house, Sally quickened her step until she stood next to Tabitha.

"Miss Tabitha, I must admit, I was quite surprised at you."

She glanced at Sally and arched an eyebrow. "You were? Whatever for?"

"You were being mighty sweet on that man. I don't believe I've ever seen you act in such a way." Sally giggled. "I was rather proud of you, in fact."

An unlady-like laugh escaped Tabitha's mouth, and she quickly covered it with her hand. "You were *proud* of me?"

"Yes. I do believe you are finally acting like a lady instead of the servant you've been for most of your life."

Shaking her head, Tabitha twisted her hands, keeping her gaze ahead of them. "I don't think I shall ever become the lady my half-brothers wish me to be. But I'm tired of trying to protect myself from men like Lord Elliot…and Lord Hawthorne." When Sally opened her mouth to talk, Tabitha held up a hand to stop her. "I know Hawthorne is nothing like Lord Elliot, but in the same respect, he is because he enjoys breaking women's hearts. Nevertheless, I'm moving on with my life and away from Hawthorne. At the moment, I find Mr. Jacobs interesting, and that's why I acted as I did while we were at his house."

A light wind blew from the east, flinging a lock of Sally's hair across her face. Swiping her finger around the curl, she hooked it behind her ear. "I think Mr. Jacobs took notice. You will see more of him, I'm quite certain of it."

Tabitha couldn't stop a grin from stretching across her face. Perhaps there was a reason she came to North Devon. For the first time in her life, she felt as if this might be where her future was. Since there was no such thing as love at first sight, she knew she would eventually come to like Mr. Jacobs and hopefully, he would create the same kind of havoc inside her body that Nic created whenever he was around.

Up the street a group of people were gathering. The closer Tabitha walked, the louder their voices grew. Confused and panicked faces were on all of them. Something was definitely wrong. When she finally reached the group, they were standing in front of the good physician's home.

Mrs. Stiles broke away from the crowd and hurried toward Tabitha. The older woman's pale face and watery eyes caused Tabitha's heart to lurch.

"Oh, Miss Tabitha." Mrs. Stiles' voice shook as she clutched Tabitha's hands. "Something awful has happened."

"Aunt Clara?" she whispered brokenly.

"No, dear." Mrs. Stiles shook her head. "Your aunt is still at home."

A wave of relief swept over Tabitha. "Then what is wrong?"

"Mr. Woodland found a dead body buried in the beach not too long ago." She brought a quivering hand to her throat. "The name of the person is still unknown. Mr. Woodland is in with Doctor Cope right now."

Both Tabitha and Sally gasped at the same time. Tabitha squeezed Mrs. Stiles' hand. "That is horrific. Poor Mr. Woodland."

The older woman nodded. "Yes, I can only imagine how it would be." She shivered and wrapped her arms around her bosom. "Actually, I don't want to imagine how it would be. I may faint dead away."

"As we all would." Tabitha patted the older woman's shoulder as she scanned the crowd again. Sickness grew in her stomach. Not another murder! After what had happened six months ago with Lord Tristan and Lady Diana, Tabitha didn't think she could stand it. She prayed they found the culprit soon, or she may have to rethink staying in North Devon.

NIC'S MIND SWIRLED in confusion. Not more than thirty minutes ago, the doctor had identified the body. David Griffin, nineteen-year-old son of Daniel and Lucy Griffin, had been the person Nic found buried in the sand. He didn't know much about David, but he seemed to be a good son and he helped his father out on their farm. From what Nic could see while in church, David had been a charming fellow and made many girls sigh with dreams in their eyes as he walked by.

Shaking his head, Nic paced the floor as the doctor continued to examine the corpse. None of this made sense. Two hours ago after he'd found the boy, he'd summoned the constable to have the body dug out of the ground. Immediately, the doctor could tell David had been strangled because of the bruises on his neck. Now Nic waited for the doctor to tell him more...and for the constable to see if they found anything else in the sand by the boy's burial.

Nic hadn't had time to hurry home and inform Frederick. He would certainly want to know since Frederick had known these people a lot longer than Nic. Would this be the thing that ended his and Frederick's switch? Naturally, the real clergyman would want to come out of hiding and do his job as the town's comforter. Frederick would know Bible verses to give to the grieving town. Nic definitely didn't know that.

"Look at this," the doctor said in a confused voice.

Nic stepped closer to the table where the body had been laid. Doctor Cope had on some glasses that magnified his view, and peered at the boy's ankle. Nic didn't really want to get any closer. The corpse was beginning to reek badly.

"What have you found, Doctor?"

"David's ankle was broken." The physician raised his head and met Nic's eyes. "I don't recall the boy breaking his leg at all. He never came to see me, anyway."

"Do you think it was done recently?"

The doctor bent once again and peered closer. "Actually, it looks like an old break. Perhaps a few weeks."

"That's very odd, isn't it? Especially since he hasn't come in to see you about it. I'd think the poor boy wouldn't be able to walk."

"Putting pressure on it would certainly make it difficult." Cope nodded. He glanced back up at Nic. "Have you been out to visit his family lately?"

Just as Nic was ready to ask the doctor *why* he'd visit the family, he stopped himself when remembering he played a clergyman. It was the man of God's duty to visit with the families. "If you had asked me this about three weeks ago, I would have given you an answer. I've been under the weather for three weeks, and I've only ventured out of my house these past few days."

"That's right." Doctor Cope nodded. "I had forgotten. Well, I suppose I shall leave the investigation to the constable. I pray they find this boy's murderer very soon."

"As do I."

He moved away from the physician and stopped at the window, peering outside. A good crowd had gathered and Nic was certain gossip was spreading like wildfire.

Way back in the crowd, he spotted a familiar bonnet, and under it was a delicate shaped face. His breathing quickened and he tried not to smile. Because of these grieving circumstances, smiling was not called for. Yet thinking about Tabitha made him grin more than he should. Especially since their luncheon.

Tabitha stood by Sally as they chatted with Mrs. Stiles and two other ladies. Concern etched in Tabitha's expression and tugged at his heart. He knew what she was thinking—the same thing he'd been thinking after finding David's body. Nic was tired of being involved one way or another with dead people, just as he was sure Tabitha felt the same way. Thankfully, she wasn't involved since she and Sally had just arrived in North Devon. Neither of them would have any reason to kill a boy in his nineteenth year, and they certainly wouldn't have the strength between the two of them to bury the poor soul.

As much as he wanted to go outside to comfort her and reassure her they'd find the person who murdered David, he didn't want to do it with everyone watching. He couldn't allow the town to think he was interested in Tabitha for anything more than friendship.

One by one, the people gathered out front swung their head in one direction. The constable and two of his men shouldered their way toward the doctor's office. The constable carried a bulky, cloth bag. They'd found something! Hopefully, their discovery would help point the finger in the direction of the killer.

Nic hurried to the front door and opened it just as the three other men arrived. As soon as they were inside the house, Nic shut the door.

"Did you find something?" he asked.

The constable was a short, squatty man with a bald head. He nodded and opened the cloth bag.

"Indeed, we did, Mr. Woodland." Sydney Burris pulled out two gold candlesticks as he aimed an accusing glare at Nic. "Do you recognize these?"

"Of course not. Why would I—" Nic closed his mouth as his recollection returned. He did recognize them. They'd been in the church for many weeks after Lord Hawthorne had arrived in North Devon. Frederick took special care of these candlesticks as they were a gift from the former clergyman. These were some of the items that had been stolen!

Nic hitched a breath as panic grew inside him. He must choose his words wisely, for Frederick's sake.

He narrowed his eyes and moved closer. "Actually, I do recognize these." He took a candlestick away from the other man. "These were in the church since before I took over. Not too long ago, they were stolen." His mind clicked things together and he released a gasp, swinging his gaze to David before quickly switching it to Sydney Burris. "Do you suppose young David was the thief?"

"Actually, that's exactly what I'm thinking." The constable arched a bushy eyebrow. "However, I'm quite sure he wasn't acting alone."

"Of course he wasn't." Nic gestured toward the dead body. "The person the boy was working with strangled him to keep quiet."

"Yes, that did cross my mind, but—" Sydney took the candlestick away from Nic—"that doesn't explain why these were buried near David's body. Why hadn't the killer taken these?"

Nic shrugged. "That's something to consider. I wish I knew the answers."

"Unless," Sydney tapped the candlestick on the palm of his hand, moving closer to Nic, "the killer wanted to make it look like the church's thief was dead." He threw an accusing glare at Nic.

Inwardly, he boiled. Was the constable really trying to make it look as if the clergyman had committed the murder? Frederick had suggested that all the robberies were making the town suspect that the clergyman had something to do with it. Apparently, Sydney also thought the same thing.

Panic expanded inside Nic's body, threatening to suffocate him. *He* was the acting clergyman, not Frederick. If the constable arrested the clergyman, Nic would be the one going to jail.

He swallowed the fear rising inside of him. Going to jail was out of the question. Nic was innocent—and so was Frederick. But evidence sure didn't make it look that way.

He hadn't prayed much in his life, but he was doing so now!

Chapter Twelve

NIC COULD *NOT* be hearing this correctly. Was the constable really accusing *him* of murder—to make it appear as if the thief was dead just so Sydney could stop the investigation? Impossible! Nic shook his head. He must not have heard right. Either that or Sydney must be addled. That could be the only explanation.

"Forgive me, Mr. Burris," Nic snapped, "but you cannot be serious. Are you actually thinking that *I* had something to do with this?" Taking a deep breath, he silently prayed he could hold his temper for a few minutes longer before using his fist to strike the man senseless. "Please enlighten me as to why a humble clergyman such as myself would steal from my own church only to turn around and kill someone to take the focus off me? Has it escaped your attention that you were the first person I had contacted after the robbery? Even you had mentioned—after looking around the church—that it indeed appeared as if someone had broken in the back door."

Exhaling a frustrated breath, Nic fisted his hands by his sides. "And let's not forget one of the items stolen was a statue…which by the way, would be too heavy for *one* person to carry."

Sydney's gaze traveled up and down Nic's frame before the constable arched an eyebrow. "Pardon me for saying this, Mr. Woodland, but lately you appear as if you are strong enough to carry a statue."

If truth be known, Nic could lift one of those statues, but that wasn't the point. He huffed and folded his arms. "Mr. Burris, you have gone too far this time! I haven't had to do this for many years, but I fear it has come down to this…" He straightened his shoulders and challenged the other man with his glare. "I'm calling you out, Sir. It's either that or fisticuffs." He lifted his fisted hands in front of him, ready to take on the other man right here and now.

"No more of this!" The doctor stood between Nic and Sydney. "This has gotten out of hand." He glanced at Sydney. "You know very well that the clergyman could not have killed anyone. And you," he swung his attention to Nic, "do not need to call anyone out or use your fists."

The scowl on Sydney's expression slowly diminished and he nodded. "Forgive me, Mr. Woodland. I'm frustrated about what's going on in our town, and I fear I'm accusing people who shouldn't be blamed without proper proof."

"Yes, well…" Nic folded his arms, "I think we should be working together to discover the killer's identity instead of arguing."

"I agree." The constable looked back at David's body on the doctor's table. "I'm just not handling my grief very well. I've known this boy since he first learned to walk. It was difficult to inform his family about what had happened." He took a deep breath. "From now on, I'll act more civilized and think before voicing my thoughts."

The doctor placed a hand on Nic's shoulder and motioned his head toward the front door. "And I think you need to go outside and give the crowd some uplifting words. They need to find comfort somehow, and they will be turning to you for strength during these hard times."

Silently, Nic groaned. Of all times to switch places with his cousin! Frederick was the one who could give uplifting words…not Nic. If only he could sneak home and have Frederick step back into his clergyman role, that would make things better. Unfortunately, there would be some people who'd notice the difference between the clergyman they saw a few hours ago, and know that Frederick was vastly different. Still, Nic didn't know what to say at all. He didn't study the Bible like his cousin had.

"Uh, yes, you are right." He nodded to the doctor. "Let me pray for a few minutes in silence before I go confront these people."

"If you would like to use my spare room, you are welcome to it." The doctor pointed at the door to the far right.

Slowly, Nic walked into the room and shut the door behind him. He searched his thoughts for anything that might help him, but after a few moments, he came up with nothing. He moved to the far wall and banged his head against it, squeezing his eyes closed. There had to be something in his memory of going to church and hearing the sermons. Even these past few months while he was learning to act like his cousin, Frederick must have said something in regards to those who have passed. Yet, Nic's mind drew a blank.

Groaning, he pulled away from the wall and went to the window. Immediately, he saw a familiar face that brought a sense of peace to his troubled heart and mind. *Tabitha.* She knew of his ruse. If he could get her attention and talk privately with her, surely she would be able to help him.

Trying not to draw attention, he slowly opened the window. Tabitha stood with Mrs. Stiles but they were closer to the house than before. More people were gathered toward the front of the house, and thankfully, only a few people stood this far back. But he only wanted Tabitha, and nobody else.

He waited, hoping she would turn and look toward him, but after a few minutes without her noticing him, he grumbled and stepped away from the window. Searching the room, he looked for something that he could throw at her that wouldn't hurt her. When he couldn't find anything, he found a blank paper and wadded it up tightly, and then returned to the window.

Keeping his aim sure, he threw the wad of paper. It missed her shoulder, and landed on the ground beside her. The two other ladies she stood by didn't notice, but Tabitha had, and that's when her head slowly turned to those around her as if searching for the person who threw the wad.

When her gaze was almost to the window, he waved his hands back and forth. The movement had done the trick and she looked his way. Quickly, he lifted a finger to his lips, silently telling her to not speak. Confusion creased her forehead, so he gestured with his hands for her to come to the window.

She whispered something to Mrs. Stiles before coming his way. He motioned his hands again to remind her to keep quiet. She rolled her eyes, but did as he requested. When she made it to the window, she knelt toward the weeds by the house and acted as if her very reason for being there was to pick them.

"What do you want?" she whispered without looking up at him.

"I need your help." He tried to keep out of everyone's vision. "You are the only one I can trust to assist me."

Suddenly, the crowd quieted and shifted more toward the front of the house. He couldn't see anything, but Tabitha had because her head swung that way.

"What's going on?"

"The constable is talking to the crowd."

"Good. That will keep everyone busy while I speak with you."

She looked back at him. "What kind of help do you need?"

"Since I'm portraying the clergyman, the constable and doctor want me to say a few words to the crowd and give them comfort." He took a deep breath to continue, but stopped when he noticed her laughing. He scowled. "This is not humorous, Tabitha."

She grinned, and the sparkle in her eyes turned them a deeper blue. Now he realized why he'd once referred to them as *amazing* eyes.

"Forgive me, my lord, but I happen to think this is very humorous." She bit her bottom lip for a moment before saying, "Unless you have forgotten, you are still a rogue no matter how hard you try to act like a clergyman. Tell me, do you not find this situation funny at all? What did you expect when switching roles with your cousin?"

"Tabitha, please," he sighed heavily, "I'm very much aware of how it looks, but I need help. I need *your* help."

"Why me?"

"Because you are the only person who knows my true identity, so you are the only one to ask."

"What do you need me to do?"

"Well, to start with," he scratched his head, "you could tell me what to say to the crowd."

Slowly, her smile stretched as a laugh bubbled up from her throat. He really enjoyed seeing her like this. Her soft expression brought an unfamiliar flip to his heart.

"You really don't know what to say to these grieving people?" she asked.

"As hard as it is for you to believe, I really have no idea."

Her lips curled as if she wanted to laugh again. "Let the crowd know how they can turn toward the Lord for comfort, and how He will always be there for them. All we need to do is come before Him in prayer. Let these people know that you will prepare a special sermon on Sunday that will calm their souls." She stood and reached through the window to touch his hand. "By Sunday, I'm sure your cousin will have put together a very touching sermon that will help everyone."

He grasped her fingers, and even after a few moments she didn't pull away. His heartbeat quickened. "You have helped me tremendously. I thank you."

"Well, I understand why you're doing this, and if I didn't help you, who else would? We don't need your true identity to be revealed so soon, now do we?"

"No, we don't." He stroked his thumb across her knuckles.

"I'm more confident to face the crowd now."

"Don't forget to take the Bible with you. Seeing the Good Book in your hands will always give people more comfort."

He smiled. "Indeed, it will."

Inhaling slowly, she withdrew her hand from his touch and stepped back. "I better go before someone notices."

"Yes, I agree. I thank you again." He closed the window as he watched her walk to the women she'd been standing by. She looked so lovely in her blue dress. But it was more than her appearance that made his heart soften. It was seeing her face all lit up and smiling…and the way her eyes sparkled.

Just before she reached the other ladies, she peeked at him over her shoulder. His heart leapt and his grin widened. Knowing she cared about him—whether or not *she* realized she cared— gave him the courage he needed to go outside and face the worried crowd.

Nic glanced around the room, hoping to find a Bible. Thankfully, the doc had one on the small table by the bed. Before leaving, Nic picked up the book and headed toward the front doors. With his head held high, confidence grew inside him.

Tabitha was one very special lady. She really did have a giving heart. She didn't have to think before telling him what to say, as if that particular subject had been utmost in her mind. She'd definitely make a clergyman a fine wife. In fact, Nic should suggest such a match to his cousin. Frederick would make her happy…

Something in Nic's gut twisted and a wave of sickness came over him. Bitterness coated his tongue, and he couldn't figure out why this had come upon him all at once. He hadn't eaten anything for a few hours. Hopefully, he wasn't getting sick. He placed his palm on his forehead. He didn't have a fever. So then why had he felt this ill all of a sudden? He'd been just fine until imagining Frederick and Tabitha married…

His stomach lurched again. Now he realized what had caused this. Chuckling, he shook his head. No, this couldn't be right. He didn't have *those* feelings for Tabitha. For heaven's sake, she and Frederick would be the perfect match.

Yet, the more he pondered the idea, the more he didn't want to see her on the arm of his cousin, presenting herself as Mrs. Woodland. Instead, he could picture her on *his* arm, as he introduced her as the Marchioness of Hawthorne.

He snorted a laugh. *Impossible!*

TABITHA DIDN'T KNOW who David was, but her heart still wrenched for these people who knew him as one of their own. She found her friends closer to the front of the house this time, off more to the side of the porch. Mrs. Stiles sniffed as tears streamed from her eyes. Sally stood next to the older woman, patting her arm.

All around her, the townsfolk were reacting the same way as her aunt's companion. Indeed, it was a shock that someone could murder a young man and bury him in the sand. The only two men Tabitha knew who had been murdered had not been good men at all, and in her mind, they'd deserved what fate had brought them. She highly doubted David's death was the same. She could tell this young man was well-liked.

"Oh, such a tragedy," Mrs. Stiles muttered brokenly into her handkerchief.

Just as Mr. Burris finished his speech about how he would continue to look for the person responsible, the front door opened and out walked Nic. She really should not want to laugh right now, but seeing him in his clergyman clothing and holding a Bible, just made her want to chuckle to her heart's content. If these people only knew…

Taking a deep breath, she tried to rein in her humor. If she even cracked a smile, the townspeople would think she didn't have a heart.

Nic stood against the outer wall until Mr. Burris was finished, and then Nic stepped up. Although his shoulders were straight and his chin was lifted slightly, she could see there was something amiss about him. Almost as if the color of his face had a green tint to it. She blinked, thinking that the sun must be playing with her vision.

"My dear friends," Nic began solemnly, "please know that God is with you...with all of us during this terrible time. He knows what is in our hearts, and he wishes to comfort us, as eh...um, like a..." He paused, his expression clouding with panic.

Tabitha held her breath, hoping he would finish his thought and not do anything to mess up right now.

He took a deep breath and dabbed the tip of his finger to the corner of his eye. She knew he wasn't crying, but she was happy to see he at least wanted to appear like he was grieving. "The Lord wants us to come unto Him in prayer. I beseech every one of you to keep the Lord in your heart at this time, and keep David and his family in your prayers as well. Let us also remember that death is part of God's plan, and that...uh..."

Panic tightened in her throat. Where was he going with this? He should have just shut up after saying what he did about David and his family. She glanced around the group and noticed confusion on their expressions as well. *Oh dear!* Nic was muffing this up greatly, and if he didn't close his mouth now, he'd only make things worse.

"Well, you see," he continued, stumbling over his words, "it's part of His plan. We live, we die..."

Groaning, Tabitha frowned. He was digging himself a deeper hole to crawl into any minute. And why didn't anyone do anything to stop him, or to offer him any words of encouragement? She couldn't be the only person who was embarrassed for him right now. Was she?

Clearing her throat loudly, she moved toward him—which thankfully, was only five steps away. Those close around her turned their heads and watched her as she stood beside their clergyman.

"Mr. Woodland," she frowned and stroked his arm, "we know what you mean. We shall keep praying for David's family."

"Uh, yes." He nodded, dabbing his finger to the invisible moisture in his eyes. "Forgive me," he said louder, "I'm very distraught over all of this. I suggest we all return to our homes to be with our families. I assure you I will be able to comfort you better on Sunday."

Relief washed over the faces of the townspeople as they turned and headed back to their houses. When Tabitha met Nic's gaze, he also appeared relieved, but there was something else in his eyes that she couldn't quite put a name to. He looked grateful, but it was more than that.

"You saved me again," he whispered and squeezed her hand. "I don't know how to thank you."

"Well, I knew that if I didn't do something, you would be showing them who you truly are sooner than planned." She pulled away, but kept her gaze locked with his as she stepped toward Mrs. Stiles and Sally who still waited for her. "And do me a favor?" she asked quietly.

"Anything for you."

Her heart tripped, making her stomach flutter. She really wished he wouldn't say things like that, especially because he didn't mean them. "Please listen more carefully to your cousin's sermons. I fear you have a lot to learn about playing a man of the cloth."

He smiled and winked. "You don't know the half of it."

"Yes, I do." She nodded, and then finally turned her attention to her maid and Mrs. Stiles.

They waited for her until she reached them, and then without a word, they turned toward the lane leading to Aunt Clara's home. The further away she walked, the more she wanted to peek over her shoulder to see if he was still watching her. Yet, she could feel his gaze upon her as if it had a touch all its own, because warmth cascaded over her back, stirring awareness inside her body. She held strong, but soon felt like screaming. Oh, drat! She must look back!

Slowly, she rolled her head and peeked over her shoulder. Sure enough, Nic hadn't moved from the porch, and his focus was on her. Quickly, she looked back at the road ahead. Giddiness danced in her chest, and she quickly scolded herself for feeling this way. Lord Hawthorne was a rogue, and he'd never change. He was trained in wooing women and charming them until they swooned in his arms. Yet knowing this didn't stop the pitter-patter of her heart from speeding up.

Blast him for doing this to her!

"Didn't you think Mr. Woodland was acting strangely just now?" Mrs. Stiles asked after a few minutes of silence had passed.

"Yes, I did," Tabitha answered. "But I think he's still in shock for finding David's body in the sand."

"Oh, that poor man." Mrs. Stiles dabbed the handkerchief to her wet eyes. "And poor David. What could possibly have happened to make someone want to murder such a kind boy?"

Sally shook her head. "I was thinking the same thing."

"I'm certain," Tabitha added, "that the constable will find the killer soon."

Mrs. Stiles' hand fluttered to her throat. "But it's unsettling to know there is a madman running around our town. What if he's not satisfied with killing one person? What if he wants more?"

"Now, now." Tabitha rubbed the older woman's arm. "Don't work yourself into a dither. Unless we know what really happened, we cannot come to these kinds of conclusions. It will make us sick if we ponder on it for too long."

"Yes, you are right, of course." Mrs. Stiles turned to Sally. "Perhaps we should make a meal and take it to the Griffin family tonight."

"Indeed, we shall." Tabitha hooked her hand around the older woman. "Cooking has always made me feel better."

"Oh, you are such a joy." Mrs. Stiles smiled at her. "I probably shouldn't say this, but I hope you never leave North Devon. I have grown fond of our times together. I was just telling your aunt earlier today that we need to find you a man to marry here in town so you will never leave us."

Tabitha chuckled, even though she really didn't like that her aunt and companion were playing matchmaker. But hadn't she been thinking about marriage as well, which is why she took that basket to Mr. Jacobs?

"In fact," Mrs. Stiles continued, "I have been noticing how much attention Mr. Woodland has been giving you. And just a few minutes ago," she motioned her head toward the doctor's office, "he was looking at you differently."

"Differently?" Panic welled in Tabitha's chest once again. "How so?"

"There was a certain twinkle in his eyes when you were talking to him." Mrs. Stiles giggled. "I think he's sweet on you."

Flipping her hand through the air, Tabitha released an awkward laugh. "No, he's not. He's kind to everyone he talks to."

"True, he is, but his eyes have never twinkled before." The older woman tilted her head, studying Tabitha a little closer. "He would be a very good husband. Any woman would be lucky to have him."

Tabitha resisted rolling her eyes. If Mrs. Stiles only knew that the wolf in sheep's clothing was really Lord Hawthorne...London's most eligible rogue.

"I think I shall talk to your aunt about having him over for supper again. After all, he's lonely, and you're lonely..." She nodded. "Yes, the two of you would suit perfectly."

Tabitha's heart sank. She couldn't have two old women doing *that*. But what kind of excuse could she give Aunt Clara, especially if Mrs. Stiles convinced her aunt that Mr. Woodland was a match made in heaven?

Chapter Thirteen

H EAVINESS WEIGHED ON Nic's chest, but then so did relief. Church was over now, and he headed back to Frederick's house. Although Nic felt he'd memorized his cousin's sermon well enough, it definitely drained him and made him want to sleep the remainder of the day. After all, didn't the Lord say that Sunday was a day of *rest*?

He opened the door and walked in, closing it behind him. As he shrugged out of his raincoat, a voice from the corner of the room startled him.

"Splendid sermon, if I must say." Frederick walked up to Nic and clapped him on the shoulder.

Confused, Nic arched an eyebrow at his cousin. "You were there? I thought you'd be sleeping."

"I shall sleep soon enough."

"Where were you? I didn't see you."

"I hid in the back classroom. Don't you think I want to make sure you are presenting yourself as a man of God?"

Nic rolled his eyes and carried his coat to the fireplace, hanging it on a nearby chair to dry. Today's weather was horrendous before church, and it surprised him to see so many people in attendance. Nevertheless, he was grateful they had turned out for the sermon his cousin had prepared. They needed the uplifting words of comfort.

"Of course I'm representing you well enough. Why do you continue to have doubts?" Nic walked into the kitchen to fix himself some tea. "Have I not succeeded in proving I can play your role?"

Frederick followed. "Actually, there were a few times you stumbled."

"Yes, and I picked myself up, didn't I?" Nic snapped.

Frederick chuckled. "Only when someone saved you."

Nic stood by the counter and stared out the window. The rain pelted the glass pane, creating a relaxing rhythm. Indeed, someone had saved him, and that one act of selflessness had warmed his heart so much he was beginning to have different feelings about Tabitha.

For three days, he'd tried to convince himself he was just grateful for Tabitha's help, and nothing else. But in the back of his mind, he knew it to be different. Had he actually come to care for the servant woman who lived a different lifestyle? He still hadn't heard from Trey or Tristan to discover why Tabitha had changed her status, but she certainly didn't act like a servant any longer. Not that she ever had. From their first day of meeting, he could see she was far too bold to be a servant. In fact, her boldness was what captured his attention. Well…that, and her beauty, of course.

Now it didn't matter about her station in life. He had indeed come to care for her, and he couldn't shake the feeling no matter how hard he tried. She was the last thing on his mind when he fell asleep at night, and she was the first thing he thought about when he awoke. Out of all the women he'd charmed over the years, none of them had taken up residence in his mind quite like Tabitha had.

Another thing that bothered him was knowing she resembled someone he knew. Sometimes her smile would have a familiar tilt to it, or her eyes would gleam in a certain way that made him think he might know her family. If he could only figure this out, perhaps then he'd know why she didn't act like a servant any longer. Maybe her family did have noble blood running through their veins. That would explain why she acted the way she did sometimes.

The constant rattle of Frederick's voice pulled Nic out of his thoughts. He quickly concentrated on what his cousin was talking about now. Never had he known another man who jabbered so much.

Nic lit the stove and placed the tea kettle on top. "Tell me you have discovered some clues," he said over his shoulder. "Shouldn't you have found something by now?"

Groaning, Frederick plopped down in a chair as a frown claimed his expression. "The only thing I have discovered is that there are many townsfolk who aren't on the up and up. Some lead double lives." He pushed his fingers through his hair. "Unfortunately, this discovery hasn't led me to the true thief."

"What about David?" Nic asked. "Do you think he was really part of the robbery?"

"Deep down in my heart, I don't think he was. I'm beginning to understand why the constable said what he had about David's death covering up the truth. I honestly think that whoever the culprit is, killed David—for some unknown reason—and then buried an item of what had been stolen to make the constable believe he was the one responsible."

"Indeed, this case is most baffling." Leaning against the counter, he folded his arms. "But I'm surprised you haven't found even one little clue yet."

Frederick shook his head. "Don't get me wrong. I have found dozens of clues, but because I have discovered so many, this has confused me more. I don't want to be making accusations before I know for certain if that person is the thief."

"I understand completely." Would Nic ever forget when he'd wrongly accused Tabitha of murder? "But I also know because of David's death, these people need you." He took the kettle of water and poured the hot liquid into a teacup.

"I have just the thing for you." Frederick tapped his finger against his chin. "There is a book in my study that will help you sympathize with these people more. I'll go get it." He stood and moved toward the kitchen door.

"But Frederick, *you* are the clergyman. They need *you!*" He didn't want to admit that playing the clergyman's role had become boring. He was eager to step back into Lord Hawthorne's boots again.

Frederick stopped at the door and met Nic's gaze over his shoulder. "Have patience, my dear cousin. Our charade will soon come to an end, but not before we find the true thief. With any luck, it'll be the same person who killed David." He walked out of the door.

Nic fixed his tea and sat at the table. Once again, his vision blurred as a stare took over. Anger swirled inside of him, looking for a way out. He had agreed to help his cousin, but because things were worse, he felt it was time to find the thief a different way. Perhaps they should try to set a trap. All he knew was that he wasn't qualified to assist the grieving townsfolk in their time of need.

The clergyman's lifestyle was quite dull. Of course, the rain lately had kept him from getting out and asking around, and now with the murder, it might be harder than before to dig into people's minds.

Grumbling, he massaged his head. It aggravated him that he couldn't be himself, except around his cousin. He couldn't even be himself around Tabitha, because his charming personality seemed to turn her away. In fact, she'd been nicer to him when he was the clergyman.

He felt torn, knowing he should help his cousin because he made a promise, but at the same time, he wanted time to be himself to just breathe. The old Nic screamed inside of him to get out and do something enjoyable. Even playing a good game of cards would be nice. But Frederick wouldn't allow that, saying that a card game was one of Satan's tools in corrupting good people.

"Here it is." Frederick brought the book to Nic and placed it on the table. "Read this and it will help you know what to say when the occasion arises."

Nic sighed in frustration. "One more week, Frederick. That's all I can handle is one more week."

His cousin scowled and shook his head. "You cannot push me. I'm doing everything I can to find the right person."

"Exactly, which means that after one more week is over and you still don't have enough evidence to have someone arrested, then there's nothing more you can do and we must bring this charade to an end."

Huffing, Frederick stormed toward the door. Just as he reached it, he snapped, "I'll think about it."

"Where are you going?"

"To my room to sleep."

Nic jumped to his feet, knocking the chair over. "How can you accomplish thinking this over if you're sleeping?"

His cousin didn't answer, just continued hurrying up the hall and up the stairs. Nic grumbled and propped his chair back in place before sitting and finishing his tea. He glanced at the book. *Dealing with Grief.* Nic rolled his eyes. He wasn't in the mood to read a book like this. For certain, reading this would put him to sleep quickly.

He was wise to give his cousin one week to fix things. But now Nic even wondered if a week was too long. He'd go insane from living this kind of life before the seven days were up, he just knew it!

TABITHA HAD BEEN surprised to see how many people attended church today because of the heavy rain. But what shocked her even more was hearing Mr. Woodland's sermon, which happened to be very spiritual and moving. Tabitha knew it was because Nic's cousin had written it. But she was happy to see Nic delivering the speech with confidence and empathy.

Aunt Clara and Mrs. Stiles had mentioned a few times during church that Mr. Woodland looked at Tabitha a little differently than he had the other single women in the congregation. Although she didn't want to believe it, as she had studied him during the sermon, and especially afterward when he mingled with the townspeople, Tabitha noticed his gaze kept wandering back to her, and sure enough, his eyes lit up with that familiar twinkle.

Once again, this action had made her heart leap, which in turn made her upset. Hadn't she talked to him about this already? Perhaps she needed to be a little more stern and forceful. She did *not* want him charming her. It might be different if she knew his feelings were sincere, but they were not. Rogues only had one purpose, and that was to win a girl's heart. Once they had accomplished this—and of course, having their wicked way with them—they'd move on to the next innocent soul.

Tabitha sat on one of her aunt's cushioned chairs by the window, and watched as the rain soaked the land. Aunt Clara and Mrs. Stiles were taking their customary Sunday afternoon naps, and Tabitha was bored out of her mind. Sally kept herself busy in her room with writing letters to her family, and Tabitha didn't want to bother her.

Reading a book was impossible, only because after a few paragraphs, visions of Nic popped into her head. She didn't want to enjoy the way he'd gazed at her with such longing, and the way he'd winked that made her heart skip a beat. She especially didn't want to delight in the way his touch had warmed her body and made her want more of his sweet attention.

Grumbling, she punched her fist into the armrest. There was no way around it. She must visit him today and let him know to cease this insanity at once! Especially since some of her aunt's friends in church had also noticed and were encouraging Tabitha to flirt with the clergyman.

The rain had eased up slightly in the past few minutes, so now was a good time to take her walk to his house. She quickly slipped on her light gray pelisse before throwing her raincoat over her shoulders. Lastly, she placed on her bonnet and tied the ribbons tightly beneath her chin. Before she left the house, she took one of Mrs. Stiles' umbrellas.

As she hurried down the street, she was vastly relieved to see that people had kept to their homes this afternoon. Just like before, she didn't need anyone getting suspicious of why she was visiting the clergyman.

She finally arrived at his house, and quickly knocked on the door. When Nic opened it, his eyes widened in disbelief. Within seconds, he scanned the street in front of the house before, gesturing with his hand for her to enter. Once inside, he closed the door behind her.

"What are you doing here?" he asked as he took the umbrella from her and hung it next to the fireplace.

"I needed to talk to you about something important." She handed her raincoat to him and he hung it next to his. She glanced around the room, listening for any more voices. "Is your cousin here?"

"Yes, but he's upstairs in his room resting."

His gaze moved to her bonnet, and he touched the brim of the hat. "Why don't you remove this and I'll sit it on the hearth. It looks a little damp."

"Yes, it is." She loosened the ribbons and lifted it off her head. "The rain fell at an angle today and I almost couldn't keep it off my face even with the umbrella's help."

He took the hat from her and placed it where he had promised. When he faced her again, his attention moved over her pelisse and lavender dress. The color of his eyes softened quite a bit and a relaxed smile touched his face. As always when he did this, her heart reacted, fluttering in her chest.

Scowling, she pointed her finger at him. "This is the reason I need to talk to you."

His forehead creased in confusion. "Because of your finger?"

"No, because of the way you look at me."

The lines smoothed out in his expression. "Pardon me? You want to talk to me because of the way I *look* at you?"

"Yes." She nodded once. "People are noticing, my lord. They see that you're looking at me differently than you do other women."

Chuckling, he folded his arms across his chest and leaned against the hearth. Curse him for looking so handsome…and desirable. Obviously, this was something he had practiced often, knowing it would make women take notice. Just for once, she wished he'd be clumsy so he didn't appear so perfect in her eyes. Inwardly, she grumbled and reminded herself that he was *not* perfect.

"Tabitha, how am I looking at you differently?"

Oh, she wanted to slap him. He really wanted her to say it? Of course he did. Men like him needed their ego stroked quite often. "Lord Hawthorne, you know exactly how you're looking at me."

"Humor me."

"My aunt and her church friends can see it as well. They say your eyes twinkle, and…um, you grin more."

His smile stretched, just as she knew it would.

"That's what they say, do they? But tell me, Tabitha, what do *you* think?"

He moved away from the fireplace, slowly coming toward her. The beat of her heart quickened and her throat turned dry. Blast it all, he's doing it again!

"My lord, this is the very reason I'm so upset." Yet, her voice certainly hadn't sounded upset just then. In fact, the volume had deepened quite a bit. "I don't need the whole town wondering why you look at me in such a tender way. You're a clergyman, for heaven's sake."

"And clergymen can't be attracted to single women?" He stopped in front of her. Slowly, his gaze moved over her face, coming to rest on her mouth. "It's hard not to look at you differently, you know." He stroked her cheek with gentleness. "Because I've been attracted to you since the first time we met."

His words, coupled with the strange feelings rushing through her, confused her greatly, and made it hard to stay mad at him. But she must. She grasped his hand, trying to move it away from her face, but either she wasn't trying hard enough or he was just too strong. Yet, his fingers were lightly touching her face. Now she knew what her problem was. She lacked willpower.

"Nic, please," she said softly.

"I love it when you say my name." His other hand joined the first, cupping her face. "There is a reason I look at you differently, Tabitha. I'm not at all embarrassed by the way I feel whenever you are near. In fact, I delight in the feelings pulsating through me."

"Nic, I don't want…this."

"Oh, but I think differently." His voice deepened. "I see a certain spark of light in your eyes whenever you look at me. My hands feel the soft quiver of your body whenever I touch you. I hear the catch in your breath whenever I'm too close."

Gently, his thumb stroked her lips. She wanted to sigh, close her eyes, and enjoy the sensations flowing through her—the ones that make her body come alive with awareness. No other man could do this to her. At least she hadn't met one, yet.

"Regardless, this isn't going to happen between us, Nic." She swallowed hard. "You are wasting your breath on me—you're wasting your charm."

"Oh, my lovely. Why do you not believe me?" He lowered his lips to hers and softly brushed them against her mouth. "I assure you, my feelings for you are real. I have never felt this way about any other woman."

She wanted to believe him, but it was so hard. Were those not the very words rogues used to get what they wanted from a woman? "No…that cannot be."

"Then let me show you."

His mouth covered hers just as his hands moved down her neck and around her shoulders as he pulled her into his embrace. A part of her wanted to fight him all the way, but that part of her seemed to have disappeared, because it surely wasn't standing in his hold right now. Against her will, she wrapped her arms around his waist as she moved her mouth seductively with his.

His lips were so very gentle, as were the stroke of his palms on her back. The warmth from his kiss shot heat flowing through her, making her heart hammer faster and her breaths quicken. The softness of his beard rubbed against her face, igniting more awareness inside of her body. Her legs threatened to crumble beneath her, so she clutched the back of his jacket. He must have suspected, because his arms tightened around her.

A sigh of delight rattled through her throat unexpectedly. He responded by releasing a groan and deepening the kiss. He kissed like a man starved for affection, and heaven help her, she answered back just as urgently.

She didn't know where the voices in her head had disappeared to, but no longer were they telling her to run away from him as fast as her legs would carry her. Instead, the voices inside of her mind were reminding her how lonely she'd been, and how she had longed to be kissed in such a passionate way that made her feel…complete.

His mouth left hers, but only to travel down her neck, leaving kisses along the way. His whiskers brushed softly against her skin. A different kind of excitement flowed through her now—one that she never wanted to end. She enjoyed the way he kissed her so passionately, she couldn't breathe, and she loved the way the palms of his hands slid over her back as if trying to enfold her tighter against his hard frame.

"Oh, Tabitha," he mumbled in between kisses, "I can't believe this is finally real." He lifted his head long enough to meet her gaze. "You don't know how long I have wanted to kiss you…hold you. You are flawless, my lovely." He placed his mouth back over hers.

Her heart soared with happiness. She wanted so badly to believe he was telling the truth. It must be because she was weak right now, but she desperately wanted his acceptance and his love. She wanted him to be the man of her dreams who would sweep her away to a world where she couldn't remember her past and where it would never harm her again.

The wild kiss sent her to that place, even if she didn't think it would be for very long. But suddenly, her limbs were weightless as if she floated on a cloud. It was then that she realized he had picked her up and carried her to the sofa. When he sat, she was still in his arms and on his lap, but their mouths had not broken apart at all.

Ahh, heaven. Could he indeed take her to a place she'd never want to leave? If Nic could erase all the pain from her past, she would do anything to keep him in her arms forever.

Chapter Fourteen

NIC KEPT WAITING for her to stop him, since that had been her habit every time he'd gotten close. But so far, she hadn't acted as if she wanted to end their passionate kiss. Indeed, this must be a dream, but he would relish in this fantasy for as long as he could.

He'd seduced many women throughout the years, and he thought himself quite good at it. Yet not once with all those others had his heart ever burst with excitement. Not once had he just wanted to hold a woman, kiss her, and…yes, even cuddle. Never had he tried so hard at getting a woman to like him as he had with Tabitha.

Several months ago she'd accused him of being after one thing…that a man of his status would never sink so low as to want a wife who was a lowly servant. He no longer thought of her in such a way. She was a woman who had been on his mind constantly. She'd been terribly abused by Lord Elliot, and Nic was determined to show her that all men were not like her former employer. Nic would shower her with love and attention, and make her feel like the most special woman alive.

As for her being his wife—he'd have to think more on that subject—but for now, he wanted her to know that he was *very* different from other men.

As much as he wanted to start doing all of that to her now, he also knew Tabitha, and taking it slowly was the best course of action. The wait would be worth it.

Breaking the kiss, he leaned his forehead against hers and sighed heavily. A quiver shook her body, but she still didn't pull away. When he finally opened his eyes and peered into hers, confusion clouded her expression. He could tell she was very leery about his next move.

"Oh, my lovely," he said softly. "I didn't want to stop. I still don't."

"Then why did you?" she asked, stroking his facial hair with the tips of her fingers.

He chuckled and straightened, but still kept his arms around her as she sat on his lap. "Because you had mentioned we needed to talk. Do you still feel that way?"

"Uh…talk?" Tabitha blinked in confusion. "Oh, yes…um, talk. We indeed need to discuss some things."

She wiggled in his arms, trying to move off his lap, but he held tight, and kept her there. "Please don't move. It feels so nice—so perfect. I don't want you to leave."

Her cheeks blossomed with color, and she shyly glanced at his chest. He wasn't used to seeing her this way. Using his knuckles, he tilted her chin up until she met his stare. He smiled and said, "Much better. Don't you agree?"

Slowly, she nodded. "I do, but it's hard to believe you share my thoughts."

As he gazed into her eyes, he realized he could stare at them forever. Whether they were lit up due to her temper or because of passion, they were still amazing, and every expressive, eyes. "So please tell me what you came to talk to me about this afternoon."

She chuckled and shook her head. "This. Us. What other people will see and what they *have* seen already." She took a deep breath. "Nic, if you continue to look at me in such a manner, people will suspect that you have feelings for me."

"But my lovely, Tabitha—I *do* have feelings for you."

The color of her cheeks darkened. "Yes, but they will think the clergyman is the one having these feelings. Unless you want the town pushing your cousin to court me...I think you need to stop this immediately."

His smile widened. "Tell me, Tabitha, are you more worried that I show my feelings or that they come from someone who is dressed as a clergyman?"

She rolled her eyes. "I'm more concerned that my aunt's friends are going to see me spending time with this clergyman, only to break his heart once you and your cousin switch roles." She took a breath. "I know the townsfolk won't like me after that."

"Ah, I see your point." Nic touched the middle of her chin. "You want to make certain people believe you are the endearing, sweet woman I know you to be."

She remained silent for a few awkward moments as her gaze slowly narrowed on him. He wasn't sure he liked her hesitation. In the past, that always meant trouble.

"Nic, I'm curious about something."

Oh, no...here it comes!

ALTHOUGH TABITHA ENJOYED the way desire hummed through her body, and the way Nic's touch and kiss could bring such havoc to her mind and soul, she wasn't foolish enough to believe any of this was real. It would eventually end. Nic would soon realize that he was just saying this to her because he was swept up in the moment. Soon, he'd find some excuse as to why he had momentarily lost his head and couldn't control the flowery words exiting his mouth.

"What are you curious about, my lovely?" he asked.

"Mainly, I wonder about your actions."

He arched a quizzical eyebrow. "My actions? Whatever for?"

"I cannot fathom why you are like this—so charming and

caring, and saying words you don't mean." He opened his mouth to speak, so she lifted a hand. "Let me continue, please." He nodded. "Nic, I've known you were a rogue even before we were introduced. You have a reputation that even servants have heard about. So I prepared myself for whatever came out of your mouth, knowing it would be a lie. Granted, you have shown me a different man since we've been in North Devon, but I'm still hesitant to believe you're sincere, since everything you do is only for your gain. Yet, just a moment ago when you could have had your wicked way with me...you stopped and wanted to talk. Now you're saying that I'm endearing and sweet, and everyone knows this. Needless to say, I'm very confused now."

He remained silent for a few more minutes before he took a deep breath and slowly exhaled. "I must admit it hurts me to hear that you don't believe me. However, I'm encouraged that you are aware of how much I've changed." He twined his fingers with hers, resting on her lap. "But I promise not to stop showing you how much I care about you."

Staring at their hands, she shook her head. "I don't understand *why* you care so much? I haven't done anything that leads you to think I'm at all interested in you."

Once more, his eyebrow lifted. "Nothing at all? The kiss you'd shared with me while at Lady Diana's cottage that one evening several months past was my first indication of your interest. And just a few moments ago you kissed me with so much passion that I didn't have a sensible thought in my head. And let's not forget," he moved his hand up to cup her face, "the time you helped me sing that song for your aunt on her birthday. Then you helped me when I was trying to give the townsfolk some comfort a few days ago." He smiled tenderly. "Forgive me, my lovely, but all of that tells me that you *are* interested in me."

Drat! He wasn't supposed to bring up those times! She released a defeated sigh. He was still missing the point to all of this—she didn't want to give her heart to a man who would certainly break it. Wasn't it bad enough that he thought of her as a servant? If he ever found out she was the illegitimate daughter of a nobleman, Nic would certainly not be able to handle a scandal like that. She couldn't even handle it. One way or another, she couldn't allow flirtation—or whatever this was that they were doing—to go any further. It must end now!

"Fine," she said. "You make a good argument, but no matter, we cannot let others notice we act this way around each other. I would rather not have gossip going around about the clergyman and Clara's grand-niece."

"Then I shall try my best to treat you as I treat other single ladies. But it will be hard." His thumb stroked her jaw. "You are so easy on the eyes and such a delight to watch."

"Please, Nic." She chuckled. "I'm no different from the other women."

"I beg to differ. They don't have your boldness." He winked as his adorable eyes twinkled again. "I don't know what other men think, but I enjoy that in a woman—mainly you."

"Yes, it's one of my worst faults."

"I think not, my dear. I don't ever want you to lose it."

She studied his eyes, and really couldn't believe how sincere he appeared. But instinct told her that this was all a front. He was in a different part of England, playing a different role. He had more freedom to act this way. If he were back home around his friends and acquaintances, he would turn into the rogue she'd heard so much about.

A portion of her heart twisted from that thought. Although she knew what kind of man Hawthorne was, a part of her wanted him to change. She wanted to be that woman who made him want to change.

When her emotions began to rise to the surface—a place they could *not* be—she forced herself to chuckle as she removed his arms still around her and lifted off his lap. Once on her feet, she smoothed out her dress. He still remained on the chair, appearing relaxed and satisfied. The gleam in his eyes and the smirk to his mouth hadn't left as he watched her closely.

"Nic, I believe you shall get your wish, because I honestly don't think I will ever be anything but bold." She straightened and arched her eyebrow. "And I'll always be a stubborn woman. That being said, I must leave now. I've been here entirely too long."

He opened his mouth to speak and reached out to try to grab her, but she moved away from him quickly, going toward the hearth where her bonnet, raincoat, and umbrella were located. As she placed the bonnet on her head, Nic came up behind her, wrapping his arms around her waist.

"I want us to meet in private again. Soon," he whispered in her ear.

As much as she wanted to give in, she couldn't. It was bad enough her heart was starting to become affected by his charm. She couldn't allow this to go on any further. For certain, in the end, Nic would abandon her and return to his normal life. Then where would she be? She'd be a lonely woman with a shattered heart.

Once again, she pulled out of his embrace as she shrugged on the raincoat. "I really don't think that's a good idea. The more we meet, the more chance we have to get caught. This is a very small town, and I don't want any gossip. I want to finally live in a place where people can get to know the real me and appreciate *me* as a person."

Confusion clouded his expression and he narrowed his gaze on her. "Tabitha, what are you talking about? Sometimes your words are so perplexing."

She took a deep breath. "I'm sure you have already noticed, but I want to start a new life—far away from my old life. I like North Devon very much, and I've been seriously thinking of staying here, which means I don't want to do anything to make these people think ill of me."

Nic took her hands in his and leaned against the wall. "Will you tell me something, my lovely?"

She cocked her head suspiciously. "What do you want me to tell you?"

"Why are you starting a new life?" His thumbs rubbed against her knuckles gently. "You're not a servant any longer, and I'm wondering why. Have you saved enough money to live on your own? Did Diana lend you some money to begin anew? Or, do you have a distant relative who left you an inheritance?" His gaze swept over her attire quickly before he met her stare again. "Your clothes are more expensive now than when you dressed as Diana's maid, so it makes me wonder what has happened in your life to make you this way?"

Her heart sank as dread passed through her. This wasn't something she was ready to share. Not with Nic. Not with anyone. The truth about her parentage still left a bitter taste in her mouth and the realization of who she really was burned her to the core.

"All I can tell you is that I'm no longer a servant," she snipped and yanked her hands away. In haste, she finished putting herself together in preparation to leave into the rainy weather.

"Will you tell me why you're not a servant?"

"No." She marched toward the door, but he was right behind her. As she reached for the knob, he pressed his palm against the hard wood, keeping her from leaving.

"Tabitha, please don't leave upset at me. I was just curious to your new lifestyle."

"Lord Hawthorne, I don't believe that's any of your business," she said between clenched teeth. "Now please let me pass."

He clutched her shoulders and with gentle care, turned her to face him. Worried lines marred his forehead, around his eyes and mouth. She wished he wouldn't look at her this way—as if he was really concerned.

"Tabitha, what has you so upset? I don't want you mad at me."

"There are just some things in my life that I don't want to discuss. This is one of them. So if you don't mind, I insist we drop the matter altogether."

He nodded. "If you wish."

"I do."

He stroked her cheek affectionately. "Forgive me for upsetting you."

Her chest wrenched with heartache. She wished she wasn't so confused. Why couldn't he just remain the selfish rogue she'd always known him to be? It would be easier to dislike him that way. Then she could just dismiss his endearing words, and not think about what those words did to her insides.

"I thank you," she said softly. "I'm just out of sorts today, and I fear I have much on my mind."

She'd realized, after saying it, that it wasn't just an excuse. Nic's attitude had caused a lot of confusion, and she didn't know what to think. Her heart didn't want to believe he'd changed. She reminded herself that he only acted this way because he was in disguise. Not only that, he acted this way because he wasn't around his friends. Nobody knew Lord Hawthorne here. A feeling of dread closed around her when she realized he would certainly turn back into the man she had known when they first met. Once he returned to his home, he would be the accomplished rogue, Lord Hawthorne.

Tears burned in her eyes, and she knew if she didn't leave now, she'd end up crying in front of him. She couldn't do that. She must remain strong and appear unaffected. Even though her heart was breaking, she couldn't let him see.

She forced herself to smile as she touched his arm. "I really must leave now. I shall see you later. I'm certain my aunt will have you over for dinner very soon."

He leaned toward her as his focus dropped to her mouth. She knew what he wanted…but she couldn't give it to him.

"Have a pleasant day, my lord," she said quickly as she pushed him aside and exited out the front door.

The rain still fell heavily, and she popped up the umbrella to help shield the water from slapping her face. Although the umbrella was helpful, it couldn't keep the tears from coursing down her cheeks as she hurried back to her aunt's house.

Chapter Fifteen

"MAY I COMPLIMENT the cook?" Nic asked as he swallowed a mouthful of the scrumptious broiled filet. "I don't think I have ever tasted anything so satisfying in my life."

Miss Talbot's face reddened, but her twinkling eyes stayed on him. "My sister and I do our own cooking," she said. "We enjoy our food better this way since we know all that goes into the meal."

Sitting beside Miss Talbot, her sister elbowed her in the arm. "Mildred, he knows this. We've told him plenty of times already."

Nic chuckled, playing along. "I certainly enjoy teasing the two of you. Of course I know you cook your own food, and once again, I'm surprised how tasty it is."

Mildred threw a quick glare at her sister before returning a much calmer gaze to Nic. "You are such a kind man, Mr. Woodland. We so much appreciate your company for dinner."

He lifted his wine glass in a salute. "Just as much as I appreciate being invited."

He sipped the liquid as he studied the two women. They were quite odd, in his opinion. Of course, he figured it was because they were such busybodies and always sticking their noses where they don't belong. Mildred still appeared to have tender feelings for the clergyman, but now Nic hesitated on trying to encourage her—for his cousin, of course. If the clergyman was going to start showing more affection toward Tabitha, he didn't want to lead Miss Talbot to believe her attention was warranted.

Mrs. Smythe offered a polite smile. "We are just so happy that your health has improved. It's so nice to see you back to mingling with the town once again."

"I'm very happy to be back and visiting once again with God's children."

"Oh, for certain." Mrs. Smythe nodded and frowned. "Especially during such tragic times such as these. It was such a shock to have one of our own murdered. Such a terrible loss."

"Yes, it was a shock," Nic agreed.

"He was such a kind boy," Mildred added. "Although, I think he might have been leading the McFadden girl to believe he wanted marriage."

Mrs. Smythe's eyes enlarged. "Mildred! Surely you jest."

"Not at all. Don't you recall how I'd mentioned last month, seeing him spending time with the Johnson girl...what's her name..."

"I believe her name is Dawn," Mrs. Smythe supplied for her sister.

The younger woman out of the two nodded, her ringlets bouncing in rhythm. "Yes, it is. Anyway, as I was returning from the market, I spotted Mr. Griffin in an alleyway standing scandalously close to Miss Johnson. They didn't see me, of course, but I could tell they were becoming very intimate."

Although Nic didn't want to hear the latest gossip, especially about a dead man, he still wondered who would want to kill David and bury him in the sand. "If you don't mind me asking, what does this have to do with the McFadden girl?"

"Well, you see," Mrs. Smythe said, "David and Sarah have been making doe eyes at each other for the past few years. Everyone in town knows it, and we all expected them to marry."

"Ah," Nic nodded, "I understand now."

"So naturally," Mildred continued in a forlorn voice, "since he was spotted with Miss Johnson, I'm certain that Miss McFadden was hurt deeply."

Nic opened his mouth to speak, but Mrs. Smythe's comment overrode his.

"But of course Miss McFadden was hurt. Mildred, you of all people know the way a woman's heart breaks when the man she loves is seen intimately with another woman. One never lives down that kind of scandal."

Once again, Miss Talbot's face reddened, but this time she lowered her gaze to her lap. "If you don't mind, *dear sister,* I would rather not talk about that time in my life."

Now Nic was beginning to understand the older—single— woman better. This was probably the reason she hadn't married. In an instant, memories flashed through his head of all the women he'd hurt over the years. He had made many women happy…yet at the same time, he'd broken their hearts. Back then, he really hadn't cared. He knew they would find another man to love eventually. Now he wished he would have been more kind and understanding.

No wonder he had such a disreputable reputation.

And it was no wonder Tabitha was having such a hard time trusting him. If he were in her shoes, he'd have the same concerns.

It was obvious yesterday while she was at his house, that she couldn't resist his charm. She felt something for him other than loathing, for which he was grateful. But it was also clear that she struggled with herself to embrace her new feelings for him. As much as he had tried to tell her how he'd changed, his words weren't enough. Somehow, he needed to *show* her. Evidently, playing his cousin's part as the clergyman wasn't enough to convince her.

Perhaps his next course of action should be wooing her like most women wanted to be courted. He also needed to prove to her that he wasn't a bad man, even if his morals had been in question most of his life. Time had changed him. Meeting

Tabitha had only changed him for the better.

"Don't you agree, Mr. Woodland?"

He was pulled out of his thoughts by Mildred's question. What was he supposed to agree on? Good grief, he should have listened closer instead of thinking about Tabitha...again.

"Uh, well of course," he stated, hoping it was what the two women wanted to hear.

Miss Talbot beamed and then focused her attention to her sister. Lifting her chin in defiance, she said, "I told you. Most men know how wrong it is to let a woman go on believing they love them even when they don't."

Inwardly, he groaned. He sincerely hoped his true identity didn't come out. For certain, he'd have these two women hating him for the rest of his life. "I think," he said quickly, "that all men *and* women should be totally honest with the people they care about. After all, that's how God wants His children to act. *Love thy neighbor as thyself.* Correct?"

Both women smiled and nodded.

Nic now wondered if playing the clergyman role had changed the way he looked at women. Well, if it hadn't before, it definitely had now. Perhaps this switch with his cousin was fate trying to tell him something.

"And what about you, Mr. Woodland?" Mrs. Smythe asked, leaning closer to him. "May I be so bold to ask when you will start looking for a wife?"

Indeed, the older woman was quite bold to be asking that. Then again, it was high time Frederick wed. Nic took a quick glance at Mildred. Her eyes were large, anticipating his answer. Her older sister kept switching her gaze between him and Mildred. It was obvious what these two matchmakers were up to.

Feeling uncomfortable, he chuckled. "I must admit, Mrs. Smythe, your question has caught me off guard, and I fear I don't know how to answer."

"It's quite simple," she said. "Do you think you will be looking for a wife soon?"

He wished it were that simple. As long as he played his cousin, he couldn't let anyone know his interest was in Tabitha Paget. "I haven't thought of it, Mrs. Smythe. Perhaps I shall turn to God and see what He wants me to do."

Both women nodded with broad smiles. "Good answer," Mrs. Smythe replied.

"Are we ready for pie yet?" Mildred asked. "I made the most delicious pie you have ever tasted."

Nic patted his stomach. "Give me another minute and I shall be ready. It would be a sin to turn down anything you cook, Miss Talbot."

She giggled like a young girl as her face flamed red. He needed to remember that he couldn't let her believe he was interested in her. He must pass out compliments to other single women, especially when Mildred was around and could hear. Maybe then she wouldn't get the wrong idea.

An hour—and a full stomach—later, Nic left the older women's house and strode toward the church. Although Frederick was keeping a close eye on the building in case of anymore thefts, Nic needed to act as if he spent a lot of time there. His cousin would have, so Nic must follow in his cousin's daily routine.

He walked inside. A few lanterns had been lit, and closer to the chapel, some candles were lit. Thankfully, Frederick did this every day because Nic would never remember.

He shrugged off his cloak and hung it on a peg by the front double doors. Silence stretched through the air, bringing peace to Nic's heart and mind. Strange to think he'd long for this solitude after the kind of life he'd led. He could only pray God had forgiven him for all of his wrongdoings.

As he neared the clergyman's private chambers, the shuffling of feet disturbed the stillness. He stopped and swung around. A young woman in a hooded cloak hurried toward him. At first, he didn't recognize her, but the closer she came, the more he realized who she was. This was the McFadden girl.

"Forgive me for startling you, Mr. Woodland, but it's important I speak with you."

She stopped in front of him and dropped her hood. Her blonde ringlets weren't wound as tight as he figured they should be. In fact, her whole appearance looked downtrodden. Sad brown eyes stared up at him, silently begging for attention.

"Why of course, Miss McFadden." He motioned his hand toward the benches. "Would you like to sit and talk?"

"Yes, that would be good."

Once they sat, she heaved a deep sigh. "Mr. Woodland, I have been completely devastated since David's death, and I needed to talk to someone."

"You know I'm always here for my parishioners."

"Yes, I know. I should have come earlier, if only to ease my sorrow, but I just couldn't bring myself to tell you…" A sob broke from her throat as she covered her hands over her face. "Oh, forgive me, for I have sinned."

Nic hitched a breath. *Sinned?* He wasn't prepared—or ordained—to help anyone who had sinned. Now what was he going to do?

"See here, Miss McFadden," he patted her shoulder lightly. "I'm sure it's not that bad. You have always been a kind-hearted, God-fearing young woman."

Slowly, her hands fell away from her face and she stared at him with wet eyes. Tears continued to fall down her freckled cheeks. "Yes, I have, but…but this time anger drove me to act out on my feelings."

A lump formed in his throat. Many thoughts swam in his head, none of which he wanted to believe. Instead, he'd be patient and wait for her to tell him her crime. "Go on."

"Well, you see, a few months ago, David Griffin and I had been talking about marriage." She wiped her eyes. "I truly believed he loved me, but several weeks ago, I saw him with Miss Johnson. I noticed the way he gazed upon her was the same way he used to look upon me. Suddenly, he was going out of his way to do things for *her* instead of me."

He nodded as his heart beat in a panicked rhythm. He prayed she wasn't going to confess what he thought…

"It hurt me, Mr. Woodland. David had broken my heart, but as much as I wanted to hate him, I still wanted to marry him. I would do *anything* to make him love me again."

"Yes, I understand." He nodded.

She licked her lips and wiped at her moist eyes again. "Anyway, I decided to confront him about his feelings for Miss Johnson. I followed him one evening and knew he left the house, so I waited for him in his barn. I knew he'd be bringing back the horse." Her shaky hand lifted to her throat. "When he returned, I stopped him. He appeared startled to see me. I could smell another woman's perfume on him, and I didn't need to ask where he'd been. I knew. Yet," she paused as a small sob released from her throat, "I still wanted him to love me and only me." She sniffed. "So I acted out of desperation." Her tears fell faster as her voice broke. "I threw myself at him, Mr. Woodland. I acted like a harlot, and…and he didn't stop me. I gave him my innocence, and he didn't try to stop me, even though he didn't love me."

Inwardly, Nic groaned. *Frederick…where are you? I can't help this young girl!* "Oh, dear," he said softly, only because he didn't know what else to say.

"When I left the barn, I wasn't ashamed of what we had done. At the time, I felt that David would do the right thing and marry me. I waited three weeks to hear from him, and when I didn't, I feared the worst. Yet, just the other day he sent me a missive, wanting to meet me in his barn at night. I thought for sure he was going to tell me that he wanted to marry me." Her lips quivered and she cried, covering her face with her hands. "But he wasn't there. It was the next day when you had found his body buried in the sand."

Nic held his breath. So Miss McFadden *hadn't* killed him? Or, had she just skipped over that part? "When you went to the barn, you didn't see him at all?"

She lowered her hands again. Tears pooled in her eyes and

streaked down her face. "No. I hadn't seen him before that, either. I only received his missive."

"Why then, are you so upset? Do you think you know who killed him?"

She shook her head. "I don't know who killed him. The reason why I'm so upset is because…because…I'm with child!"

Groaning, Nic scrubbed his palms over his face. Good grief, he hadn't seen that coming. There was no way he could help this young woman. He didn't even know where to begin. Frederick would, though. The *real* clergyman was needed now!

"Oh, Miss McFadden. This is not good." He shook his head.

"I know." She tugged on his sleeve jacket. "That's why I'm here. I don't know what to do. Please help me."

"Yes, yes, of course, my child." He took her hand and squeezed it. "But what I need for you to do is return home and pray. I will pray tonight as well, and I shall have an answer for you tomorrow." At least, he hoped he'd have one. Frederick better know what to do in this situation.

"I will." She nodded. "I thank you, Mr. Woodland." She stood and lifted the hood back over her head before leaving the church.

As soon as she was out of the church, Nic leaned his forehead against the bench in front of him. Frederick had said them switching roles would be easy. He'd said that nothing would go wrong.

Frederick was very wrong!

Another noise disturbed his thoughts and he jerked up, listening closer. It sounded more like footsteps, but they were coming from the clergyman's private chambers. He jumped to his feet and hurried toward the room. It'd better be his cousin, because he was *not* in the mood to meet up with any thieves right now.

Chapter Sixteen

N IC THREW OPEN the door and barged inside. The woman standing by the desk froze. In her hand was a piece of paper. Wide, frightened eyes stared at him. Within seconds, she sighed in relief, placing her hand on her bosom.

"Oh, Nic. Why did you frighten me so?" Tabitha asked.

His body relaxed and he breathed a heavy sigh. Happiness welled inside him, erasing all the confusion he'd felt only moments ago. She looked so lovely in her beige dress with white over-lace. Her hair was in ringlets today, and he wished he could stroke her curls as he kissed her passionately. With any luck, he'd get his wish.

Quickly, he stepped inside and closed the door. "You don't know how pleased I am to see you."

"Yes, well…you could have shown it differently instead of bolting in here like you had fire on your heels."

He chuckled and moved closer to her, but she stepped back around the desk, keeping it between them. "I thought you were a thief." He shrugged. "I didn't know what else to think of the noise inside this *private* chamber."

"Oh, that." She placed the paper on his desk. "Well, I didn't want to interrupt the meeting you had with Miss McFadden." She arched an eyebrow. "Shame on you, Nic, for making that girl think you could help her."

"You heard?" His hopes lifted.

"That was not my intention. I had come to see you, and I figured this room would be the best place we could talk. But then Miss McFadden arrived before I could make my presence known. I was just about to leave you a note." She pointed to the paper. "I'm sorry I overheard her confession, but really, it was unavoidable."

"That's very understandable. Let me reassure you, I don't plan on taking care of this. I'm not qualified to act as a clergyman. This is Frederick's job, and I will relate Miss McFadden's story to him and encourage him to take care of the poor young woman."

She nodded. "That is a very unfortunate thing that happened to her. My heart goes out to Miss McFadden."

Although he wanted nothing more than to take her in his arms and kiss her, it was obvious she was keeping her distance from him for a reason. So he must not act like the overeager lover. Casually, he sat on the edge of the desk and gently swung his leg.

"My heart goes out to her, as well. I cannot even comprehend what must be going through her mind right now. I wouldn't know what kind of advice to give her."

Tabitha folded her arms and leaned against the wall. "Really, there's not much that can be done. If she stays here to have her child, her family will be embarrassed and greatly shamed. If that happens, she'll be shunned by Society. If she wants to continue to live a normal life, she can either find another man to marry, or she can have her family send her to the countryside someplace out of the way to have the baby. If Frederick knows of any childless couples, he can arrange an adoption that way. If not, the child will have to go to an orphanage."

"You are very knowledgeable on the subject. I'm sure you have known other young girls who were in the family way without a husband."

Irritation creased Tabitha's face and she curled her lip in disdain. "Lord Elliot had impregnated many of his servants, that's how I know. In fact, Sally was one of them."

Nic gasped and rose to his feet. "Sally?"

"She was pregnant when Lord Elliot nearly beat her to death. We thought she might lose the baby, but she didn't. She delivered two months ago and gave her child to a couple who couldn't have children. Servants don't have to suffer being shunned from Society, but we still are shamed beyond belief. Sally is taking this very well, and has seemed to flourish here in North Devon. I think it's because nobody knows her."

He moved slowly toward Tabitha. Thankfully, she didn't try to get away. Sadness clouded her pretty face, and he would do anything to remove it. When he stood in front of her, he lifted her hand to his mouth and brushed his lips over her knuckles. "Please forgive me for making you relive a time in your life you'd rather forget."

She released a slow breath of air. "I wish it had never happened, but it's part of my past whether I want it to be or not. However, being in North Devon, I have felt a sense of freedom I thought I'd never have. Sometimes I actually feel normal."

"No, my lovely." He shook his head and cupped her face. "You're far from normal. You're exceptional…an astonishing woman that lights up a room just by entering. Don't ever forget that."

The corner of her mouth quirked up in a grin. "As always, Lord Hawthorne, you're saying words I don't know if I can believe."

"You can believe them." He winked.

As much as he wanted to kiss her right now, he found the courage to step back. It was hard, but it must be done. He needed her to make the next step in their relationship. How else would he know when she was ready to love him and give him her heart? "So tell me, what brings you to my office today?"

She appeared bewildered for a moment, but then blinked and shook her head. "Oh yes, I remember now. I wanted to talk to you before you come to have lunch with my aunt tomorrow afternoon."

"Is something amiss?"

Chuckling, she rolled her eyes. "I would think it was, considering both Aunt Clara and Mrs. Stiles are playing matchmaker. I warned you about this, remember?"

He grinned. "Yes, you did. So what do you want me to do about it?"

"I want you to convince them that we don't suit. Somehow, you need to make them believe that you don't find me interesting in the least."

"Oh, my lovely Tabitha." He laughed. "It would take a true performer to pull that off. Even a blind person would be able to tell how much I care about you, because I'm sure they'd hear it in my voice."

"Please, Nic." She walked to him and laid her hand on his arm. "We must do something to stop them. Have you forgotten our talk yesterday?"

"No. I'll never forget the times we spend together or what was said."

"Then you see why we need to do this."

"Yes, but I'm just saying that it's going to be hard."

She nodded. "I understand, but I want you to try, anyway."

"Of course, my lovely. I'll do anything for you."

She tilted her head, studying him for a few moments. He hoped it didn't take her long before she realized he was being truthful.

With a nod, she stepped away from him and breathed a heavy sigh. "Well then, now that I have said what I came to say, I'll be leaving."

She lifted her cloak off the chair and proceeded to wrap it around her shoulders. He moved closer and assisted. Once she had her bonnet on, she strode toward the door.

"Wait," he called out, stopping her. "Let me go out to see if anyone is out there. We don't want anyone witnessing you leaving my private chambers."

"Oh, yes. Thank you for remembering."

As he passed her, the urge to take her in his arms and hold her was strong. But unwavering, he walked out of the room without touching her. He gazed around the chapel area and couldn't see anyone. Still, he felt she shouldn't leave out the front doors. She'd been seen right away.

"Tabitha," he said softly. "Why don't you use the back door? That way nobody will see you. The thicket of trees out back should block you from being seen leaving the church altogether."

"That is very wise. Thank you, Nic." She moved passed him, then slowed down her steps as she peeked at him over her shoulder. "I shall see you tomorrow afternoon. Don't forget to be on your best behavior."

"I shall do my best." He winked.

He watched her leave with a grin. He would do his best, but he feared the evidence of his feelings would be seen through his eyes when he gazed upon her, and in his voice whenever he spoke to her. Truly, Aunt Clara and Mrs. Stiles would have to be blind not to notice.

TABITHA DIDN'T BELIEVE him one bit. He'd do his *best*? She highly doubted he knew what that meant.

Grumbling, she made her way through the thicket of trees before finding the path leading to the main road. When she reached it, she slowed her steps and smoothed out her cloak. She didn't want anyone to think she was in a hurry. If they noticed her, she prayed they would think she was doing her daily walking.

But walking made her think, and she couldn't believe the conversation with Nic, or his actions. Not once did he try to kiss her. Although, when he'd cupped her face, she wondered if he was thinking about it then. Yet, he never did. He never even said anything along those lines, either. He still hinted about his feelings for her, but for some reason, it was different this time.

The Nic she knew always wanted to convince her of his affections by using his mouth in a wild kiss.

Not this time.

Dare she hope he was having second thoughts, just as she knew he would eventually?

As soon as she thought it, her chest grew heavy with sorrow. She didn't like the fact that she enjoyed his attention, and especially that she enjoyed his kisses. She even hated the fact that he made her feel so special. But what she hated even more was feeling sad with the mere idea of him giving up on her.

She shook the thought from her head. No, he must give up on her. They were not meant to be together. He was a marquess, and she just a lowly woman who'd been a servant for most of her life until recently. Her world was far different from Nic's, and because of that, they could never be together.

Perhaps in a small way Nic had come to realize this as well. That could have been the reason why he didn't try harder to steal a kiss or to wrap his arms around her. Dare she hope that he finally realized his mistake in saying those words to her? Had he come to realize their worlds were too different?

Taking a big breath of courage, she held her shoulders straight, continuing toward her aunt's house. Out of the corner of her eyes, she saw Mr. Jacobs and his daughter coming from down the street. He still leaned heavily on a cane as his daughter skipped around him, laughing.

When they noticed her, he raised his hand in greeting. Tabitha waved back. Little Joanna squealed and ran toward Tabitha. Her heart grew warm from the girl's endearing response.

"Miss Paget," Joanna said out of breath, "it's so nice to see you again."

Tabitha smiled as she tapped her finger on the girl's nose. "And I'm happy to see you, too."

"Would you like to join my father and me for a walk?"

Tabitha lifted her gaze as Mr. Jacobs neared. He gave her a nod as his eyes gleamed with excitement.

"Good day, Miss Paget."

"Indeed, it's a very pleasant day, and now that I have seen the two of you, my day is much brighter."

Joanna clasped her father's hand. "Papa? I asked Miss Paget to join us in our walk."

He bobbed his head. "Yes, that would be very enjoyable."

Although Tabitha really should accept their offer—mainly to keep her mind off Nic—she really wanted to be alone right now. "As thrilling as that sounds, I'm actually on my way back home. I've done my walking this morning and I find myself exhausted."

Mr. Jacobs' smile waned. "I understand. Perhaps another time."

"Yes, that would be wonderful, thank you."

He nodded again. "Then I wish you a good day." Taking his daughter's hand, he turned and limped away.

Guilt gnawed at her gut, and she felt sorry for turning him down. He might not be the man who'd take away the memories of Nic, but what if no man could do that? If that's the case, then maybe she should give Mr. Jacobs a chance. From what she knew about him, he seemed genuinely nice. He wasn't bad on the eyes, either.

"Mr. Jacobs," she called out, stopping him. "I was wondering…my aunt is having a luncheon tomorrow and I would like for you and Joanna to join us."

Happiness brightened his face once more and he nodded. "We would be delighted to come."

"Splendid. I shall inform my aunt. The two of you will be my special guests."

Joanna bounced. "Thank you, Miss Paget. I cannot wait."

Tabitha smiled at the little girl. "Neither can I. The luncheon is at one o'clock."

"We shall be there," he announced with much enthusiasm.

As Tabitha headed back to her aunt's house, she realized

she'd been inspired to invite Mr. Jacobs. Now Aunt Clara and Mrs. Stiles would release the silly notion of getting Tabitha and Mr. Woodland together. When they saw how sweet Mr. Jacobs was on Tabitha—and she would do her best to be just as nice in return—the two old ladies would finally know that Tabitha and the clergyman would never be together.

It hurt to admit that to herself. Dominic Lawrence would have been very loving and attentive, she was sure. Well, for as long as she kept his interest, anyway. But in the short time they've been together in North Devon, he had showered her with affection and kindness…even if they were not going to last. Never in her life had she experienced such feelings. She prayed there would be another man out there who would show her half of what Nic had shown her. Maybe then, she could convince herself that it would be enough.

Lord Hawthorne would always be that one man she could never have. As long as she held the memories close, she was sure it would help her survive when she had to go through life without him.

It didn't take her long to reach Aunt Clara's house. Once inside, she went straight to the older woman's bedroom. Aunt Clara was propped up in bed with pillows stuffed behind her, assisting her to sit up. Mrs. Stiles sat in the chair next to the bed, reading aloud from a book. When Tabitha entered, they both lifted their gaze to her.

"Did you have a nice walk, my dear?" Aunt Clara asked.

"Yes, I did. I saw Mr. Jacobs and his darling daughter on the way, and I stopped and chatted with them for a minute."

Mrs. Stiles smiled. "He's such a nice man."

Tabitha nodded. "I agree, which is why I invited him and his daughter to the luncheon tomorrow."

Both women gasped and their eyes widened. Aunt Clara slowly shook her head. "Why did you do that when you knew Mr. Woodland was coming?"

"Because I knew you wouldn't mind." Tabitha challenged

sweetly. "Two more people for the luncheon will not make that big of difference. Besides," she quickly continued before her aunt or the companion could interrupt, "Mr. Jacobs is a lonely man. He's been cooped up in his home far too long without company. All I wanted to do was give him and his daughter a well-deserved outing. Is that so much to ask?"

Mrs. Stiles swung her head toward Aunt Clara as if waiting for the other woman to say something first. Tabitha could tell the companion wanted to talk, but hesitated.

Aunt Clara licked her dry lips and swallowed hard. "You have such a kind heart, Tabitha. Indeed, it's not too much to ask. Mr. Jacobs and his daughter may come." She met Mrs. Stiles' gaze. "Will you make sure to add more food to our list? I'm sure it won't be much trouble."

"Uh…none at all, Clara."

"I thank you, Aunt Clara." Tabitha grinned. "I shall find Sally and she'll be delighted to help you with the luncheon."

Tabitha turned and hurried out of the room, not giving the ladies any opportunity to stop her. However, she did hear them chatting in low voices, but knew not what they were saying. Tabitha chuckled. Actually, she could guess what they were saying, and she'd be correct, too. The two meddlesome old women were probably not very happy that Tabitha had ruined their matchmaking plans for tomorrow.

After looking throughout the house and not finding Sally, Tabitha wandered out back. Sally stood by the gate, gazing at the sea in the distance. She held a red tulip and twirled the stem between her finger and thumb. The closer Tabitha came to her friend, she suspected something was bothering Sally. Her shoulders were drooped, and from her profile, Tabitha noticed a frown marring her face.

Stopping beside her, Tabitha leaned against the gate. Sally straightened as if she tried not to let her see how sad Sally had been.

"Gazing at the ocean," Sally said, "is very soothing, I think. I could become very attached to feeling this relaxed."

Tabitha nodded. "As could I." She turned her head and looked at her friend. "Is something amiss, Sally?"

Her maid chuckled and shook her head. "What could possibly be wrong with staring at the calming sea?"

"Sally," Tabitha said in a motherly tone, "you know what I'm talking about, so don't play coy with me." She bumped her elbow against Sally's. "I've known you long enough to know when something is wrong."

The maid released a heavy sigh which brought a frown with it. "I'm just feeling melancholic. I suppose I'm a little jealous of your life. I wish I could find something to make my life happy."

"Pardon me?" Tabitha's voice lifted as she grasped Sally's arm and turned her. As she studied the other woman's eyes, she could see sadness. "You think my life is happy?"

Sally shrugged. "Things seem to be going well for you. Because your half-brothers are accepting you, they have helped you to become a better person. You will never have to be a servant again."

Tabitha nodded, her heart aching for her friend. "I must admit, I never thought this would happen to me."

"And now you have a handsome, wealthy man who adores you. The way I see it, you are on your way to having a happy life."

"What are you talking about, Sally?" Tabitha shook her head. "I do *not* have a handsome, wealthy man who adores me."

The maid arched an eyebrow. "Lord Hawthorne isn't wealthy and handsome?"

"Well of course he is, but he doesn't adore me, and I for certain don't believe his flowery words are sincere. It's very hard to trust that man." She flipped a hand through the air. "Besides that, he is only acting this way because nobody here knows him. When he's with his friends again, he'll turn back into the accomplished rogue we remember."

Sally's gaze narrowed. "Are you certain? He certainly acts sincere."

"That's why he's an *accomplished* rogue. He knows just what to say to make a woman swoon."

"Yes, you are probably right." Sally's gaze dropped to the tulip. "I suppose I'm still wishing for a man to take notice of me and fall in love with me."

"It will happen." Tabitha patted her friend's shoulder. "Be patient and things will happen for you." She gestured her head toward the house. "But let's put our worries aside for now and help my aunt and Mrs. Stiles prepare the luncheon tomorrow. I invited Mr. Jacobs and his daughter to join us, as well."

Sally's eyes enlarged. "Mr. Jacobs? Why did you invite him when you know *why* your aunt is having this luncheon with Mr. Woodland?"

"That's exactly why I invited Mr. Jacobs." Tabitha grinned. "Because I don't want my aunt or Mrs. Stiles to think there's a chance that me and the clergyman…" She grimaced. "No, I'm sorry, but it will not happen that way. Not if I have anything to do with it."

Laughing, Sally kept in step beside Tabitha on the way to the house. "Poor Mr. Jacobs. Does he know what he's in for?"

"Probably not, but let's not tell him. I fear he'll run away and never return." Tabitha snickered. "But it will be entertaining, nonetheless. I, for one, cannot wait to see Nic's reaction."

"Me, either."

Tabitha grinned all the way to the house. Perhaps she shouldn't be toying with these two men's affections the way she was, but she couldn't help it. Indeed, tomorrow afternoon would be most entertaining.

Chapter Seventeen

"WHERE HAVE YOU been?" Nic raised his voice to his cousin. Standing in the kitchen, Nic folded his arms across his chest and glared. "I haven't seen you for over twenty-four hours. I was beginning to suspect something terrible had happened to you."

With one elbow leaning on the table as his hand held up his head, Frederick gripped his coffee cup with the other hand. "Forgive me, dear cousin, but I had thought I found a clue and I was hot on the suspect's trail. Unfortunately, it turned out to be nothing."

"What did you find?" Nic asked in a calmer voice as he walked closer to the table.

"The Griffin's houseguest—whom I'd suspected—left and I followed. Their houseguest had been with them for a few months, and I had begun to wonder about this strange man. When I saw him packing his carriage bright and early yesterday morning, I decided to follow." Frederick shook his head. "Apparently, the man was just returning home. He didn't meet with anyone, and he traveled directly home—which, by the way was nearly a half-day's journey up the coast. I stayed and watched his house for a few hours, but when I realized nothing was going to happen, I left to come home." Frowning, he shook his head. "I'm beginning to believe I will never find the true thief."

"Why did you suspect him?"

"Because he was limping as if he'd sprained his ankle. Right now a man with an injured leg is the only lead I have." Frederick sipped his coffee cup.

"David Griffin had a broken ankle. Don't you recall that's what the doctor had found?"

With his eyes closed, Frederick nodded. "Yes, but I still don't believe he did it. He has no reason to steal from the church."

Grumbling, Nic sat in the chair next to his cousin. "Perhaps we should look at this from a different angle."

Frederick gave Nic a dubious stare. "Pray tell, my dear cousin, what angle are we supposed to look at it?"

"Do you know for certain that it was a man? Or, by chance, do you think it could have been a woman?"

Frederick rolled his eyes. "A woman? Why would a woman want to steal from the church?"

Nic held up his hand, palm facing his cousin. "Just listen to me." He took a deep breath. "Today I had Miss McFadden come into the church to confess her sins to me."

Frederick gasped and shook his head "Oh, please tell me you didn't give her any guidance."

"Of course not. I had no idea what to say to the poor girl." Nic scratched underneath his ear where his beard had been bothering him since he grew facial hair. "But what she told me made me start looking at this theft situation in a whole new light."

Nic continued to tell Frederick about what happened to Miss McFadden. As he explained, his chest tightened as he thought of the poor girl's circumstance. In the back of Nic's mind, he hoped he'd never had to put a woman through this. Then again, if he had, the woman should have had the decency to come tell him. He would have done the proper thing, even if he didn't love the woman. Which made him realize he'd better not be doing *that* with a woman unless he wanted to marry her.

Frederick squeezed his eyes closed and shook his head but

didn't say anything. Nic waited a few seconds in silence before adding, "I tell you, Frederick, I really believed she could have killed David Griffin—although I had no idea how she could have buried him in the sand. Nevertheless, the idea struck me as odd that perhaps we haven't been looking in the right direction."

Opening his eyes, Frederick stared at Nic. "So have you seen any woman limping around lately?"

Nic held his breath as his mind skimmed over everyone who had been at church last Sunday. He frowned. "Actually, no, but that still doesn't mean it wasn't a woman. All that means is that if the thief is indeed a woman, she doesn't attend your church."

Frederick groaned and stood, taking his cup to the sink. "No, I honestly believe the thief is a man. I know it was dark, but the figure that I saw leaving the church was that of a man. He was tall and large, but not really fat, and neither was he muscular. Perhaps a mixture of both."

"So tell me," Nic propped his leg over his knee, "if you did see a man and he sprained his ankle…and he knew you saw him…why would he show himself at all? He would know you'd be looking for a man with a limp. What if the thief is still in hiding for fear you'll see him limp when he walks?"

Slowly Frederick turned and faced Nic. His eyes grew wider. "You know, that does make sense."

Nic shrugged. "Thank you. Every once in a while I will say something noteworthy."

Chuckling, Frederick shook his head. "So true, cousin."

Nic left the chair and strode to his cousin, and then rested his hand on Frederick's shoulder. "Don't get discouraged about not finding the thief. This is a pretty big area, and some of the neighboring towns are closer than you think. Anybody could have done it."

"But why steal from a church?" Frederick sighed. "That just doesn't make any sense."

"Apparently, this person doesn't fear God like the rest of us. And, after all, if he's thieving, he's not a good Christian person, anyway."

"Every criminal has a reason."

"Then I suggest," Nic said, "we look at everyone. Men *and* women."

"Fine." Frederick rubbed his eyes. "But I'm exhausted and need some sleep. I fear your guest yesterday morning kept me from receiving a sound sleep."

Nic's attention perked and he froze. "My...guest?"

"Yes." Frederick threw Nic a curious stare as he made his way to the stairs. "A woman, if I'm not mistaken. I didn't have the energy to wander downstairs, but I suspect it was Miss Paget. After all, what other maiden would be coming to the clergyman's house alone?"

Clearing his throat, Nic nodded. "Yes, Tabitha did visit me yesterday morning. We had much to talk about." He flipped his hand. "The visit was very important, and we were finally able to talk about our feelings for each other."

Frederick grasped the railing on the stairs, but didn't climb them. His eyes stayed on Nic. Unease ran through him, and he wished his cousin wouldn't give him that degrading glare.

"Your *feelings*? Pray tell, Lord Hawthorne, what type of feelings does a marquess have for a servant girl—besides the improper kind?"

Growling, Nic folded fisted his hands by his side. "I'm a normal man and she's a normal woman. That's how I see her now. No longer is she a maid." He shrugged. "Besides that, something happened in her life and she no longer has to work as a servant."

"That doesn't matter, Nic," Frederick came toward him, "because *you* are still a marquess, and her station will always be beneath yours."

Emotion choked Nic's throat, and he wanted to tell his cousin to mind his own business. Yet, Nic knew his own family would see the situation just as Frederick. They'd think Tabitha was just trying to worm her way into Nic's life for the chance of a title.

"And I'm telling you, it doesn't matter," Nic snapped.

"It had better. Your family expects you to find a suitable wife. A marchioness must be dignified and elegant. She must have the proper training, too, or she'll become a great disappointment." He shook his head. "My cousin, I tell you this because I care about your future. Please thoughtfully consider what I have said, and remember…you're not the only one who will be affected by this marriage. Your family will, also."

Gritting his teeth, Nic watched his cousin proceed upstairs to his bedroom. Although Nic wanted to argue, he knew he'd be wasting his breath. Frederick wasn't ready to hear what was in Nic's heart, and his family for darn sure wouldn't be prepared, either.

Nothing matters but my heart. Nic marched into the front room and to the front window. He'd seen too many men not follow their hearts, and look where it led them. They were miserable. Yet, his three good friends, Trevor, Tristan, and Trey Worthington, all followed their hearts and married the most amazing women. This was what Nic wanted, and he wouldn't settle for anything less!

THE MORNING WAS too lovely not to take a walk by the beach. Of course, Tabitha couldn't sit still at home, either. Today was when Mr. Jacobs and Nic would be in the same room while she tried to act as if she wanted the blacksmith's attention and not the clergyman's.

Would she be able to pull it off? Or would her heart betray her and show the others in the room that she really had deep feelings for Nic?

So nervous, she couldn't concentrate on anything, and trying to help Sally and Mrs. Stiles in the kitchen had become a disaster because Tabitha kept spilling things. Finally, Mrs. Stiles suggested that Tabitha take a walk by the beach. How could she turn down such a tempting idea?

The sky was so clear and so very blue this morning. A small wind teased the curls hanging from beneath her bonnet and the ties at her throat, but that was all. The sun seemed brighter today, and it definitely brought with it more heat. She should have brought a parasol to keep the sun's rays from her face, but the warmth against her skin felt too nice to block.

She didn't need a jacket this time, and her bright yellow day dress with short sleeves fit her chipper mood immensely. Outward, she knew she appeared happy, but inside, doubt and heartache intertwined, making her stomach twist in nausea.

Several people had the same idea—to stroll along the beach. There were many couples, a handful of families, and even more who walked by themselves. She nodded a greeting to those she'd met, but nobody had stopped to chat with her. Normally, this would have bothered her, but not this morning. She needed time to sort out her thoughts.

If only she could.

As she walked closer by the water, she noticed several children splashing in a section of ocean. In the distance, she saw three young women wading in the water, splashing each other and laughing. Smiling, Tabitha recalled when she had done this as a child and young woman. Would it hurt to wade through the water right now, especially if others were doing it?

Cautiously, she stepped into the cold water. She sucked in a quick breath from the chilling temperature, but within seconds, her body became used to it. Gradually, she wandered a little deeper until the water reached her shins.

As much as she enjoyed this, she *must* make sense of her thoughts. Unfortunately, they had been jumbled since she first saw Nic as the clergyman. If she really looked back on it, she'd been confused from the first time they'd met, especially after their first kiss.

They'd been at Diana's grandmother's cottage, and Nic and Lord Tristan had shown up unexpectedly. Neither she nor Diana realized that the men were suspicious of Tabitha and wondered if she had been the one murdering the lords of the realm in the middle of the night.

Tristan had asked to speak with Diana in private, so that left Nic alone with Tabitha. The rogue was charming with his words until soon he'd convinced her that she had wanted his kiss. To this day, she didn't know how he was able to accomplish that, but the kiss had been more thrilling than she'd expected. His passion literally left her mindless. The thing she remembered most about that kiss was how good it felt, and how she'd wanted it to go on and on.

LATER, SHE'D DISCOVERED Nic had only kissed her to distract her from what Tristan and Diana were doing. The whole night had been nothing but a farce; accusations flew, and feelings were hurt badly.

When coolness touched her knees, she stopped. Blinking out of the haze her thoughts had put her under, she realized she'd ventured out into the water a little deeper. Heavens! Why hadn't she realized?

She glanced behind her, scoping out the others who she'd greeted along the way. Only a few couples had noticed her, and they just smiled and waved. The others that she'd noticed earlier who were playing in the water were looking at her as well. Goodness! What could they possibly be thinking of her?

She tried to smile under the embarrassing situation, as she waited for them to leave. Wading through the water became bothersome now that most of her dress was wet. Although the sun was warm, the water was still cold on this spring day.

The roar of water rushing toward her had her jerking toward the loud sound. A wave came her way, and her heart dropped. She didn't know how to swim!

Turning, she tried to hurry toward the shore, but the weight of her dress kept her from moving fast. Closer and closer the wave came. Knowing it would soon hit, she clenched her fists and held her breath.

When the water rushed over her, it pulled her down. Before she knew it, her feet were swept up and she couldn't feel anything under her. Continuing to hold her breath, she flailed her arms and legs, trying to find something solid to hold her.

Her chest burned as panic filled her, but she couldn't take a breath until her head was above water. When her life flashed before her, she feared the worst. She might not survive.

Oh, Lord! Help me!

NIC COULDN'T RUN down the slope fast enough.

A moment ago he'd spotted Tabitha wading knee-deep in the water. At first, he'd chuckled, wondered why she'd do such an outlandish thing, but within seconds the wave had swallowed her.

As he tore down the side of the hill toward the water, he ripped off his clergyman coat, and yanked off his cravat. These would only pull him down when he dove in the water to find her.

He didn't bother to take off his boots. That would only slow him down. She had already been in the water for a good ten seconds. He prayed she had taken a deep breath before going under.

His long legs ate up the distance between the sand and the water until he was to the point that he could dive in and swim. He'd been watching the wave to see where it might have taken her. Pushing his arms to the limit, he swam in the water, searching for her.

From the corner of his eyes, he noticed something bright yellow just underneath the water. Moving in that direction, he forced his arms to go faster. The moment he was within reach, he grabbed at the dress and yanked her to him.

Immediately, his hand held her head above water. They were in a deep spot, but he could still stand, thankfully.

Her eyes were closed, and her body felt limp. His heart sank. "Breathe, Tabitha," he commanded and shook her.

Tabitha's head rolled forward, resting against his chest. His arms tightened around her waist. Her chest expanded and released. He sighed heavily. "Tabitha, take a breath. You're all right. I have you." He turned and headed back to shore.

Coughing, she slowly opened her eyes. Color gradually seeped into her face. Tears stung his eyes as joyful reprieve overwhelmed him. "Oh, Tabitha. I almost lost you." Groaning, he buried his face in her neck and held her closer. She still seemed weak and unmoving, which worried him.

When they reached the shore, he dropped to his knees and laid her on the sand. Her eyes closed and once again, panic whipped through him like a tornado. "Tabitha? Please say something."

Her eyes flickered open and she nodded. "I'm…fine."

Relief poured through him, and he gathered her in his arms, pulling her close to his chest. Nuzzling his face against her ear, he felt the urgent need to kiss her—to show her how grateful he was that she was responsive. If she had drowned, he didn't know what he would have done.

"Mr. Woodland?" The high-pitched sound of a woman's voice rented the air. "Is Miss Paget all right?"

Realizing where he was at—and what he'd almost done—brought him out of his shocked state. He lifted his head. Immediately, he noticed the small crowd that had gathered. Mrs. Smythe and Miss Talbot were the ring-leaders out in front. From what he could see, most everyone wore an expression of worry, but not the two busy-bodies. They appeared appalled.

Groaning, inwardly, he knew he had to say something to dig himself out of this quickly before these people got the wrong idea…which of course was the *right* idea, he just couldn't let them know it.

Chapter Eighteen

"Uh…" Nic glanced down at Tabitha, who he was still practically laying on. Her eyes were now wide and the color was leaving her pretty face again. But this time, he knew it was for different reasons. *Drat!* He needed to say something quickly.

"Um, Miss Tabitha? Oh, thank heavens." He slowly lifted himself off her, but rested on his knees. "You're breathing. I thought you had—had—" He made his voice choke on purpose as he blinked back pretend tears. At least he'd hoped the onlookers thought that he was trying not to cry.

Taking a deep breath, she nodded and placed her hand to her bosom. "Yes, Mr. Woodland. I'm breathing fine now. I thank you for rescuing me." She struggled to sit up, so he helped by taking her arm and pulling her to an upright position. She glanced at the people around them. "I'm fine now, thanks to Mr. Woodland."

Sighs of relief passed through the crowd. Some people even stepped forward to pat Nic on the shoulder and congratulate him. Soon, they started leaving, but the two older women remained, unmoving…and gaping. Nic wanted to hand them back their noses and tell them to keep it out of his business, but he was supposed to be the kind, forgiving, clergyman, and Frederick would never say such a thing to these women.

He stood and brushed off the sand from his trousers. "Allow

me to help you up." He reached his hand for Tabitha to grab.

"I thank you, again." She clutched his hand and stood. She released him and swiped the water off her face and hair. "I...I don't know what happened." She glanced at the ocean, shaking her head.

"I was wading through the water, and the next thing I knew a wave had hit me and pulled me under."

"It was the most frightening thing I'd ever seen," Mrs. Smythe said, breathless.

"Indeed, it was." Nic nodded. "I saw her go under, and I didn't know if I would be able to reach her soon enough."

"But Mr. Woodland," Miss Talbot spoke softly, "I thought you told us you couldn't swim. Yet," she pointed toward the water, "I watched you swim out to Miss Paget."

Growling under his breath, he glanced at Tabitha. Her eyes were large and frightened. He was going to ruin the disguise, he just knew it. Yet, it had been worth it to save Tabitha.

"Oh, my," Tabitha gasped. "Mr. Woodland, you don't suppose..."

Confused, he shook his head, wishing he could read her thoughts right now. "What?"

"Do you suppose the Lord had wanted you to save me, so He helped you to swim because you don't know how?"

He wanted to hug her for her quick thinking. He'd do it later when they were in a private setting.

Sucking in a quick breath, he laid on the dramatics, mainly for the two older women. He glanced up into the sky and steepled his fingers against his lips. "Miss Tabitha, I believe we have all witnessed a miracle just now." He swallowed hard. "Thank you, Lord, for strengthening our faith."

When he finally tore his gaze away from the heavens and looked at Miss Talbot and her sister, he was relieved to see they wore different expressions. Apparently, they had believed the ruse and figured they had just been witness to a miracle. But in truth, this had been a miracle. God *had* helped Nic to find Tabitha and save her.

"Miss Tabitha?" he asked, turning his attention back to her. "I think I should get you home before you catch a chill."

Nodding, she wrapped her arms around her chest, hugging herself. "Yes, I believe that's wise."

He bowed to the two older women. "If you will excuse us."

"Of course, Mr. Woodland. Take care, Miss Paget."

He found the clergyman coat and draped it over Tabitha's shoulders. Before leaving, he scooped up his cravat and folded it.

Both he and Tabitha's steps were hurried as they headed toward Mrs. Burls. When he knew they were far enough away from curious ears, he said softly, "I'm so very grateful I was able to get to you in time." He glanced at her.

She sneaked a peek, but then quickly looked back at the road. "Nic, you…you almost caused suspicion." She looked at him again; her gaze slowly wandering over his wet shirt that melded to his frame. "I think Mrs. Smythe and her sister will be thinking of you differently now. Unless of course, your cousin is as muscular as you are."

Chuckling, he shook his head. "No, Frederick is not. I do realize that I could have given away my true identity, but…I had to save you. I don't know what I would have done if you had—" His voice choked for real this time, and he breathed deeply, calming his emotions. "I would do it again in a heartbeat, my lovely. I'd do anything to protect you."

"Thank you, Nic. I—I—don't know how to thank you enough."

"Well, for now, just resting and not becoming sick will be thanks enough."

When she glanced at him again, he winked. A smile tugged on the corners of her mouth. Heavens, he loved seeing her this way. "Is the luncheon still planned for this afternoon, or do you think your aunt will cancel it now?"

She shook her head. "I won't let her cancel it."

When he walked her to the doorstep, he stopped and faced her. "Then I'll see you this afternoon."

"Yes." She shrugged out of his coat and handed it back to him.

He bowed. "Until later, then."

He turned and strolled back toward the street. He didn't hear her open the door, so he knew she was watching him. Happiness grew in his chest and he nearly burst with excitement. Perhaps she'd now realize how much he had changed, and in doing so, her heart would soften and allow him to court her properly.

In due time, he told himself. Everything would work out, he was certain of it.

WITH HER HAIR dry and restyled, and wearing another dress, Tabitha perched upon the edge of the chair, sitting with a straight back and hands folded in her lap as she conversed with Mr. Jacobs. She'd tried to relate what had happened to her this morning without worrying the elder ladies, but Aunt Clara was in a dither. Even Mrs. Stiles wanted to cancel their afternoon activities, but Tabitha wouldn't have it. She felt well enough to have company. Not only that, she needed a distraction from her confused thoughts.

Before today, she was determined to put Nic from her mind. She'd convinced herself that his feelings for her weren't real. Yet this morning's rescue only proved to her that she didn't know what to think of Lord Hawthorne.

The tenderness and care in his eyes had been real. His endearing words made her heart clench, and she wanted to cry. And he risked exposing his true identity to save her...yet he wasn't upset over it, either.

She inhaled an uneven breath. Oh, why couldn't her heart and her mind meet so that she wasn't so torn over this?

She focused back on Mr. Jacobs, smiling her best for him. Even through all of this turmoil, she still felt Nic's station in life was too above hers, and it would be hopeless to dream of a life with him.

No matter, she must see if she and Mr. Jacobs suited. Tabitha was saddened when he'd told her his daughter had caught a chill and couldn't attend the luncheon. Nevertheless, she'd get to know Mr. Jacobs a little better without his daughter present.

For some reason, he seemed more charming today. Tabitha wasn't sure if it was because she decided to give this man a chance to impress her, or if Mr. Jacobs was actually different from the man she'd talked with before. Either way, he made her laugh, and at this time in her life, that was something she needed.

Nic makes me laugh, too... Quickly, she stopped the thought from going any farther. It wasn't wise to have such hopes.

Unfortunately, Aunt Clara and Mrs. Stiles didn't look very happy with the attention she gave to Mr. Jacobs. They both sat on opposite chairs, watching her closely with critical eyes. Whenever Mr. Jacobs said something to them or glanced their way, they'd quickly change their dark expressions to a happy one. But the second he took his focus off them, their analytical stares returned.

It worried Tabitha that Mr. Jacobs would see—or feel—the uneasy current in the room, but he was polite and didn't say anything. He didn't even act uncomfortable, for which Tabitha was relieved.

Her gaze moved to the door. Where was Nic? She expected him to arrive early for the luncheon, mainly because of the way he'd acted this morning. Although he knew she was fine, she thought for sure he'd still come to check on her.

Concern rooted deep into her chest. Had something bad happened to him? Hopefully, he hadn't caught a chill from rescuing her. Or perhaps his lateness stemmed from something else. After all, he and his cousin were looking for a thief. What if something unexpected happened? What if Nic was lying injured somewhere and nobody knew?

The knock on the door startled her, and she jumped in her chair. Sally walked slowly into the hall and to the door and let Nic in. A mixture between happiness and relief rushed through Tabitha and she became anxious to see him again. She sat a little taller and smoothed her hands down her gold dress with white-laced bodice and underskirt. Nervously, she reached up to her ringlets before remembering she'd restyled her hair after her near-drowning experience. Instead, she had swept her hair into a chignon, and only wisps of curls hung near her ears.

From the hallway, Nic's voice boomed through the air. Delightful shivers cascaded over her and she found herself smiling broader. She swallowed hard as butterflies danced in her stomach. When Sally showed him into the room, Tabitha's heart melted. Just as handsome as always, his gaze locked immediately to hers and he smiled. In his hand, he gripped the stems of several blue irises. She hitched a breath. Had she ever told him that flower was her favorite?

"Oh, Mr. Woodland, you are here." Aunt Clara stood and leaned heavily on her cane with one hand, while holding the other hand outstretched to Nic. "How glad I am to see you here, especially after this morning's upset at the beach. And oh, look…you brought flowers."

Nic walked to Aunt Clara and took her hand. "I know these flowers will never be as lovely as the women in this room, but I thought they came close."

Mrs. Stiles giggled and Aunt Clara laughed. "Oh, Mr. Woodland. You are such a tease." She gestured to Sally. "Would you please take these and place them in a vase?"

"As you wish." Sally curtsied and then took the flowers from Nic before leaving the room.

When Nic took his focus off Aunt Clara and swept it around the room, it came to a startling halt on Mr. Jacobs. Nic's eyes broadened and a faux smile touched his face.

"Ah, Mr. Jacobs. It's good to see you again."

"And it's nice to see you too, Mr. Woodland. I heard you saved another person from drowning this morning. You have definitely been busy lately."

Nic shook his head. "God had me in the right time at the right place."

He moved to the other man who rose to his feet, and the two shook hands. Tabitha found it surprising that neither of them appeared to be very happy about *seeing* the other as they had proclaimed.

Once Nic released Mr. Jacob's hand, he turned toward her. The irritation she'd detected in his gaze only moments ago had disappeared. His eyes twinkled in that familiar knee-weakening way.

"Good afternoon, Miss Paget. I see your lovely complexion is back and your blue eyes are looking more alert." His gaze swept over her yet again. "And you appear much drier than the last time we spoke."

Once more, his words melted her heart. "You are such a flatterer, Mr. Woodland." She grinned, although she tried not to make it too big. "I am feeling better. I had worried you would be the one catching a chill."

He shook his head. "I'm very well, thank you."

"Well, now that we are all here," Aunt Clara announced, "let's adjourn to the veranda out back and partake of our luncheon."

Mr. Woodland offered his arm to Aunt Clara, who beamed excitedly as she hooked her hand around his elbow. Mr. Jacobs quickly offered his arm to Tabitha, who accepted his escort. Mrs. Stiles and Sally strolled behind.

Although Tabitha could see her aunt talking to Nic, she couldn't quite hear what they were saying. She just prayed he would stick to his promise and not make her aunt or Mrs. Stiles suspect anything was going on between her and the clergyman.

"Miss Paget," Mr. Jacobs said softly.

She pulled her gaze away from the couple in front of her and focused on the man by her side. "Yes?"

"Mr. Woodland was right, you know. You are very lovely today."

It wasn't until now that she realized how brown his eyes really were—like melting pools of chocolate. She wasn't naïve to the way he was peering at her. Most assuredly, he was interested in her. She just wished his gaze would warm her as Nic's could.

"I thank you, Mr. Jacobs. You're very kind." She smiled. Perhaps it didn't matter if her body had a different reaction with Mr. Jacobs than with Nic. Mr. Jacobs was still a kind man—a man closer to her station in life, she reminded herself.

The tables were set up under the canopy, blocking the sun from their food. Chairs were placed in a half circle around the veranda as well. The weather was perfect for an outdoor luncheon. No wind to disrupt their meal, and the temperature was warmer than it had been lately. Tabitha didn't even need a shawl.

Tabitha filled her plate and found a chair. Within seconds, Mr. Jacob sat beside her. She glanced across the veranda at Nic, who was clearly watching her as he pretended to listen to the chattering Mrs. Stiles. Tabitha wasn't certain if she liked the disapproving look he gave her, but she definitely enjoyed the jealousy he displayed.

"Miss Paget," Mr. Jacobs said. "Would you tell me a little about yourself? Where did you grow up?"

She tore her attention from Nic and focused back on Mr. Jacobs. Smiling, she scrambled to think of something she could tell him. Was she ready to admit to being a servant all her life? Even though it was the truth, she worried about that dreaded question that would follow—about how she was able to overcome that status and be on her own without a husband to support her. She wasn't ready to tell him—or anyone—about that secret.

"Most of my life, I worked beside my mother as a maid for a wealthy woman. We lived in York." She shrugged. "I fear I don't have a very exciting life to tell you about."

"Is your mother still alive?"

She shook her head. "She died several years ago."

He sipped his punch. "I take it you don't still work for the wealthy woman any longer."

"No, I don't. Within this past…uh, year, my life has changed drastically. No longer do I have to work as a servant, thanks to my relatives."

Mr. Jacobs glanced at Aunt Clara who was just settling into her cushioned chair as Nic assisted. Tabitha wondered if Nic had heard because he kept throwing glances at her. But most assuredly, Mr. Jacobs would assume her aunt was the *family* she'd referred to.

"Well, whatever it was that brought you to North Devon, I'm most grateful. I don't think I have met anyone as gracious and sweet as you."

"Again, I thank you for your kind words, Mr. Jacobs."

"I hope you decide to stay in North Devon. I'm sure by now you can see it's a more relaxed place to live than York."

Chuckling, she nodded. "Indeed, it's very relaxed here."

Mrs. Stiles walked to the chair next to Mr. Jacobs. Just before reaching it, she stumbled and her foot kicked against Mr. Jacob's ankle. Groaning, he quickly pulled it away, but his hand shot out to steady the older woman.

"Oh, forgive me, Mr. Jacobs. I didn't mean to hurt you." She glanced at his foot. "Are you all right?"

"Not to worry, Mrs. Stiles. I'm on the mend."

"Mr. Jacobs," Nic said in a rush. "I thought it was your knee that you had injured."

Nodding, Mr. Jacobs turned to look at Nic. "It was my knee."

"But Mrs. Stiles bumped into your foot and you grimaced. Have you by chance, injured your ankle as well?"

During the disturbing pause, Tabitha gritted her teeth. What was Nic getting at now? His tone of voice was most accusing, too. She glanced at Mr. Jacobs who appeared at a loss for words. After a few awkward moments passed with nothing said, she held her breath. Was Nic precise in accusing Mr. Jacobs of something?

Chapter Nineteen

NIC WAITED PATIENTLY for Mr. Jacobs to answer, but as each second passed, curiosity built inside him. Mr. Jacobs was now climbing to the top of Nic's suspect list of being the church's thief.

Finally, the other man pulled back his shoulders and raised his chin stubbornly. "Mr. Woodland, I'm not quite certain what you're asking. I had injured my knee while working in my barn, but not too long ago, I sprained my ankle as I tried to rescue my daughter when she fell in a hole." He arched an eyebrow. "You were there and saved Joanna. Do you not remember?"

"Of course I remember." Inwardly, Nic kicked himself for *not* remembering, but he wasn't going to let Mr. Jacobs know.

"I had twisted my ankle at that time." He glanced at Tabitha. "Miss Paget and her maid assisted me home because I had a hard time walking."

"Forgive me then," Nic said. "I didn't realize your ankle was still sore."

Mr. Jacobs shrugged. "It's starting to feel better. However, whenever it's bumped a certain way, it does sting."

"Once again, Mr. Jacobs," Mrs. Stiles said, frowning, "I'm truly sorry for knocking into you with my foot."

He reached over and patted her hand. "No need to apologize. It was an accident."

The air seemed to crackle throughout the group, and Nic realized he should start a new topic. Tabitha wasn't looking at him any longer, and although he wanted her attention more than anything right now, he knew it wouldn't be wise to obtain it yet. Not when his feelings were ready to burst from his chest whenever he looked at her. She was so very lovely this afternoon, it was extremely hard not to stare. If only they were alone.

"Mr. Woodland," Mrs. Burls said, finally breaking the silence. "I want you to know I've noticed a change about you lately."

Alarm rattled through Nic and he froze. From the corner of his eyes, he noticed Tabitha snap her head toward her aunt, as well. If Mrs. Burls had seen a change in him, then who else had wondered about the clergyman?

"Uh…you have?" he asked the older woman as he lifted his punch to his mouth and sipped.

"Oh, yes. Of course everyone has noticed how much weight you've lost since you were sick, but it's more than that." She narrowed her gaze on him. "I have noticed a twinkle in your eyes that hasn't been there before." She grinned. "Am I correct in assuming you have finally decided to start looking for a wife?"

The drink caught in his throat and he choked. He lifted his hand to his mouth, and covered his coughing fit. His eyes watered, so he quickly blinked away the liquid.

"Are you quite all right?" Mrs. Burls asked in a concerned tone.

He nodded. "Yes." His voice broke, so he cleared his throat. "Your question caught me off guard, I'm afraid."

"Oh, dear." The older woman's cheeks reddened. "I do that sometimes. It's my worst fault. But when a question comes to mind, I can't help but blurt it out."

"I understand." He smiled. Now he knew where Tabitha got this trait.

"So?" The older woman arched an eyebrow. "Have you de-cided to start looking for a wife?"

Chuckling, he shook his head. Good grief, this woman was

forward…or just being too curious for her own good. "Actually, I haven't decided anything, Mrs. Burls. In fact, the thought hasn't come to me as of yet."

"Oh, don't you be saying that, Mr. Woodland." Mrs. Burls wagged her finger at him. "I'm wise beyond my years, and I can see a spark in your eyes…the kind of spark that only a woman can create."

He grinned. "Then it must be you that creates that certain gleam, Mrs. Burls, because I assure you, no other woman can make me smile the way you can."

She giggled, her cheeks flaring red once again. From the other side of the veranda, Mrs. Stiles even let out a giddy laugh. Tabitha, however, offered a small smile. She must have not seen the humor in the subject as much as the other two women.

Mr. Jacobs leaned closer to Tabitha and whispered something to her. Suddenly, she beamed and laughed. Jealousy ate away at Nic, making him want to march over to them and break up their little private session.

He gripped his drink with one hand and the plate with the other as irritation simmered inside of him. How could he stop this anger flowing through him so that the older women didn't notice his jealousy? Tabitha didn't want them knowing his feelings, and he did make a promise—although at this point he wasn't sure he'd be able to keep it.

Especially after this morning. For a few brief and heart-wrenching moments, he'd thought he'd lost Tabitha. When she started breathing on her own, his heart soared, and emotion filled his chest. He couldn't deny his feelings for her now. Indeed, he loved this woman more than life itself. This was probably the reason that Mr. Jacobs' presence grated on Nic's nerves. Was the man trying to win Tabitha's hand? And what was she doing encouraging the blacksmith's attention?

Out of the corner of his eyes, Sally walked slowly to the buffet table. She stirred some dishes and even covered them with lids. Six months ago, he didn't get to see much of her while she stayed with Diana and Tabitha at their cottage hideaway. Sally had been abused severely by her former employer, Lord Elliot, so she had stayed in her room recuperating. Now as he really studied the younger woman, he realized she was quite attractive. The maid was possibly in her nineteenth year, but she had the prettiest blonde hair and bright gray eyes. And her eyes…were constantly moving toward Tabitha and Mr. Jacobs.

Gradually, he released a sigh of relief. Perhaps there was a way around his jealousy with Mr. Jacobs after all. As he studied Sally, he could see her fascination with the other man. If Nic could somehow make Mr. Jacobs aware of Sally, with any luck, the other man would turn his attention to the young maid, instead.

Nic stood and moved to the table. Sally's gaze snapped to him before she retreated to the corner of the veranda. He'd seen her act this way before. Once he stopped at the table, he pretended to look over the several plates of dishes as if seeing what he wanted to eat. He peered up at her, meeting her gaze, and smiled.

"Sally, what are you doing over there? Have you eaten yet?"

Her eyes grew larger and she shook her head. "Of course not, my lo—uh, Mr. Woodland. I will eat afterward, as most servants do."

He was relieved she didn't say *my lord,* which it sounded like she was going to.

"But why? There are just a few of us, and I don't think any of us will mind you eating now." He glanced over his shoulder at the others. Tabitha watched him with a curious gaze, and the older women appeared shocked that he would suggest such a thing. Mr. Jacobs looked mildly interested in what was going on though, and that's what mattered to Nic. He glanced back at Sally. "Please, get yourself a plate and come sit with us. In fact, you can sit by me."

Sally's face paled as her gaze darted to everyone in the group. Nobody said anything, and Nic hoped the older women wouldn't try to talk him out of it.

"But…" the maid said softly, "I'm a servant."

"Oh, come now, Sally. We are all equal in the eyes of the Lord." He tried not to grin. That line just popped into his head. Strange to think he was acting more and more like a clergyman the longer he portrayed one. Frederick would certainly get a good laugh over this one. Nic turned to Mrs. Burls. "Am I correct?"

"Uh…about what, Mr. Woodland?" the older woman asked with great hesitation.

"That we are all equal in the eyes of the Lord, and because of that, I think Sally should be able to eat with us this time."

Mrs. Burls' throat lurched as if she had swallowed something hard. Slowly, she nodded. "I think you are correct. Sally is like family anyway, so I believe she can eat with us." She turned her attention to the maid. "Sally, please don't be shy. Fix yourself a plate and come sit with us, just as Mr. Woodland has asked."

He glanced over his shoulder at Tabitha. Worried lines creased around her eyes and mouth as she looked at the maid.

Finally, Tabitha nodded. "Yes, Sally. Please join us." She stood and set her plate on the chair, and then strode to the table to assist Sally.

After a few minutes, Tabitha returned to her chair with Sally following. She sat between Tabitha and Nic. He waited for her to start eating before speaking to her. Everyone seemed to be at ease, as well.

"So Sally," he said, turning in his chair to face her, "are you from York like Miss Paget?"

She dropped her gaze to her plate as her cheeks turned red. "No. I'm actually from Mayfair."

"Oh, what a nice place. I know a few people from there, too."

Shyly, she glanced at him before her gaze fell to her food again. "Indeed, it's a very lovely place to live."

"Are you enjoying yourself in North Devon?"

She bobbed her head. "Immensely."

"Well, you picked the perfect host to stay with. Mrs. Burls is one of the sweetest women I know."

Beside him, the older woman laughed. "Oh, Mr. Woodland. You are such a charmer."

Nic noticed that Mr. Jacobs had his focus on Sally now. Of course he was also paying more attention to the conversation as well.

The other man nodded as he met the maid's gaze. "I must agree with Mr. Woodland. Mrs. Burls is a wonderful woman. Both she and Mrs. Stiles are very generous. You are truly fortunate to be staying with them."

Sally's face darkened with a blush, and Nic held himself back from grinning. Indeed, he was correct when assuming the maid had taken a fancy to the blacksmith.

For the next little while, the group didn't talk as much as they finished their meal. Nic kept his eyes on the woman next to him, and especially Mr. Jacobs. It relieved Nic that the other man didn't try to talk privately with Tabitha now, but included Sally in on the conversation.

"I hope you don't mind," Mrs. Burls announced as Mrs. Stiles took her empty plate back to the table, "but I would like us all to play a lawn game. I have good memories of playing Bowls when I was a child, and it still brings me joy as an old woman." She looked at the maid. "Sally, I would like you to join us, if that is all right."

"Yes, Ma'am," Sally muttered, keeping her gaze down.

Once everyone returned their empty plates to the table, they strolled out to the lawn that was set up for the game. It relieved Nic when Mrs. Burls didn't pair anyone up or put them in groups—only because he knew the old woman would put him and Tabitha together. Clara was definitely one sneaky aunt.

Everyone selected their ball, but only Sally appeared confused as she held hers against her bosom. Nic walked to her. "Is something amiss, Sally?"

"I, um…I don't think I know how to play."

It never occurred to him that servants weren't able to play the game, but perhaps Sally was never given the chance. Nevertheless, it was his civic duty to teach her. Unless…

He took a quick glance at Mr. Jacobs who stood entirely too close to Tabitha, smiling much too wide, and laughing more than Nic thought the other man should. In an instant, an idea popped into Nic's head. He now knew the perfect solution!

TABITHA COULDN'T BELIEVE how much she enjoyed Mr. Jacobs' company. He really was a nice man, and he was trying hard to charm her. True, he couldn't compare to Lord Hawthorne's knee-weakening charm, but Mr. Jacobs was doing his best, and she appreciated that he was more entertaining than she expected him to be. The longer he was with her, the more he relaxed and she could actually see his true nature.

But Nic kept drawing her attention as well. Some of the things he had said and done already this afternoon caused her to be wary. What she wouldn't give to know his thoughts. Then again, she didn't need to read his mind to know how it had irritated him because she was so chummy with Mr. Jacobs. Yet, that didn't explain why Nic was being so nice to Sally.

"See, the object of the game is to throw our ball and try to hit those at that end," Nic explained to the maid as he stood very close to her. "In the many years I have played this game, I have found that holding the ball the right way is the key to making it go farther."

What is he talking about? Tabitha narrowed her gaze on the pair. Nic tried so diligently to show Sally how to hold the ball, it was almost comical. There was no *right* way to hold the ball. Not really. The key was how to throw it with the correct amount of strength.

"See, you put your hands like so…" Nic instructed as he tried in the most proper way he could without actually putting his arms around Sally.

Beside Tabitha, a low grumble released from Mr. Jacobs' throat. She swung her gaze to him. He was watching the odd pair as well, shaking his head. Expelling a heavy sigh, he muttered an apology and left Tabitha to go assist Sally and Nic.

"If you will permit me to show you," he said to Sally, "I would gladly assist you in any way I can."

Sally's cheeks turned a bright pink when she stared into Mr. Jacob's face. Slowly, the maid nodded as she handed him the ball. When he moved beside her to display the correct stance, Sally couldn't take her eyes off him. When the man moved behind the maid and moved her arm in the correct position, Tabitha was surprised to see how much Sally was enjoying the attention.

Shock splashed over Tabitha as she witnessed the subtle way her maid flirted with Mr. Jacobs. It wasn't outright obvious that Sally had taken a fancy to the other man, yet Tabitha could read her friend's expression perfectly. The huge eyes and fluttering eyelashes told the story, as well as Sally's gracious smile that gradually grew the longer she stared at Mr. Jacobs. Even the light laughs bubbling up from the girl's throat let Tabitha know how smitten the maid was for this man.

Tabitha grinned as happiness filled her and she wanted to shout with joy. Finally, after all this time Sally felt relaxed around a man. Ever since their former employer had beaten Sally within an inch of her life, the girl had not wanted to get near anyone of the male gender, let alone speak with them. But now, the maid practically glowed while standing so close to Mr. Jacobs.

The longer Tabitha studied him, the more she could see that he was quite aware of Sally's interest. Of course he was. There was nothing more attractive to a man than to have a woman doe-eyed and giddy with infatuation. When he talked with Sally, his gaze held hers longer than normal, and the color in his eyes even softened quite a bit. A few times a red hue would light the man's cheeks as well.

Never had he been that way around Tabitha.

After she had a minute to think about it, she realized her

initial reaction was changing quickly. Doubts lingered in her head. *Why* hadn't he acted that way around her? Was it because she'd never acted as giddy and innocent as Sally was doing? After all, she'd never been infatuated with the blacksmith. Well not yet, anyway. But given some time, maybe she would have been.

The longer she watched the two, the more she realized Mr. Jacobs was becoming smitten with Sally—*not* Tabitha. She knew when to step back and allow another woman to try to catch a man, and she would gladly let Sally be the one who was happy right now. Mr. Jacobs and Sally suited each other perfectly.

Of course that only meant that Tabitha needed to find another man who *might* take her mind off Nic. There were several men in this township, so she was certain she could find someone.

She glanced at Nic. He watched Sally and the blacksmith with keen interest. A grin pulled at the corners of his mouth, growing wider as each second passed. Slowly anger filled her head. Nic had this planned all along! Obviously, he was behind putting the blacksmith and the maid together. *Ohhhh!* Tabitha fisted her hands. He had interfered in her life on purpose! Was he going to do this with all the men she tried to take an interest in? Of course he would! Somehow, some way, she needed to tell him to stop meddling in her life.

"Now do you understand how to play," Mr. Jacobs asked Sally with tenderness coating his voice.

The maid stared at him with a starry-eyed gaze and nodded. "Indeed, I do. I thank you for your help."

He flashed her with a teasing grin. "Think nothing of it. Let me know if you have any more problems with the game."

Using the anger flowing through her, Tabitha put all of her emotions into the game. One by one, she knocked all the other balls aside, which put her in the lead. Not once did anyone inquire as to what was wrong with her, which suited her just fine right now. She would definitely become too vocal if anyone asked.

Nic, however, noticed. Although she didn't want to look at

him very much—for fear she'd give away her annoyance for him at this time—she still could see how he gloated on his recent victory. She didn't have to ask him if this had been his plan all along. The triumphant smile on his face said it all. He even chatted more playfully with Aunt Clara and Mrs. Stiles, proving his jovial spirit. Once in a while, his gaze connected with Tabitha and his impish grin softened. The look in his eyes became more affectionate…which made her even angrier.

She spun around and put her focus on Aunt Clara who was in the process of throwing her ball. The older woman didn't have a lot of strength, but she tried her best. After throwing the ball, Aunt Clara stumbled.

Tabitha rushed to her side and grasped her elbow. "Are you all right?"

"Yes, dear. Although this is my favorite game, I just don't have the strength that I used to have." Clara frowned and shook her head. "But I'm enjoying myself nonetheless."

"Mrs. Burls," Nic said as he stopped beside Tabitha, "you appear exhausted. Would you like me to take you back to the veranda?"

"Heavens no, Mr. Woodland. I would rather you stay right here by Tabitha and play. I can see myself to the veranda just fine." She straightened and smiled. "And I give you permission to visit with my grandniece for a little while, as well."

Aunt Clara turned and made her way back toward the house. Tabitha wondered if her intrusive aunt had planned this, too. This afternoon was full of plans; Tabitha trying to become interested in the blacksmith, Nic trying to get Mr. Jacobs more aware of Sally, and of course, her wonderful aunt and the companion who just didn't know when to stop trying to find Tabitha a husband. Hers was the only plan that hadn't worked out well.

She glanced at the others. Mrs. Stiles now stood by Mr. Jacobs and Sally roughly ten steps away. Tabitha knew if she and Nic talked in low voices, nobody would hear them.

She switched her gaze back to Nic, who as always, wore a

self-assured grin…the kind she wanted to slap off his face right now. "Mr. Woodland," she snipped. "I would appreciate it if you would stop sticking your nose into other people's lives."

Confusion replaced his self-assured look as he slowly shook his head. "I fear, Miss Tabitha, that I don't quite understand your meaning."

"Nic," she growled quieter. "I think you most certainly do understand what I'm saying." She threw a quick glance at Mr. Jacobs and Sally. "I believe that you are trying to keep me from getting to know other men."

Chuckling, he shook his head and turned to toss his ball at the other balls on the grass. "My dear, sweet woman. If you can't see how your maid looks upon that blacksmith with adoring eyes, then I'm afraid you're a lost cause. However, I can see that Mr. Jacobs is just as interested in your friend."

Tabitha tried hard not to stomp her foot—or clobber the man beside her. She prayed that she could keep her wits about her and not lash out her frustration on the man who'd ruined her afternoon. It would be hard, though, and she feared by the end of this luncheon, one of them would be sporting a bruise.

Chapter Twenty

TABITHA TOOK A deep breath and prayed for more patience, but it seemed God had other things to do and couldn't help her. "I can see very clearly that my maid and Mr. Jacobs are enamored with each other, which I think is just wonderful. But what I don't understand is why you thought it necessary to intrude in my life and decide what man I can or cannot get to know better. Is it so terrible to believe that I might want to get to know a man and perhaps have him court me?"

A serious expression came over Nic and his smile disappeared. Confusion and hurt coated his eyes, making the color darker. "Obviously, I don't understand what you are thinking, my lovely. Why would you want a blacksmith when you can have me?" He moved closer. "Tabitha, why can't you see that you already have me? You need not look for another man at all. The last we had spoken on this subject, you were very much aware of my feelings for you. In fact, you had given me the impression that you returned them…quite eagerly, if I remember correctly."

Her heart sank, and her chest tightened. It had become hard to breathe. This time it had nothing to do with Nic's nearness. It was the catch in his voice that let her know she'd just hurt him.

Now was not the time to explain in full detail why she couldn't love him—why it was impossible for him to love her. But she must say something.

"Tabitha?" he asked again when she hadn't spoken for a few minutes. "Please tell me."

She heaved a heavy and difficult sigh. "Oh, Nic. It's true that I led you to believe I had wanted to be with you, but since then I have done a lot of thinking." She took a quick glance over her shoulder to see if the others were coming. Thankfully, they still stood in the same spot, chatting away. She walked closer to the ball she'd just thrown. "I have come to realize that there is no way we can ever be together."

Nic kept in step beside her. "I'm not going to play the clergyman role forever, you know. You and I can—and will—be together soon."

"No, Nic." She faced him and stared deep into his eyes. "A marquess and a servant woman can never be together. Not the right way."

"But, for some reason which you haven't quite explained, you're not a servant any longer."

"That doesn't matter. Because I've been a servant all my life, my status is different than yours. We come from two different worlds—worlds that will never allow a servant to love a marquess. The decision is out of our hands. As much as it pains me to say this, I know I must look for another man. I must find one more to my class, just as you should find a woman closer to yours."

The voices from the others grew louder, and Tabitha blinked back the tears that were going to make their debut very soon. Out of the corner of her eyes, she saw Mr. Jacobs walking toward her—without Sally. Taking a deep breath to refresh her emotions, she turned just in time as he stopped beside her.

"I see you are doing very well in this game."

She forced herself to smile. "But of course. I have played this sport many times, and just like my aunt, this is one of my favorites."

She peeked over her shoulder at Nic. He wasn't smiling as he'd been doing since arriving for the luncheon. Pain was evident on his face, especially in his deep frown. It hurt to know she was the cause. But really, there wasn't anything she could do to change it. She was who she was, and he would always be a marquess. Neither of them could change their stations in life.

Sally came closer and Tabitha turned her attention toward her friend. The maid's smile was much brighter than Tabitha had seen before. Another pain sliced through her heart. How could she have been so jealous of her friend when Sally deserved happiness just as much as the next woman?

Tabitha would happily surrender Mr. Jacobs over to Sally. As much as she liked the man and thought him a pleasant fellow, he couldn't take her mind off Nic, and after all, that was one of the reasons she searched for a man. Now she was beginning to believe there was no such man out there. Nic would be a hard person to forget.

As the others continued to play, helplessness grew heavy within Tabitha. Was she destined to be the only one who would never find happiness? Although it was within grasp, she couldn't snatch it. The *ton* dictated what class of person was allowed to marry a servant, and Nic was definitely not in that category.

Tabitha hurried the others in the game, mainly because she couldn't wait for this luncheon to end. She needed to be by herself. Seeing how much Nic appeared wounded by her confession, it nearly destroyed her. She couldn't take it anymore.

Finally, the luncheon came to an end. Nic was actually the first one to leave. He talked to Aunt Clara and Mrs. Stiles, but not once did he look Tabitha's way. That injured her heart more than she was prepared for. Tears stung her eyes, but she blinked quickly, refusing to shed them.

Soon afterward, Mr. Jacobs made his excuse to leave, and within minutes, he was gone. Sally appeared much too happy, and even though Tabitha should be elated over her friend's joy, that emotion just was not there.

"Sally, I would stay to help you clean up the dishes, but I fear I have a terrible headache, and I need to lie down."

Sally shook her head. "You don't need to help me. I can do this myself."

Mrs. Stiles and Aunt Clara didn't say anything to Tabitha as she made her way back inside the house. Of course, they didn't hide the sadness in their eyes as they watched her depart, but thankfully, they didn't comment about it, either.

When she reached her room and closed the door, the tears she'd been holding back rushed forth. None of this was fair. As much as she wanted to change things, she couldn't. Frustration built inside of her, making her want to lash out at something—or someone.

She paced the small space in her room, but that only aggravated her more. Outside was where she needed to be—outside breathing in the fresh ocean air that had brought comfort to her since her arrival here.

She grabbed her shawl and flung open her bedroom door. She flew down the stairs in a whirlwind of confusion and rage, and left the house as if the devil himself were on her heels.

Before reaching the gate, someone called her name from over by the shade tree. Her heart sped faster, recognizing the sound of his voice before she was able to see his face. Nic leaned against the tree with his arms folded over his chest. Sadness encased his face, tearing at her heart even more.

She clutched her hands against her middle and walked to him. The tall hedges around the fence would help block anyone passing by on the street from seeing and becoming curious. When she reached him, she stopped.

"I have just one thing to ask," he said softly.

She nodded, but didn't dare speak for fear her voice would crack with emotion.

"Do you love me?"

She sucked in a quick breath of air. *Love?* Why would he ask such a question? "My lord, I don't understand why you need to know that. After all, you have not confessed to me anything of the sort. True, I know you care about me, as I care about you, but…love?"

His expression didn't change; he only blinked a couple of times. "Tabitha, you didn't answer the question. Do you love me?"

"I—I—um, I don't know." Confusion strummed through her, making her want to cry. Although she might love him, she didn't want to. Loving him would only break her heart. "Oh, Nic, I just don't know what I feel anymore. I know you think I don't know my own mind, and maybe I don't." She rubbed her forehead. "Perhaps all I need is to just get away from you for a few days to think—" She shook her head, knowing that wasn't the answer. "But really, I don't hear *you* confessing words of love toward me." She took a deep breath and quickly continued, "And do you know why you don't? It's because deep down inside, you *know* loving me is impossible. We are from two different worlds and we can never be together."

His jaw hardened and he nodded once. "That's all I need to know." He moved away from her, his feet tearing up the grass as if he couldn't wait to put distance between the two of them. Soon he was out of the yard and storming down the street toward his cousin's house.

Agony wrenched her heart, and tears came once again. Sobs escaped her throat as her legs took her in the opposite direction toward the ocean. A small wind blew, but the coolness against her skin refreshed her slightly. Tears streamed down her face in buckets by the time she reached the beach, but she didn't care if anyone saw. Thankfully, the only people out for a stroll this afternoon were farther up the beach and wouldn't disturb her.

She found a sawed off tree trunk by the grassy cliff and sat, gazing out across the ocean. Closing her eyes, she took deep breaths and literally felt herself becoming calmer. The sound of the rushing water and the waves of the ocean did that to her. This morning's accident had scared her and her life did flash before her eyes, but she was glad it didn't take away her love for the soothing waters.

Thinking back about her days here, she realized she really loved this place, but if Nic remained close by, it would be impossible to stay here. She prayed he'd help his cousin find their thief so that the marquess could return to his own home in Mayfair.

"Oh, Nic," she muttered. "Why are you doing this to me?"

She covered her hands over her face and sobbed, body-shaking, heart-wrenching cries. Resting her elbows on her knees, she continued to let her grief out the only way she knew. Yet, no matter how hard she cried, grief still stayed inside her. She would never be able to remove Nic from her thoughts or her heart. She'd always remember his endearing words. Her mind would never forget the way his eyes lit up when he smiled and winked at her. And his kiss was permanently branded on her mouth. Life as she knew it would be miserable from this day forward.

Behind her, the leaves of the bushes rustled, startling her. Within an instant, her sobbing stopped as she spun around to see what had made the noise. Through her teary vision, an older woman came toward her, brushing her sand-covered hands against the skirt of her dress.

"Miss Paget? Is that you?"

Inwardly, Tabitha groaned. She didn't want to speak to anyone, especially the meddlesome Miss Talbot. Quickly, Tabitha turned her head to wipe the tears off her cheeks and in her eyes.

"Oh, dear. You are crying."

Tabitha didn't look at the other woman, but continued to fight her emotions from boiling over again. She must stop this madness. Crying wouldn't do her any good at all. "I shall be fine, I assure you." Her voice squeaked.

Miss Talbot placed a soothing hand on Tabitha's shoulder. "Now, my dear, it'll help you more if you let it out. You can talk to me. Everyone knows I'm a good listener."

Tabitha wanted to chuckle, but she stopped herself. She wondered where the older woman had gotten that bit of information. Not once had Tabitha heard that Miss Talbot was a good listener.

"I really appreciate the offer," Tabitha said, "but I don't wish to talk about it."

"Now, Miss Paget," Miss Talbot grasped one of Tabitha's hands and squeezed, "you can tell me anything. In fact, by the forlorn look on your face, I think you have had your heart crushed by a man. Am I correct?"

Surprise washed through Tabitha that the maiden woman would know such a thing. But instead of being too stunned to speak, the tears fell freely once more and she couldn't stop them. She covered her face and sobbed into her hands. Miss Talbot's arms circled around her shoulders as a hand coaxed Tabitha's head toward the other woman's bosom—which seemed to have beads of sand on the material of her dress.

"There, there, my dear. Just let it all out now," Miss Talbot cooed.

Tabitha didn't know why she felt this way. Perhaps she just needed the comfort an older woman could bring—even if she didn't think Miss Talbot had ever experienced this kind of helplessness.

"Am I correct?" the lady asked. "Is this all because of a man?"

Sniffling, Tabitha pulled away and gazed up into the caring eyes of the older woman. "I shouldn't bother you with my problems." She skimmed over the woman's dress. "Were you digging in the sand? I don't wish to disturb you."

"Do not worry about me." She flipped her hand in the air. "One of the things I enjoy doing is collecting seashells. But I'm here for you now. Please tell me what is wrong. Did a man break your heart?"

"In a way, but it's really more than that. I'm very upset with how unfair life can be at times."

Nodding, Miss Talbot stroked a palm down Tabitha's arm. "I feel your frustration. Indeed, life is not fair. But we must continue on. We must pick ourselves up, lift our chin, straighten our shoulders, and keep looking for that one person who will love us forever."

"But I think I've found him. It's just…" Tabitha took a deep breath. "It's just that Society won't approve."

The older woman arched an eyebrow. "And why not, may I ask?"

"Because Nic is a marquess, and I'm but…a servant."

"You're not a servant." Miss Talbot looked her over once.

"Not now, but I grew up as one. It hasn't been until recently that I discovered a family I never knew would accept me. This family gives me a yearly income so I don't have to work as a servant anymore."

The woman pursed her lips together and nodded. "I see. So you are worried about what the *ton* will say if you fall in love with a marquess?"

"I already know what they'll say." Sadness clenched Tabitha's chest so tight she could scarcely breathe. "They won't approve. Nic deserves a *noble* wife. He doesn't deserve a woman who was the by-product of an affair, and then worked as a servant all of her life."

"Oh, my dear, dear, girl." Miss Talbot shook her head. "Do you know what you need? You need to come with me and let me fix you some relaxing tea. We could sit in a room without anyone bothering us, and talk over tea and treats."

Tabitha tried to smile, but failed miserably. "I appreciate your hospitality, but I really don't wish to bother you, nor your sister. I'm sure Mrs. Smythe is there and I don't want anyone else knowing about my problems."

"Not to worry." Miss Talbot slid her arm around Tabitha's shoulders and urged her to walk away from the beach. "My sister is out visiting friends this afternoon. We shall have the house to ourselves."

Tabitha glanced up the beach, but didn't immediately recognize anyone. Of course, through her teary gaze, she was certain she couldn't see that well, anyway. As much as she wanted to stay right here, the older woman was correct. Out on the beach Tabitha would risk the chance of running into someone—even

Nic. All she wanted to do was be alone, but at least Miss Talbot offered her an afternoon to do nothing but talk out her problems. Tabitha would have to be careful not to let the other woman know about the role Nic played right now, but perhaps talking to another woman would help her feel better. The way it appeared right now; Miss Talbot was the means of an escape, both mentally and physically.

"All right, I shall come with you." Tabitha tried to smile again, and finally managed a weak one.

"Splendid. Just this morning, our cook made a batch of the most delicious cookies you have ever tasted. We shall munch on those and sip our tea, and you will feel much better within a few hours, I assure you."

"Thank you, Miss Talbot."

Taking a deep breath, Tabitha wiped her eyes again. She prayed that this heartache would soon leave so that she could return to her life once again.

NIC WANTED TO leave this place. Now! Unfortunately, Frederick wasn't here, and so Nic had to wait for his cousin's return before packing up and leaving North Devon. At this point, he didn't care to help his cousin catch the thief. He was certain that one day the sinner would make a mistake and get caught.

Impatient for Frederick's appearance, Nic rushed up the stairs to his room and started packing his trunks. It didn't take long before the afternoon ended and night crept upon the land. With nothing to do now, Nic was beside himself. He was ready to leave, yet where was his cousin?

Threading his fingers through his hair, he left his bedroom and wandered downstairs, hoping to find a flask or bottle of whiskey—or anything that could be used to dull his mind. The only strong drink that Frederick had in his house was wine. That would certainly not do!

He was tempted to dress in his own clothes and go to the local tavern. He paused in thought, and then growled, scrubbing his hands over his bearded face. Unfortunately, he wasn't able to shave off this bothersome facial hair, and because of that, everyone would think he was the clergyman. And men of God definitely didn't get drunk…in front of others and in a local establishment, anyway.

He stopped near the window. Shadows gradually grew on the ground as the sun slowly disappeared on the horizon. His mind wouldn't stop reliving the conversations with Tabitha this afternoon. Why had he given his heart to the woman in the first place? Hadn't he learned years ago that loving a woman made men vulnerable? Obviously, Nic had forgotten that hard lesson in life and decided to try his luck at love once more.

Groaning, he closed his eyes and pressed his head against the window frame. Tabitha had hinted not once, but a couple of times, that *he* hadn't confessed to loving her. Yet, deep in his heart, he had definitely reached that point. So why hadn't he said those three important words to her? Had she been correct to assume the reason he didn't voice his feelings was because deep down he realized their love could never be? A marquess and a servant could never marry.

As much as his mind wanted to argue the point, he knew she had been correct.

He cursed fate for handing him a raw deal. He'd watched his friends fall in love and marry the perfect woman, so why couldn't Nic? Perhaps he was destined to be a rogue forever. He glanced down at his clergyman clothes and plucked at the black jacket. If he was meant to be a rogue, then why was he still dressed like this?

Suddenly, a knock pounded on the front door, breaking the stillness of the evening and jarring Nic away from his thoughts. He cleared his throat and went to the door to open it. Sally stood on the porch, wringing her hands against her middle.

"My lord," she said softly, "forgive me for coming to see you, but I'm wondering…do you know where Tabitha is?"

His mind jumped back to the last time he'd seen Tabitha by the tree in front of her aunt's house. She'd been so very lovely wearing that gold and white gown with her hair done up beautifully, making her look like a regal woman. The emotions he'd experienced while gazing upon her during that time also returned. It had been so hard not to take her into his arms and hold her the way he'd wanted…and to kiss her with so much passion.

A throb began in his forehead and he rubbed it with two fingers. "The last time I saw her was at the luncheon."

A deep frown pulled on Sally's mouth and she released a heavy sigh. "Oh, dear."

"What's wrong, Sally?"

"We haven't seen her since the luncheon either. The last we knew, Tabitha had gone to her room. Yet when I checked on her an hour ago, she was not there. Her bed hadn't even been touched."

His first instinct was to worry, but then he recalled her words while they were by the tree.

"Tabitha was upset and confused. I did speak briefly with her after the luncheon before I came home, and she'd mentioned she wanted to be by herself for a little while and think." He shook his head. "I wouldn't worry too much, Sally. Tabitha will return tonight, I'm sure of it."

Nodding, the maid stepped backward as if preparing to flee. "I thank you, my lord. I shall inform her aunt."

As Nic closed the door, he wondered why Tabitha wouldn't have said something to her maid about leaving. Tabitha seemed like a responsible woman, so why didn't she tell someone where she was going?

Once again, he felt as if he should worry about her welfare, but his broken heart and confused mind didn't want any more complications. The best course of action would be doing nothing.

Tabitha had wanted some time alone. He understood that better than anyone, especially now.

And as soon as Frederick came back from wherever he was, Nic would load the trunks on his coach that had been hidden inside his cousin's barn all this time, and leave as soon as he could to return to Mayfair.

The past reminded him how long it would take to mend his broken heart.

Chapter Twenty-One

B Y LATE AFTERNOON the next day, Nic was ready to strangle his cousin. Again! Where could that blasted man be? Where on earth could he have been all day *and* night? Of course, Frederick had done this before, which really hadn't bothered him, yet because he now wanted to leave this place, he wished his cousin would come home immediately.

Nic had paced the length of the entire house at least a hundred times, but that only made him more impatient. Now he feared that when his cousin finally did walk through the front door, Nic would feel the need to wrap his hands around his cousin's throat and squeeze.

The sound of a carriage pulling up to the front of the house jarred him out of his harmful thoughts. If he succeeded in choking his cousin—a man of God—Nic would certainly *not* be going to heaven.

He hurried to the window that overlooked the front yard and peered out. There were actually two coaches that had stopped in front of the house. As the door to the first vehicle opened and a head poked out, his breath caught in his throat. What in the devil was *he* doing here? Within minutes, several more familiar people had exited the conveyances.

His heart flipped with excitement and he rushed to the door, throwing it open. His best friend, Trey Worthington, and his lovely wife, Judith, led the promenade of Worthingtons from up the drive. Trevor and Louisa came next, followed by Tristan and Diana.

Stepping out on the porch, Nic folded his arms across his chest. When Trey's attention landed on Nic, the man stopped in his tracks as his eyes widened. Behind him, his brothers did the same, and even had the same dumbfounded expressions. Gasps escaped all of them, sounding like a choir.

"I say, my good man," Trey began in a teasing voice, "but I fear the world has indeed come to an end." He glanced up at the sky. "In fact, I wouldn't be surprised to see pigs flying, either." When he met Nic's gaze, Trey grinned. "But I admit, I find myself intrigued to discover why my wayward friend is dressed like a clergyman and is sporting a beard."

"I must add my interest, as well." Trevor nodded.

Tristan chuckled. "Actually, nothing that Hawthorne does surprises me anymore."

Nic laughed, suddenly feeling lighthearted again. "Actually, I'm not Hawthorne, here. I'm Mr. Woodland, the good clergyman of this parish."

Trey arched a dark eyebrow. "Oh, now I *am* intrigued…and slightly worried at the same time." He glanced at his wife. "My dear, we didn't come soon enough, I fear. Hawthorne is a lost cause."

Nic gestured his hand toward the house. "Please come in and I shall settle your worries."

Trey walked up to Nic and threw his arms around him, giving him a bear hug. "It's been too long, my friend."

Nic pulled away and nodded. "Indeed, it has." He took Judith in a small hug and placed a kiss on her cheek. She, out of all the Worthington wives, he felt comfortable enough to do this. They had become close while she was falling in love with Trey. "My lady, you are practically glowing. I swear you grow more beautiful every time I see you."

She rolled her eyes. "And you, my lord, grow bolder with

your flirtation every time I see you."

"Only for you." He winked.

Once they walked in, Trevor stopped in front of Nic and hugged him. "I must admit, I have missed seeing you as well." He shrugged. "Your personality rather grows on a person, you know."

Chuckling, Nic nodded. "I've been told that many times, Your Grace." He took Louisa's hand and kissed her knuckles. He really hadn't gotten to know Louisa that well, but she made his friend very happy, and that was good enough for Nic. "It's a pleasure to see you again."

"And you as well, Lord Hawthorne." Louisa displayed a caring smile.

When Tristan walked up to Nic, the two men embraced as if they hadn't seen each other for years…but in reality, it had been about six months. "It's good to see you, my friend," Nic said.

Tristan's gaze swept over Nic. "I sincerely hope you are keeping out of trouble."

Diana bumped her arm against Tristan. "Come now, my dear husband. You know Hawthorne better than that. He's *always* in trouble." A twinkle lit her eyes when she grinned at Nic.

He laughed and nodded. "Listen to your wife, Worthington. She knows what she's talking about." He took Diana's hand and kissed her knuckles. "It's good to see you again." Seeing Diana made him think of Tabitha, and once again, heaviness grew in his heart.

Once everyone was inside and seated, Nic stood against the hearth. "I still can't believe you *all* came to see me."

The brothers exchanged glances before Trey cleared his throat and looked at Nic. "The letter you had sent me was what encouraged us to come and visit."

Confused, Nic tilted his head. "My letter?"

"Yes, about Tabitha." Trey nodded.

"I'm aware what I wrote in the letter, but I'm not sure why my questions had all three Worthington brothers—and their wives—coming to see me."

Trevor chuckled. "Well, when our wives discovered we were planning this trip, they convinced us they needed an outing as well."

"That makes sense," Nic said, "but I find I'm still confused as to why you just couldn't reply in a letter. Why did all three of you have to come see me? Not that I'm complaining, of course, it's just that...I'm confused."

"Obviously you're *very* confused," Trey answered as he motioned his hand toward Nic's attire. "Look at the way you're dressed. Now, I'm wondering why we didn't come sooner. I fear, my good man, you have absolutely lost your mind this time. There is no way *you* could be a clergyman."

Shaking his head, Nic flipped his hand in the air. "Long story short, my cousin—the clergyman—convinced me to help him catch a thief. Part of his plan was for me to play the clergyman role so that Frederick could sneak around after dark and spy on people." He shrugged. "So that's the reason for the facial hair, and for this ridiculous outfit."

"Thank heavens you had a reason." Tristan nodded. "I wouldn't have ever believed you had given up your title as an accomplished rogue."

"For the right woman, I would." Nic practically whispered his answer, but he could see the others had heard. All three brothers wore shocked expressions—again, and their wives...well, they were women, so naturally, they appeared very pleased to hear him say that.

"So tell me, Hawthorne," Tristan said. "Why do you want to know about Tabitha? Your letter to Trey was very...eh...different."

Nic narrowed his gaze on the middle brother. *"Different?* What do you mean by that?"

"Well, you see," Trey answered for his brother, "your letter led me to believe that you might have feelings for Tabitha."

A quick breath caught in Nic's throat and this time, he nearly choked on it. Instead, he swallowed hard and shrugged. "As Tristan and Diana can probably tell you, I had gotten to know the young maid not too long ago. And of course, I wrongly accused her of murder, for which I will be forever ungrateful. When Tabitha arrived here in town, my first point of business was to make sure she knew how sorry I was. After that, we became friends, and I'll admit that I began having feelings for her."

"What kind of feelings?" Diana asked quickly. Her eyes were larger and locked on to Nic.

"I cared about her. Deeply."

"Cared?" Diana continued her questions. "As in past tense? Do you still care for her now?"

Gritting his teeth, Nic raked his fingers through his hair. Why did he suddenly feel as if he were on trial? All of them looked at Nic as if they were appalled he could have feelings for a mere maid. "Actually, Diana, I still do have feelings for her, although she has already told me it could never go any farther. Simply put, she doesn't want my affections."

Although it hurt him to confess the truth, these people were his friends, especially the brothers. They would understand Nic's heartache. Apparently they had liked Nic's answer, because their shoulders gradually relaxed.

Confusion filled Nic once more. None of this made any sense. He could understand Diana's concern, because Tabitha was a close friend, but why the others? Why *all three* Worthington brothers?

Taking a deep breath, Nic moved away from the hearth and to the window. He leaned against the wall and folded his arms. "Now will someone be so kind as to tell me why this matter is so important to you? Why does Trevor and Trey care about how I feel in regards to Diana's friend? And why did you all feel it important enough to travel all this way to come talk to me?"

Tristan stood and hesitantly moved toward Nic. The middle brother's eyes never left Nic's face. "Well, you see, Hawthorne." He scrubbed his hand over his chin. "About six months ago Diana and I discovered a secret about Tabitha. In fact, it was the very evening I was stabbed. Remember that?"

Nic nodded. "Yes, I recall you telling me about that night."

"Well, Tabitha saved me, along with my beautiful Diana, but Tabitha had been harboring a secret for many years. That night was when she told us about who she *really* was."

Nic wasn't sure he liked the direction this conversation was taking. The beat of his heart pounded a different rhythm. Even the palms of his hands were moist with uncertainty. Did he really want to know? Would it change his feelings at all? She had been hiding something from him, but obviously, she didn't feel it important to tell him. "What's her secret?"

Tristan stopped in front of him. "You remember when my father was alive and all the scandals he'd created and all the affairs he'd been in?"

"Of course. I think all of London knew about that man."

"Well, you see," Tristan continued, "Tabitha came from one of our father's affairs. She's our half-sister."

Nic gasped for air as his mind tried to absorb what Tristan had just confessed. Glancing at the others around the room, Nic realized this information was true. All of them nodded as they met his gaze.

"She's your sister?" he asked his friend.

"She is." Trey moved from his spot beside Judith and stood beside his brother. "Believe it or not, we are very happy to finally have a sister. In fact, we had arranged a story that would welcome her into our family, but Tabitha was the one who needed more time to deal with everything."

Tristan nodded. "We had planned to tell everyone that she was Father's recently acquired ward, and that she had come to us to launch into Society. By telling Society that story, we knew they'd accept her without questions asked."

Nic remained silent for a few awkward minutes as he tried to grasp the shocking information. This was the reason her status had changed from being a maid to *having* a maid beside her. This was the reason Tabitha's wardrobe looked more expensive. He was certain his kind and benevolent friends would have given their sister a yearly allowance. And...this explained why he always felt he'd known her—that she looked familiar.

Yet it didn't explain why Tabitha still thought of herself as a maid. She kept repeating how a marquess and a maid could never love each other the right way. So what was really keeping her from following her heart? Was there something about him she didn't approve of? Could it be possible that she still hasn't forgiven him from when he accused her of murder?

He shook that thought out of his head. That couldn't be it. She did have feelings for him! Her body had responded to him like a woman who was attracted to a man. Her passionate kisses had told him how much she desired being in his arms, and even her tears had told him how heart-broken she was over the thought of a marquess and maid not being able to love each other.

So why had she ended it with him? Unless...

He held his breath. Perhaps she wasn't as worried about being a maid as being an illegitimate child from a duke. She was probably extremely embarrassed.

Chuckling, he shook his head. "The puzzle pieces are starting to come together now. Tabitha is a secretive woman and would never tell me why she came to North Devon looking like a true lady with a maid by her side. She even held herself a little straighter than she had as a maid. Of course, her charming sense of humor and attitude didn't change much from when I'd first met her."

"Lord Hawthorne," Diana said, coming to stand by her husband, "I'm still very apprehensive about your feelings for Tabitha." She laid her hand on Nic's forearm. "She was treated badly while working for Lord Elliot, which I'm sure you're aware of, but she has a very tender heart, nonetheless. She doesn't need it to be broken again. Please understand."

He smiled at her. "Actually, I do understand. However, she

was the one who ended everything. Yesterday, in fact. She doesn't want to see me again, I'm afraid. She wants to find a man to marry that's closer to her station in life. She made it perfectly clear that I wasn't going to be that man." He threw up his hands in surrender. "So you see, your worry and your trip, was wasted, because nothing will ever become of my feelings for Tabitha. Ever."

Diana gave him a pathetic smile and squeezed his arm. "No, Lord Hawthorne, our trip was not wasted. It's good to see you again, and having the Worthington brothers visit with you is what they've wanted to do for quite some time."

The tenseness in the room seemed to disappear as the brothers all started talking at once, and to each other. Laughing, they each put blame at the other for the reasons they had to come see Nic. He, however, didn't believe a word of it. Obviously, they were very content with being married and having happy homes filled with children, so why should they worry about Dominic Lawrence at all?

He laughed and participated in the banter going around the room, but deep in his heart, he felt lost and lonely. Seeing his friends and their wives again reminded Nic of what he'd wanted—what he'd been thinking about having with Tabitha lately. And how he was never going to get that with her.

A knock came upon the front door, and he excused himself and went to see who had come. When he opened the door and peered into the frightened eyes of Miss McFadden, his heart dropped. Why would she seek out the clergyman at his home instead of waiting for Sunday to speak with him?

"Good morning, Miss McFadden. What a surprise to see you."

"Yes, I suppose it's wrong of me to come to your home, but I really needed to see you." She glanced over her shoulder at the coaches. "I fear I've come at a bad time, too." She moved her stare back to him and continued, "But it can't be helped. We really need to talk."

He didn't want to walk all the way to the church, so hopeful-ly because he had guests here, it would be proper to take her into Frederick's study and speak privately with her there. "Of course. Please come in."

Once she stepped inside and he closed the door, he turned and led her to the study. As he passed the sitting room, his guests looked his way with curious eyes. He paused at the doorway and told them, "Please excuse me for a moment. Something im-portant has just come up and I need to speak with this lady." He looked at the girl. "Come, my child. Let's adjourn to my study."

Murmurs from the brothers echoed in the room. Nic took a peek inside once more before walking away. He noticed how hard it was for his friends to keep a straight face. Trey and Tristan held grins behind their hands, and the women had turned their heads so their snickers were not noticed. He tried not to grin, himself. If the roles were reversed, he'd have been cackling with laughter and rolling on the floor by now.

He hurried the girl into the study before she noticed his friends' reaction and commented on it. Once inside the room with the door closed, he sighed and folded his arms. "Now tell me, what has you in such a worried state?"

"My family has decided to send me to my aunt's place in North Yorkshire until after the baby is born, which is the right thing to do."

He nodded. "Yes, that is very good."

"But as I have pondered this and everything else that has happened with David, I realized something that might be important. That's why I knew I must tell you. I'll be leaving tomorrow morning for my aunt's, and that's why I'm here now."

"Go on." He steepled his hands against his chin.

"While I was having problems with David, I confided in an-other woman…one that I knew would hold my secret. This morning when I went to tell her about me leaving for North Yorkshire, she said something that made me very curious." She rubbed her arms. "Thinking about it even now makes my skin crawl."

"What did this other woman say?"

"She reassured me that none of this was my fault…that going to North Yorkshire was the best thing to do to have my baby. When I made a comment about missing David, even though I know he'd wronged me, she told me that David was Satan's spawn and that David deserved dying in such an unnatural way. She believed it was her duty in life to weed out men like David and make them pay for their sins."

Nic could now understand why Miss McFadden's skin had crawled after hearing this, because his was doing the same thing. He tried shaking off the feeling. "Indeed, that isn't natural for someone to say. Will you tell me who this woman is? Perhaps this information should be given to the constable."

Her head bobbed quickly, making her ringlets bounce in rhythm. "Yes, that's what I thought as well. It was Miss Talbot who I had confided in; who had said those most disturbing things to me."

"Miss…Mildred Talbot? The spinster sister of Mrs. Smythe?"

"Yes of course. Is there another Miss Talbot you know?"

"Actually, there isn't." Slowly, he shook his head. "That does surprise me that she'd said such things about David."

"Apparently, many years ago when Miss Talbot was younger, a man had broken her heart, as well."

"Yes, I did hear about that." This tale was becoming very interesting now, and he was eager to find out more. "Well, I do appreciate you coming to me first. Please don't say anything to anyone right now. I'll take this up with the constable and let him see if it needs further investigating."

"I thank you, Mr. Woodland." She stood and walked to the door.

"Miss McFadden," he stopped her from opening the door. "Please remember that God does love you, and your sins can be forgiven."

Tears collected in her eyes. "Yes, I know."

He nodded. "I'll pray for you while you're gone."

He walked her through the house and to the front door. As he opened it, Sally stood on the other side, her hand raised and ready to knock. She hitched a breath but didn't say anything. Miss McFadden mumbled something and hurried off the porch and down the drive. Sally watched the other girl leave and didn't turn back to look at Nic until Miss McFadden was gone.

"Sally? What do you need?" he wondered.

"Oh, Lord Hawthorne. We are most distressed. Tabitha is still missing," she cried out before placing a hand to her mouth.

Quick footsteps from the other room came toward the entrance. Nic glanced over his shoulder to see Tristan and Diana ahead of the others.

"Sally?" Diana exclaimed and rushed to her, taking her shaking hands. "What is this about Tabitha?"

"She's gone, my lady. She disappeared and nobody knows where she went."

Tightness enclosed around Nic's heart. "She never returned last night?" he asked the maid.

She looked at him with watery eyes and shook her head. "No, she didn't. Today we all asked around town to see if anyone had seen her. Nobody had seen her since yesterday. The only person who confessed to being with Tabitha after the luncheon was Miss Talbot. She said she noticed Tabitha strolling alongside the ocean, but that's the last time she saw her."

His head throbbed with panic. Miss Talbot? Could the woman be as insane as Miss McFadden made her out to be? He prayed the girl was wrong about the spinster, because if she was correct then Tabitha might be in grave danger.

Chapter Twenty-Two

SLOWLY, TABITHA CAME awake. Immediately, a pain shot through her skull. She didn't dare open her eyes yet, but being careful, she lifted her hand to her throbbing head. Why did her arm ache, too? Softly, she patted her head, but couldn't find where she might have injured herself to have that kind of pain.

As she came more alert, a different scent hung in the air, making her want to sneeze. The dusty, unclean scent reminded her of being in Lord Elliot's attic on those occasions when he'd placed her there as punishment. Wherever she was now, she was certainly not in the room where she stayed at her aunt's house.

As she tried to remember what she'd been doing last, the memories spinning in her head seemed fuzzy. She recalled her talk with Nic and how much it hurt to say those things to him and to see the pain in his eyes. She remembered going to the ocean and meeting Miss Talbot—Mildred, the woman had asked Tabitha to call her. And she recalled the special kind of tea the older woman had served that made her feel very tired and sick to her stomach. Mildred had suggested Tabitha lie down, and…

That's all she could remember clearly. But then there were those disjointed flashbacks that didn't make any sense. Mildred had carried—almost dragged—her to another house up on a hill. Tabitha knew she'd been there before but couldn't pinpoint the location. Once inside, there were stairs going up, a hidden trap door, and darkness as they carefully made their way down another set of stairs into a musty, cellar with little to no light.

Mildred's voice echoed in Tabitha's mind, but her words didn't have any meaning. She'd said something about *justice being served* and made mention about how all *heartless men* and the jezebel women who led them astray deserved to die.

It took a few minutes of breathing deeply, but soon the pain in Tabitha's head lessened enough for her to open her eyes. A small amount of light shone through the cracks on the wooden door at the top of the stairs, but it didn't highlight the room very well. Thick shadows floated everywhere. She could barely see the stairs she'd come down from the hidden trap door. She rested upon a mattress covered by one woolen blanket, and she was thankful that she had this much. It was then that another scent assailed her senses, smelling like strong urine and…manure. Her stomach lurched. What was down here that had this kind of aroma?

Listening closely, she hoped she could detect any sounds from outside. At first she heard nothing, but soon there was a sound from within the room. The muffled cries were barely audible. Fear of the unknown escalated through her, but then she felt as if she wasn't the only one in the room. She trusted her instincts that this was a good thing.

"Is anyone there?" she said in a low voice.

A distinct gasp echoed and the rustling sound in the other corner of the room stirred the silence. "Who is here?" The voice belonged to a woman.

Relief swept through Tabitha that she was not alone. "My name is Tabitha Paget. I'm visiting my great aunt, Mrs. Burls."

"Oh, Miss Paget." The woman didn't sound very old. Perhaps still in her twentieth year or thereabouts. "Why are we here?"

"Where is *here*?" Tabitha wondered.

"I don't know, but it's an abandoned house. I've been here almost a week." A shaky breath rented the air. "At least I think it's been a week."

Slowly, Tabitha's memory opened. She now remembered the house. This was where she and Nic had met that one afternoon. "Have you seen anyone come here?"

"Only Miss Talbot. She's the one holding me prisoner."

Tabitha's head pounded harder. "Do you know why? I cannot imagine that sweet, old woman doing this."

"Looks are deceiving. Miss Talbot is not the sweet, old woman she has portrayed. She drugged me with her tea that first day, and since I've been here, she continues to put something in the food that makes me sleep. I eat it, only because I'm hungry, but I know it will put me to sleep."

A bitter taste coated Tabitha's tongue and mouth. She swallowed hard. There had been something in the tea, to be sure. Maybe even in the cookies she'd fed her. It made sense now as to why Miss Talbot kept urging Tabitha to partake of the refreshments.

"I wish I knew why she's doing this," the other woman said. "All I know is that she's not happy with me for making David Griffin fall in love with me."

Tabitha sucked in a quick breath. "Are you Miss Johnson?"

"Yes." The younger woman's voice shook.

"Keep talking. I'm going to crawl over to you."

"All right."

As Miss Johnson told Tabitha about how Mildred had brought her here, Tabitha scooted across the dirty floor on hands and knees toward Miss Johnson's voice. When she reached her, she grasped the other woman's hands. Sobbing, she fell against Tabitha.

"Oh, Miss Paget, I didn't think anyone else would be here. I thought I was going to die in this abandoned house…alone."

A chill passed through Tabitha and she tried to shake it off. She would *not* accept death. Especially not now. Not when she had lived through Lord Elliot's beatings and had begun living the kind of life she'd always dreamed about having. "Nobody is going to die if I can help it."

Memories resurfaced of those times Lord Elliot took her out in the barn and beat her with nothing but his iron fist. During all of her beatings, he'd been drunk, but the man still retained his strength. The few times he tried to rape her, he'd been too drunk to follow through with it. Thankfully, God was watching out for her then. So she must believe God would help her now.

"How often does Miss Talbot come to check on you?"

"Twice a day. She brings me food, but very little." A whine escaped the woman's throat. "I think she's trying to starve me to death. Oh, Miss Paget, I don't want to die." She sniffed. "Miss Talbot blames me for David's death. Can you believe that?"

Tabitha stroked Miss Johnson's matted hair in hopes of calming her. "How so?"

"She told me that if I hadn't flirted with David, he would still be alive."

"You don't suppose..." Tabitha held her breath. No, she shouldn't even think such a thing. The very idea was preposterous.

"Suppose what, Miss Paget?"

"That Miss Talbot...killed David."

"Oh, yes. I do think she killed my David. I don't know why, but she's very capable of murder. The grip she had on my arms was very strong, and I recall when she brought me here, I was surprised by her strength. She even kicked me a few times while I was on the ground. Indeed, that woman has the strength to end someone's life."

Miss Johnson started crying again as she leaned against Tabitha's shoulder. Each sob from the other woman broke Tabitha's heart. Miss Johnson was probably very weak and wouldn't be much help if Tabitha tried to go up against the spinster, who for some reason was set on revenge. But she couldn't understand why Miss Talbot would want Tabitha. What had she done to the older woman to upset her?

The only way she was going to know would be to ask her. Hopefully, Mildred would come soon. Tabitha didn't want to be in this dark, smelly room any longer.

Although her head was still spinning from that tea she'd sipped, Tabitha had to find a way out of here. Blinking, she tried to adjust her blurry vision enough to map out the room, but unfortunately it was too dark. But, from the small amount of light coming from the hidden trap door above them, she could barely see an outline of the stairs.

"Miss Johnson? Has Miss Talbot been here today yet?"

"I don't know. It's hard to tell when it's day or night. All I know is that she brought me some food, which of course made me sleep, and when I awoke, you were here."

"I'm going to try to crawl to those stairs." Tabitha studied the pathway she'd have to take. "I want to see if I can open the trap door."

"It's locked. I tried doing that the first day I was here, but I'm not very strong, and I couldn't get the door to budge."

Tabitha frowned. "Have you searched the room to see if there are any boards or sticks, or rocks? I'm wondering if there is anything in here we can use to defend ourselves from when she comes."

"No." Miss Johnson shivered. "I hate dark places like this. I haven't left my mattress, except of course to do the womanly necessities."

Bile rose in Tabitha's throat. Now she knew why the room smelled so wretched. "Well, I'm determined to break that door open. I still have a little strength, so I must try."

Miss Johnson squeezed Tabitha's fingers. "May God be with you—with us."

"Yes, I pray for that as well."

Taking a deep breath in hopes of clearing her mind a little better, she moved away from Miss Johnson and slowly scooted across the floor toward the stairs. Dizziness assaulted her, and she paused, trying to control the feeling consuming her body. She closed her eyes and breathed steady again, but her world still continued to tilt. *No!* She must not allow this to happen. She must be in control.

She had something to live for, and she would fight every second to keep alive. Regrets surfaced in her mind, and saddened her. Perhaps she shouldn't have been so ashamed over her parentage and allowed the Worthington brothers to introduce her to Society as their sister. After all, it wasn't *her* sin that she was born out of wedlock. It was their deceased father's sin.

And then there was Dominic, Lord Hawthorne—the only man who had achieved making her feel like a desired woman. At first she hadn't taken his flirtations seriously, because he was, after all, a gifted rogue. But he was still able to make her weak in the knees, and yearn for his passionate kisses. He'd accomplished making her fall in love with him.

She should have done things differently with Nic. Instead of trying to hide her feelings for him, she should have embraced them, and let him know how she'd fallen in love. She should not have pushed him away. Instead, she wished she'd have cherished every day—every moment—he'd made her happy and complete.

If she got out of here… No, *when* she got out of here, she'd find him and apologize and tell him her feelings. Hopefully, he would return them.

She started out toward the stairs slower this time, and focused on her destination. *I will do this!* When she bumped against the bottom step, she heaved a relieved sigh. "I'm to the steps."

"Oh, Miss Paget. Please be careful."

At this point, Tabitha didn't dare stand, so she bunched her gown to her knees and proceeded up the stairs in an unhurried pace. Right away, she could tell the steps were very rickety and old. She would definitely have splinters in her palms and knees once she was finished. But she'd worry about that later.

When she placed her weight on the next step, it creaked and wobbled. She held her breath, praying that it wouldn't break beneath her. Then she realized if Miss Talbot's large frame hadn't broken the piece of wood by now, there was no way Tabitha's small body would, either.

Continuing on her way, she crawled slower. She discovered that hurrying only made the dizziness in her head worse. But she was almost to the top of the stairs, so she couldn't stop now. As she climbed the next step, it trembled more than the first had. Reaching her hand out, she tried to grasp something to hold onto. Wasn't there supposed to be a railing? But she couldn't find it. Blindly, she searched for something to stop her—to keep from tumbling down the steps, but her hand came up empty.

God, please help me!

FOR SOME REASON, Frederick was also missing.

But Nic was more worried about Tabitha. Unfortunately, in order to find her, Nic needed his cousin to make an appearance and take over the role as clergyman. This way, Nic could go and do as he pleased without people thinking he was the man of God.

While the Worthington brothers and their wives settled in their rooms at the inn, Nic went out in town dressed as the clergyman—since he felt he needed to play this part. His main purpose was to find Miss Talbot. He didn't know what he'd say to her when he found her, but if she did take Tabitha, he wouldn't stop hounding the spinster until he received some answers.

His walk through town was more hurried than before, and some of the people who waved, gave him a curious stare. He could tell some of them wanted to talk, but Nic wouldn't stop for anyone but Miss Talbot.

Ever since his conversation with Miss McFadden, he wondered why the spinster would act in such a way. He knew about having her heart broken by a man in her younger years, but why would she think that men like David didn't deserve to live? Why would Miss Talbot make it her duty in life to weed out men like David and make them pay for their sins?

His gut feeling told him Miss Talbot was not right in the head. Something sinister was afoot in this town, and he needed to find out what it was. Because of Miss Talbot's anger toward David Griffin, Nic wondered if she had anything to do with the young man's death. Was the spinster insane enough to kill? She was a tall, stout woman—whereas David was thin. Did the woman have the strength to carry a dead body to the sandy beach and bury him by herself? Or had she enlisted help?

And did this even relate to the theft at the church? Frederick had remembered seeing someone who was thin twist their ankle as the suspect fled the scene of robbery. Frederick also recalled seeing a larger man who'd sprinted out the back door first. By these descriptions, Nic wondered if it was Miss Talbot and David. After all, when the doctor had examined the young man's body, he'd mentioned a broken ankle. What were the odds Miss Talbot was dressed as a man? But more importantly, *why* was she doing this? What were her reasons?

These questions and more would be answered if he could find the blasted woman!

The house she shared with her widowed sister was finally within view. He quickened his step until he stood in front of the door. He knocked hard, and then grimaced. Perhaps he shouldn't have pounded on the door with so much force.

The door was answered by Mrs. Smythe. When she looked at Nic, her eyes widened.

"Oh, Mr. Woodland. What a wonderful surprise to have you visit."

He smiled the best he could under these circumstances. "I hope you don't mind me coming unannounced. I'm actually looking for your sister."

She gaped for a few awkward moments. "Mildred? You wish to see her?"

"Yes, of course. Is something wrong with that?"

"Of course not, Mr. Woodland. In fact, I'm very happy that you would want to see my sister. However, she's not here right now, and that upsets me greatly."

He arched an eyebrow. "You're upset that she's not here?

Why, may I ask?"

She chuckled. "Because after all these years a man comes calling on her, and she's not here to receive him."

Oh, for goodness sake! She thought Nic—or the clergyman—wanted to *court* the spinster? Well, he supposed miracles did happen, but it was still quite humorous. Unfortunately, now was not the time to laugh. "By chance, do you know where she's at?"

"I do not. My sister enjoys walking along the beach and finding seashells. Other than that, I cannot possibly imagine where else she'd be."

"I thank you, Mrs. Smythe. I shall go down by the beach to look for her." He turned to leave, but the older woman grabbed his arm, stopping him. He peered into her mischievous eyes.

"Mr. Woodland, if I might suggest something." She grinned. "I think you should find some daisies to take with you. She loves daisies."

He gritted his teeth and counted to ten under his breath. It wasn't wise for Dominic Lawrence's true nature to come out right now, but Nic's impatience was having a hard time staying hidden. "Indeed, that's a good suggestion. Thank you."

When Mrs. Smythe released his arm, he breathed a sigh of relief and hurried away from the house. He turned in the direction that would lead him toward the beach, but something halted his progress. It was almost like an invisible force moved in front of him, keeping him from going any further. How strange…

Closing his eyes, he rubbed his forehead and took deep breaths. The afternoon sun shone warm upon him, and he realized summer would be here soon. The birds squawked as they flew by. In the distance, the splashing of waves hitting the rocks was heard. Closer to town, children played and laughed. But there was another sound…something that he didn't normally hear, and it was coming from behind Mrs. Smythe's house.

He turned his head and peeked in that direction. There was nothing behind the house except for the yard. And the only building behind that was up on a hill. It was the old abandoned house where he'd met Tabitha that one afternoon. That was the first time he'd heard her jovial laugh. The musical sound was still in his memory, and he could hear it now.

But that wasn't the sound he heard a moment ago. It was more like a loud...cry. Almost as if someone were pleading for help. How odd.

Shrugging off the feeling, he turned back toward the ocean and took another step, but once again, the same sensation washed over him, holding him from going any farther. What in the blazes was wrong?

Once more, something tugged on his conscience and made him look toward the abandoned house up on the hill. An eerie sense of remembrance came over him, and for some reason, he pictured him and Tabitha exploring the inside of that house. It was empty, which he had found strange at the time, but there were unexplained footsteps in the corner of the room that had disturbed him more.

Usually, he allowed his feelings to guide him in the direction he needed to go, and right now, his feelings told him to look inside the house again. The more he studied the place, the stronger the urge became. He couldn't ignore it, yet he wanted to because searching for Miss Talbot was top priority—and finding Tabitha.

Oh, bugger! He grumbled and sprinted toward the house on the hill, praying that he'd find something important. He didn't want to waste any time on something useless. And right now, he feared going to the abandoned house would indeed take him on a goose-chase.

Chapter Twenty-Three

"MISS PAGET? ARE you all right?"

Miss Johnson's panicked voice rang through the stillness. Before answering, Tabitha wanted to wait until the room stopped spinning, but it wasn't happening any time soon. The tips of her fingers dug into something hard and the pain was almost unbearable, but she refused to let go. At least she hadn't fallen. That was a good thing.

She breathed deeply, praying her mind would become clear again. Slowly, she opened her eyes and gathered her wits. She was still on the steps, thank goodness. Her limbs shook, but she couldn't tell if she was losing her strength or if it was her nerves causing the problem. Either way, she must ignore it. She must keep moving.

"Miss Paget," Miss Johnson's voice strained with panic. "Please answer me!"

"I'm all right. I'm just a little dizzy."

"Whatever it is that Miss Talbot adds to her tea, it has a lingering effect. It's just awful, I tell you."

"Be that as it may, I cannot allow it to stop me."

Tabitha pushed herself until she teetered on the top step. She didn't want to give into her sigh of victory—not yet. Things were definitely not over. This was just one small obstacle she had to hurtle over, she was certain.

Moving her hands up the wall, she felt for the door opening. The large piece of wood jiggled slightly, but it was obvious that there was a hooked lock on the other side. Straining her eyes, she followed the seam between the trap door and the wall until she saw the exact point where the hook was located. If she had something thin enough to slide between the seam in order to unhook the latch, perhaps she could open this door after all. But what could she use?

Immediately, her fuzzy mind knew. For the luncheon that her aunt had, Tabitha had tried to make herself lovely by fixing her hair differently. She'd used several pins to hold the coil together.

Excitement rushed through her as she fished through her hair to locate the pins. One by one, she pulled them out until her hair tumbled down her shoulders. She clutched the hair-pins tightly and looked back at the seam again. Now, she had to stand. *Oh, heavens*. This would be difficult, only because she was still very dizzy.

Using all of her strength, she leaned against the wall as her legs pushed her up. While one hand clutched the hair-pins, the other assisted in balancing her against the wall as she made an upward climb. When she was finally standing, her legs shook terribly. Staying against the wall, she slid one of the pins through the seam. Her hand trembled, making it hard to focus. When the pin reached the hook located on the other side of the wall, she pushed with all her might to get the object to move.

Tension from the other side resisted her efforts, which made it difficult to wiggle the hair-pin. She gripped harder, hoping it would steady her hand better. But the pin slipped from her fingers and fell to the other room. Groaning softly, she took another hair-pin and tried again. Just as she connected with the hook, the pin slid from her fingers and fell just like the one before it had.

Frustration filled her, but she couldn't give up. She still had two more hair-pins left. She must keep trying!

Taking a deep breath and repeating in her mind *I can do this,* she took hold of another pin and pushed it through the seam. Trying to keep her hand steady, she wiggled the pin against the hook. Something moved on the other side, but yet the door remained locked.

Hope sprang inside her. Maybe, just maybe she was getting closer to removing the obstacle. She tried it again, but the pin bumped against something hard and flipped out of her fingers. As she tried to grab it, the last pin fell from her hand as well.

Her hopes fell to the ground along with the hair-pins, and her heart shattered.

"No!" Tears burned beneath her eyelids. She knocked her forehead against the door as she pounded her fists against the wood. How could she have lost all of the pins? If she had only tried harder. Things would have worked. Why couldn't her hands be steadier?

"What's wrong, Miss Paget?"

Defeat overwhelmed Tabitha and she sank to her knees. "I cannot open the door," she told the other woman in a choked-up voice.

Miss Johnson's heartfelt sobs rang through the room. The tears Tabitha had been holding back slid from her eyes and streamed down her cheeks.

Their future looked grim.

THE CLOSER NIC walked to the abandoned house, the more anxious he became. Something told him this was where he'd find answers.

What could he say to Miss Talbot when he finally found her? He could demand she tell him where she was keeping Tabitha, but then if Miss Talbot were truly innocent, she would be put off by his rude behavior. But making small talk with her was out of the question. Tabitha needed to be found, and quickly. Yet, if

Miss Talbot was responsible, then he needed to somehow get on that topic.

As he neared the front door, he scanned the perimeter and slowed his steps. If this place was supposed to be abandoned, then why did he feel as if eyes were watching him? The chills running up and down his spine testified to the fact that something was sinister about this place. Surprisingly, he hadn't felt that way when he met Tabitha here for lunch. So perhaps it was only lately that this house had turned very disturbing.

Just as he placed his foot on the front porch step, the rustling of bushes sounded from the corner of the house. He froze, keeping his gaze fastened to that spot. Miss Talbot bustled from around the corner, brushing off her gardening gloves. Her focus was on her gloves and she didn't see him. Quickly, he stepped away from the porch and stood still, waiting for her to notice his presence. When she finally looked up and saw him, she stopped dead in her tracks. Her mouth dropped open.

"Mr. Woodland? What....are you doing here?"

He could ask her the same question, which he would after he figured out a reason for being here. "Well, you see, I was at home studying the Bible, and I had a strong impression that I needed to come to this house." Not bad, if he had to say so himself, especially since a little of it was true. "What are you doing here?" He glanced from her dirt-smudged gown, down to her mud-crusted shoes, then up to her gardening gloves.

"Oh, well...I have been tidying up the yard lately." She shrugged. "It gives me something to do, and I'm helping Mr. Lancaster take care of his property while he's away."

"I haven't seen Mr. Lancaster around for several months. Do you know where he went?"

"I believe he's living with his brother now. Mr. Lancaster was getting on in years and could not afford to take care of the house, nor did he have the strength to care for himself."

"Yes, I suppose, but..." Nic scratched his chin and narrowed his gaze toward the house. "I'm still wondering why I received such a strong impression to come here. It was as if the Lord was trying to tell me something."

"Oh, dear."

Miss Talbot had said it so softly, he wasn't sure he'd heard her correctly. "What did you say?"

"Uh, well…I just don't know why you were prompted to come here." She shook her head. "It's just me, and I'm fine. Unless—" She batted her eyes as if she were a young flirtatious girl once again, and moved closer. "Perhaps you came to help me."

He arched an eyebrow. "Help you do what? Tidy up the yard?"

She chuckled and flipped her hand in the air. "Heavens, no. I'm doing well enough by myself. However, I would love some company. If you'd come inside," she motioned her head toward the house, "I will fix you some tea."

He was about ready to ask her where they'd sit since the last time he was here, there was not a stitch of furniture in the house, but then he quickly decided against saying that. He didn't need her asking questions as to why he was in the house. "Well, I suppose. But I cannot stay long. I'm preparing Sunday's sermon."

"Oh, how nice. Perhaps you can tell me all about it over tea."

She walked past him and up the porch steps. When she turned the knob and opened the front door, he wondered how she was able to accomplish that since the door had been locked a few weeks ago. Unless, she had taken over the inside of the house as well as the outside.

Hesitantly, he followed her in…and halted in shock. Two couches and one small table stood in the room. Curtains even hung on the windows. Where had all of this come from?

"Mr. Woodland, please come in the kitchen with me. It's cozier in here. I haven't been able to keep the sitting room clean."

Cautiously, he stepped into the kitchen, and once again, surprise washed over him. There was a table and two chairs, and even some pots and a kettle on the stove. A scent of roast beef hinted the air. Food? She was cooking food? Here instead of her own house? Definitely, something was afoot here.

She went to the cupboard and withdrew two teacups before moving to the stove. Suspicious, Nic narrowed his gaze. What was going on? None of this was in the house when he and Tabitha had walked through a few weeks ago.

"So, Miss Talbot," he began, hoping he'd know the right words to say to get her talking about Tabitha. "I noticed you with Miss Paget yesterday afternoon down by the beach."

Her body stiffened as she stood in front of the stove. "You did?"

"Yes. She's a lovely woman, don't you agree? So kind and caring. Did you know she and her maid have been assisting Mr. Jacobs and his daughter?"

"Uh, no…I wasn't aware of that. She hadn't told me." Miss Talbot glanced at him over her shoulder. "Do you think Miss Paget is seeking Mr. Jacobs out for marriage purposes?"

He could see by her hopeful expression that this was what she'd wanted. Instead of going along with the idea, he decided to shake things around. Frederick might hate him, but it's something Nic felt he had to do in order to get answers.

"Actually, I think she was just helping him out of the kindness of her heart. Not only that, but the other day, I noticed the way Mr. Jacobs was eyeing Miss Paget's maid, so I think there might be a marriage soon between the blacksmith and the maid." He wagged his eyebrows. "That being said, I must confess that since Mrs. Burls' birthday party, and since the song Miss Paget and I sang together, I have been thinking of her more and more. And then when I rescued her from drowning, I felt differently about her. Something special warmed my heart." He sighed heavily for dramatic purposes, and smiled. "I'm thinking of seeking her out for marriage, myself."

Slowly, Miss Talbot turned toward him. Her expression changed from light-hearted to sour in the course of a few seconds. Lines of anger creased her forehead, around her eyes, and mouth.

Even the color of her eyes had changed, growing a darker brown.

Good heavens, if he wasn't mistaken, he had finally found the words that brought out the devil in her. Literally!

"You don't say," she spat.

The tone of her voice grated on his nerves. He watched her closely, wondering if her fingernails would turn into claws and horns would sprout from her head, but so far they hadn't. But her whole countenance had shifted. No longer did she appear the kind older woman he'd been visiting with these past few months. Instead, she looked like a beast; evil and menacing.

"Is something wrong, Miss Talbot?" Of course, he acted as if he didn't notice her sudden change.

"Wrong? Of course not, Mr. Woodland. What could possibly be wrong? After all these years, you are finally thinking of marriage once again. How lovely for you."

The tone of her voice didn't match the sweetness of her words. But he still acted as if he didn't notice. "Indeed, it is. And Miss Paget is a very stunning woman. I have talked to her a few times, and she has been very perceptive to the subtle hints I've been dropping her about wanting to court her."

"I'm sure she is aware of your interest, and returns your feelings. What woman in their right mind wouldn't find you attractive and charming?"

He forced a laugh, shaking his head. "Miss Talbot, you are too kind. But I've heard that about you. Miss McFadden mentioned to me how very generous and helpful you've been toward her. I'm so grateful there are women in the world like you, Miss Talbot."

"Uh…yes, Miss McFadden is a most unfortunate girl. My heart goes out to her. But I must say, I'm very glad she never got the chance to wed that horrible Mr. Griffin's son, David." She turned back to the stove to prepare the tea.

"Really? And why not? David seemed like a fine man, and would have made Miss McFadden a good husband."

"Then you didn't see the man I knew him to be." She lifted

her chin, stubbornly, bringing their cups of tea over to the table. She placed his in front of him before taking hers to the other side of the table and sitting. She continued, "David Griffin was a chameleon. He lied to our dear Sarah, leading her to believe he loved her when in fact, his eye was turned by another stunning female." She gave a sharp nod. "Indeed, that man deserved his fate."

"I'm sorry to hear you say that. In fact, I'm rather shocked to hear those words come from your mouth. It's not very Christian of you to think in such a way."

"Then forgive me for this sin, but I cannot forgive men like David. They care about no one but themselves."

"Is it because the same thing happened to you?"

Her jaw tightened as she fisted her hands on the table. Yet her gaze wasn't laced with malice. Instead, he saw sadness coating her eyes.

"Yes, the same thing happened to me. Kent's actions ripped out my heart. The experience left me a broken woman, and I have truly never recovered."

"I'm sure the experience was troubling, Miss Talbot." He took a sip of the tea, but it was still too hot to drink. "Tell me, what did you do when you discovered the man you loved being unfaithful?"

Her eyes watered, and he almost kicked himself for being so mean and pushing the issue. Yet instinct told him this was the only way he was going to get answers.

"I made things right," she said, staring at her teacup. "I will always make things right." The tone of her voice had started out in a whisper but was growing louder the more she talked. "Men like David and Kent do not deserve happiness. I won't allow it."

She pushed away from the table and moved to the cupboards behind him. Once she was in back of him, he didn't turn to see what she was doing. Obviously, he made her uncomfortable, but he'd keep on pushing for answers.

"Miss Talbot, did you have anything to do with David's death?"

Silence stretched through the room. Occasionally, he heard her deep breaths, but that was all. He lifted the teacup to his mouth and sipped once more. The liquid wasn't as hot, so he swallowed more. A bitter taste coated his tongue. Grimacing, he set the cup back on the table. This was the most disgusting tea he'd ever consumed.

Finally, she released a rush of air. "Mr. Woodland, you will never know what it's like. You are handsome and charming. I'm sure women have flocked to you, and you haven't even needed to lift a finger to encourage them. People like me are not anything like you. We aren't as attractive. We don't possess any charm. We must do all we can in order to win those we fall in love with. And because we put so much effort into it, when we get our hearts broken, it turns us into monsters."

Once again, chills ran up his body. He still didn't dare look at her, but her tone of voice let him know he was conversing with a half-crazed woman. He should get out of here immediately, and summon the constable. However, Nic needed more answers before he left. He couldn't leave without knowing where Tabitha was being kept. Deep down in his heart, he knew something was wrong—that she was in danger.

"I'm sorry, but I must disagree with you. Beauty is in the eye of the beholder. My wife was not the most beautiful woman I'd met, nor was she the most charming. But what drew me to her was her kindness and the way she loved unconditionally. Her personality made her the loveliest woman in the world to me." He recalled his cousin speaking of his deceased wife this way. "Most men look for those qualities in a woman, and if they don't, then they aren't good men at all. What I'm trying to say, Miss Talbot, is that Kent might not have been a good man, but there are others out there who are. If you hadn't hardened your heart toward men, I'm sure you would have found the right one, just for you."

"I don't believe you."

Her tone of voice sounded foreign with so much anger behind each word. He turned to look at her, and she stood over him wielding a butcher knife high in her hand. Her eyes were so dark they were almost black as she stared at him.

Startled, he jumped out of his chair, knocking into the table. The teacup spilled over, but he didn't care. He needed to stop this madwoman before she plunged the sharp blade into his chest. Yet, as he stepped back, dizziness assailed him and he stumbled. Why was he feeling this way?

As each second passed, the dizziness in his head worsened. The room tilted, and he grasped the counter to hold himself up. "Miss Talbot, what have you done to me?"

"I'm going to dispose of you the same way I got rid of Kent and David. Then once you are laid to rest, I will torture the women who are responsible for luring the men away from us. Miss Johnson and Miss Paget will soon die slow and very painful deaths."

Nic fought the cloud of darkness trying to fill his head. He couldn't let her get him. He had to save Tabitha!

Chapter Twenty-Four

NIC BLINKED QUICKLY, trying to keep his vision clear. If she made a move toward him, he had to prepare for it; to block the attack. "Miss Talbot, would you think of what you're doing?"

She sneered. "I know exactly what I'm doing." She stepped closer and raised her knife. "I either kill you with this weapon, or I whack you over the head with a shovel like I did David."

Nic's stomach lurched. Neither way sounded good. "But...I'm a clergyman. Surely, if you kill me, the Lord will strike you down and your life will end." He wasn't sure that would happen, but he must implant fear in her one way or another.

"I don't believe you, Mr. Woodland." She shook her head. "I also didn't believe Tabitha when she was relaying her sad story to me about not being able to love a marquess. At first I thought she was being truthful, but then I realized she was substituting names to protect you. When she referred to a man named Nic, I knew she was thinking of you. She just didn't want me to know the truth, but I have a sharp mind."

"What...did Tabitha say about loving a marquess?" he wondered. Although he wanted to know, he mainly wanted to keep Miss Talbot busy so he could think of a way out of this mess—while his head swam in a fog, no less.

"She wailed on about how life was unfair. She called herself a servant—which I knew she wasn't—and that she was in love with a marquess, but she knew Society wouldn't approve."

For a moment, happiness bounced in his chest with the knowledge that Tabitha was indeed in love with him. "Was that all she said?"

"Did you know that she was born out of wedlock? How revolting!" She shook her head. "And apparently, because of her status in life, she felt you—her imaginary marquess—deserved a better wife."

Just as he had suspected. That was the reason she had pushed him away. "Actually, she wasn't imagining anything of the sort. She is in love with a marquess, just as the marquess is in love with her."

Confusion crossed Mildred's face and she scowled. "What are you talking about?"

He brushed his hands through his powdered hair, removing the white color. Then he shrugged out of Frederick's jacket that was nearly two sizes too large for Nic. He tightened the material of his shirt around his waist, showing the older woman that he wasn't fat. Of course if she remembered how he looked when he was wet the other morning, then she'd know something was off about him. "I'm not the clergyman. I'm his cousin, Dominic Lawrence, Marquess of Hawthorne. We first met approximately five months ago. Do you not remember?"

"I—I—I don't understand." She clutched the knife with both hands now, still holding it toward him.

"My cousin and I switched roles. For approximately two months Frederick feigned sick so that I could grow a beard, which would help me look more like my cousin. Then I told everyone I had lost weight due to my sickness."

"You're lying."

"I'm telling the truth, and if my cousin were here now, he would prove to you that he's the true clergyman, and not I." Hesitantly, he reached out his hand toward her. "Miss Talbot…Mildred, please give me the knife. Nobody needs to die over this."

Shaking her head, she slashed the knife toward him. He jumped back and stumbled again. The wooziness in his head was still in control. Blast it all! Glancing down at his shirt, he noticed she had ripped the material. Thankfully, though, the knife hadn't touched his skin.

"Don't call me Mildred. You do not have the right."

"Miss Talbot, please let me help you."

"You want to help me?" Tilting back her head, she cackled with laughter. "Then stand still so I can push this knife into your deceiving heart."

"Why do you want to kill an innocent man? You thought I was the clergyman, and I'm not. I know you are in love with my cousin, but I'm not him. So in reality, you haven't been hurt in the least. I love Tabitha, and so you can still love Frederick."

"Oh, you think I'm obtuse, don't you? If you are indeed Lord Hawthorne, then I remember well about your reputation as a rogue. And since you are a rogue, then you must die because I'm quite certain you have broken many hearts along your journey."

"But Miss Talbot, you're forgetting something else. Because I'm not Frederick, Tabitha hasn't betrayed you in any way. Tabitha loves *me*, not my cousin. I pray, let her go, because she's innocent…more so than I."

Miss Talbot hesitated. A different emotion crossed her face, making her appear more forgiving and understanding. He hoped she at least pondered on this good and hard—for several minutes would be nice, since he still hadn't figured out a way to defend himself.

He glanced at the stove which was close to him. The tea kettle was still there, and the water would be hot. Perhaps this was the answer. Now he could only hope his movements were faster than hers.

From somewhere in the house, a loud crash shook the walls. Mildred gasped and swung toward the hallway, but her gaze moved up to the ceiling. Something—or someone—was upstairs. *Tabitha?*

With the spinster's back toward him, he took the opportunity and grabbed at the tea kettle. In one smooth movement, he turned the kettle and let the water splash on Mildred. She dropped the knife and screamed. Taking several steps backward, she staggered and fell to the ground. When her back touched the floor, she screamed louder and rolled to her front. Nic knew she'd received some burns, which was why she reacted in such a way.

He reached for the knife that was by his feet, but tripped. Thankfully, though, he was still able to grab it.

Miss Talbot glared at him and struggled to stand. He held the knife toward her and shook his head. "I wouldn't do that if I were you."

"Nic? Is that you?"

An angelic voice drifted from the hallway and softened his heart. He lifted his gaze just in time to see Tabitha peek around the corner as she leaned against the wall. His heart soared with gladness. She wasn't hurt…although she did look as dazed as he felt. If Miss Talbot overcame her pain and turned on him, would they be able to fend her off in their state of lightheadedness?

"Tabitha, my love. I'm here."

Tears streaked down her face as she moved slowly toward him, but then stopped when she noticed Miss Talbot on the floor.

"She won't hurt you. I have the knife," he told Tabitha. "Keep coming toward me."

Instead of watching Tabitha, he kept his eyes on the spinster just in case she tried to grab the woman he loved. Mildred glowered at him. She must have realized he'd do anything to protect Tabitha.

When she reached him, her body fell against him, which knocked him off balance against the stove. At least he was in an upright position. He gathered her in a tight embrace.

"Oh, Nic. I thought I'd never see you again."

He kissed her forehead, but quickly looked back at Miss Talbot. "Tabitha, my lovely, you should have known I would search everywhere for you until you were found. There's nothing I wouldn't do to show you my affections."

"I have been so wrong," she muttered against his chest. "I should have never told you the things I did. I love you, Nic, and I always will."

"And I love you more than life itself." He kissed her forehead again. "Don't ever leave me. We will *make* it work…our love will prevail."

"Stop it!" Miss Talbot screamed, holding her hands over her ears. "I don't want to hear another word. Do you realize what this is doing to me?" Slowly, she dropped her hands as tears filled her eyes. "All you're doing is reminding me of a love I will never have. Mr. Woodland will never want me now, and I tried so hard and for so long. I had it all worked out, too." She wiped at her eyes as she sat up, but still hunched her sore back. "I wanted to show Frederick what a wonderful woman I was. I wanted to do something for him to take notice of me. So one night, I snuck into the church, and I stole one of the statues. When I realized I could get away with this, I decided to steal more. I hired David Griffin to assist me since he was looking to earn money. Of course, I thought it was so that he could purchase Sarah McFadden a wedding ring." She huffed. "But when we tried to steal more things from the church, we were almost caught, so I decided not to do it again."

"I don't understand," Nic said. "What did you think to gain by doing this?"

"Because I was going to hide them somewhere and then let Frederick know I'd found the missing items. He would think I was trying to help him, and in doing that, he'd see me for the loving and kind woman that I really want to be." More tears fell. "But now I can't do that. You will tell him that I'm a killer, and he'll never love me."

Tabitha turned her head and looked at Miss Talbot. "I feel sorry for you, Mildred. You are truly one demented woman."

"Now, now, my lovely." He squeezed Tabitha's arm. "We should not judge. That's the Lord's job."

Tilting her head back, she gazed up into his eyes and grinned. "You are turning more and more into a clergyman every day. Imagine that."

He could see how she struggled with consciousness even now. Mildred must have drugged Tabitha just as the spinster had drugged him.

"Nic, Miss Johnson is in the hidden room as well. We must get her out."

He threw Mildred a glare before meeting Tabitha's tender gaze once more. "We will, my lovely. As soon as help arrives."

"Are others coming?"

He shrugged. "I can only pray they are."

From his mouth to God's ears... Outside the house, men's voices grew louder, and more urgent. Footsteps pounded up the front porch mere seconds before the door flew open and hit the wall.

"Hawthorne? Are you in here?"

Relief washed through Nic. "Trey, I'm in here."

Trey rushed into the room first, followed by the constable. Behind them were Tristan and Trevor. All the men held pistols.

Another pair of heavy footsteps ran inside the house and into the kitchen. Frederick's face was pale, his eyes were wide with worry. He glanced from Nic and Tabitha, down to the floor at Mildred.

"What is going on here?" the clergyman snapped.

Nic pointed the knife toward Mildred as he glanced at the constable. "There is David's murderer." He switched his focus back to Frederick. "And she is your thief, as well. She confessed everything."

Frederick scowled. "But you aren't a clergyman! You cannot listen to confessions."

Tabitha chuckled very weakly. "No, Mr. Woodland. Miss Talbot admitted her crimes to both of us after Nic told her he wasn't the clergyman."

The constable grabbed Miss Talbot's arm and Frederick

helped the wounded woman, taking hold of her other arm. She cried out, but finally stood.

"Frederick, you might want to have the doctor examine her back. She has severe burns," Nic told him.

Trey and Tristan hurried over to them. Tristan took Tabitha's hand in his. "Are you all right?"

Sighing heavily, she glanced up at Nic and smiled. "I am now."

Nic winked at her. "So am I."

Tabitha grew weak in his arms. Obviously, she was dazed worse than he was. "Tristan, we need to lie her down somewhere. She's been drugged."

Between him and Tristan, they helped her into the other room to lie down on the couch. As soon as her head hit the cushion, she closed her eyes and her head rolled to the side.

"Poor girl." Trey shook his head. "I've never seen anyone in such a state before."

Huffing with exertion, Frederick entered the house again and stopped next to Nic. "Can you please explain what happened here? I was only gone for one day, and I return to—" he swept his hand through the air, "this mayhem!"

Nic scowled. "Exactly! You were gone for one day and you didn't tell me where you were going or when you'd return. *You* could have been the one to handle all of this, not me. *You* are the clergyman, after all."

Frederick nodded and pushed his fingers through his hair. "Yes, and I'm deeply sorry for not being here." He heaved a breath. "But I'm glad it's over and our thief was discovered."

Irritation flowed through Nic and he rolled his eyes. "*You* are glad? Pray, what were you doing all this time? You were supposed to spy on people, and yet I was the one who discovered everything." He glanced at the Worthington brothers who all stood with their arms crossed, glaring at Frederick as if they waited for his answer.

Frederick frowned. "Yes, I'm aware of that, and I apologize

again. I had really been spying, but perhaps not as much as I could have been doing. You see," he released another loud sigh, "I've met someone, and I felt compelled to get to know this person a little better."

Nic arched an eyebrow. "Why? Did you suspect them of being the thief?"

"No." Frederick scratched his chin. "But I met her when I'd followed the Griffin's houseguest home the other night. She lives in the same township. I feel like a different man when I'm around her, and well..." he shrugged, "after all these years I've actually considered courting again."

Nic gaped at his cousin. He wasn't sure whether to become upset at the man for doing that instead of what Frederick had said he'd do...or become happy for Frederick because he was finally going to find a wife.

"Well, I suppose I should congratulate you instead of trying to wring your neck." Nic nodded.

Frederick chuckled. "Yes, I'd greatly appreciate that, my good man. I'm rather fond of where my head attaches to my body."

He clapped his hand on Nic's shoulder, which threw him off balance again. He stumbled, but then grasped on to his cousin's arm. Dizziness flowed through Nic. Groaning, he rubbed his forehead. "Good grief! I wish I knew what was in that tea that Miss Talbot fixed for me, because it has made me very lightheaded."

Trevor chuckled. "Perhaps, Hawthorne, you are lightheaded for a different reason?" He gestured his head toward Tabitha asleep on the couch.

A grin stretched across Nic's face. He just couldn't help it. He was very much in love and wanted everyone to know it. "I'll admit, Your Grace, that I do love her with all my heart and I can't live without her."

Trevor groaned loudly. "This is just great. All these years Hawthorne has acted like part of the family, and now he's actually going to marry our sister just to become one of us." He shook his head and grinned.

Laughter filled the room quickly. Love spread through Nic's heart, easing all his fears. Once again, everything was right with the world.

Chapter Twenty-Five

I N QUIET SOLITUDE, Tabitha sat on the couch with her legs tucked under her as she stared at the low burning fire. Her aunt and Mrs. Stiles had left her alone to her thoughts this morning, which was what she truly wanted. Yesterday had been a very long day, most of which was spent wondering whether she'd live or die. Now she was content to think back on the horrors she'd experienced, realizing that she was a stronger woman than she first imagined—not only physically, but mentally.

Lord Elliot had tried to instill vulnerability in her mind by telling her that weak women should always be controlled with an iron fist. Now she knew differently, and the realization was like a new world opening her eyes to everything and everyone around her, and especially, to her own feelings.

Of course, her new world had a lot to do with Nic. If not for him, she would have never known love and acceptance. He had known she was a maid but still allowed his heart to soften for her. Now there was just one last test Nic had to pass. Deep in her heart, she prayed he would still love her when he discovered her true parentage. She wondered if her meddlesome brothers had said anything to Nic about it, but he acted as if he didn't know.

Although...why did her brothers choose to come to North Devon for a visit? Was it to see her or Nic? She had yet to hear their explanation for that.

Smiling, she rolled her head on the back of the couch. Never had she been this happy before. Everyone should be able to experience such joy. According to what her aunt had said this morning, Sally and Mr. Jacobs were hitting it off splendidly. Tabitha was certain she'd hear a wedding announcement in the near future.

A knock came upon the front door, and moments later, she heard Mrs. Stiles' cheerful voice. Soon footsteps thudded on the hallway floor, coming closer to the sitting room. Tabitha dropped her feet to the Persian rug and quickly slipped into her shoes before the visitors arrived. Just as she straightened, Mrs. Stiles and Miss Johnson entered.

"Tabitha, my dear, you have a visitor." She motioned her head toward the younger woman. "I knew you wouldn't mind if she came to see you."

Smiling big, Tabitha rose from the couch and held out her hands for the younger woman to grasp. "Not at all. I will always welcome your company, Miss Johnson."

After slipping her hands in Tabitha's, the other woman shook her head. "I thought I told you to call me Dawn."

"Indeed, you did. Please forgive me."

"After all we have been through together; I think it's only right. Don't you?"

Tabitha nodded. "Yes, of course."

This was the first time she was able to see Dawn in the daylight, and without feeling dizzy. Although she was certain they had been introduced before, Tabitha hadn't remembered the girl. Now she realized Dawn was a very stunning young lady. Her curly blonde hair had streaks of brown flowing through it, more noticeable in ringlets. But it wasn't just the woman's hair that made her lovely, it was her bright blue eyes; clear like the ocean on a cloudless day. No wonder David Griffin had been taken with her.

"Would you care to sit?" Tabitha turned to the furniture.

"Let me fetch some tea," Mrs. Stiles said. "I'm sure that

would be refreshing—"

"No!" Both Tabitha and Dawn shouted. Mrs. Stiles' eyes grew enlarged as her hand flew to her throat. "Forgive me, Mrs. Stiles," Tabitha quickly added. "Miss Johnson and I aren't ready to drink tea any time soon."

"Oh, of course not, my dear." Red blotches appeared on the older woman's cheeks. "Forgive me for not remembering. Then I shall just bring cookies."

"Actually, Mrs. Stiles," Dawn interrupted, "I won't be here very long at all. I just wanted to see how my friend was faring."

"Well, all right. I'll let you two be alone then." Mrs. Stiles turned and left the room.

Still holding onto Dawn's hands, Tabitha pulled her to the couch to sit. "It seems as if it were several days ago instead of just yesterday that we were together in that dreadful cellar, doesn't it?"

"Yes. It truly was a nightmare. I'm grateful you didn't have to be there as long as I was."

"Are you feeling better? Have you gained your strength back?"

"A little." Dawn shrugged. "I know I should have stayed home and rested today, but I just had to come see you…and thank you for all you did."'

"Oh, Dawn. I didn't do anything special. Any woman would have done that. I'm sure you had tried to break down that trap door, too."

Dawn ducked her head and frowned. "Actually, I was too frightened to leave the mattress. I've always been afraid of the dark, and I was literally frightened to death." She looked up. "You really did save me." She glanced down at Tabitha's hands. "You were so brave pulling that nail out of the piece of wood so you could use it to unlock the hook. It was pure brilliance on your part."

Chuckling, Tabitha shook her head and looked at her fingers. The scabs were still visible, and her fingertips would be tender for a few days, she was certain. "When I had lost all my hair-pins, I fell into despair and sank down the wall. That's when I felt the nail sticking out of the board as it scraped my arm. I knew it was there for a reason…to help us escape. I just feel bad that when I finally opened the door, I was so dizzy I fell inside the room. I thought for sure Miss Talbot would hear the noise and come running."

"Oh, me, too. Those were the most terrifying moments of my life. I waited for her to bring you back down, but I was vastly relieved when help came for me. Who were those men, anyway?"

Tabitha grinned and puffed her chest. "Those were my brothers; Trevor, Tristan, and Trey Worthington."

"I shall never forget their kindness."

"Yes, all three of them have the kindest hearts."

Dawn pulled away and stood. "Well, I'm starting to feel tired again, so I'd better return home. But please come visit me. I don't have many friends, and I hope now to consider you one."

Tabitha rose to her feet and hooked her arm through Dawn's, turning them toward the door. "I shall be proud to call you my friend. And, as the first order of our friendship, I shall help you to the front door."

Dawn laughed and patted Tabitha's arm, walking beside her up the corridor. Just as she opened the door, a man stepped up to knock, his fist still raised in action.

Tabitha gasped at the incredibly handsome man. Gone was the clergyman's disguise, and in its place was the lord who'd stirred her heart several months ago. Clean shaven and wearing clothes that fit his muscular body well, Dominic Lawrence, the Marquess of Hawthorne stood before her. Never had she seen him more breathtaking.

"Nic—um, Lord Hawthorne," she sighed.

He quickly dropped his hand to his side, and then offered a nod. "Miss Paget. Miss Johnson. I hope I'm not interrupting anything."

"Of course not, Lord Hawthorne." Dawn smiled. "I was just

leaving." She started to step past him, but she stopped and met his gaze again. "I hope you don't mind me saying that you look much better without the beard."

Nic threw back his head and chuckled. "I don't mind it at all."

"Good day, my lord." Dawn hurried toward her buggy.

Nic's warm stare captured Tabitha's heart once more, and stirred feelings inside her that gratefully, hadn't disappeared. "I'll add my vote to Miss Johnson's comment. I think you're much more handsome when you're clean-shaven."

He took her hand and lifted it to his mouth. As he brushed his lips across her knuckles, his gaze darkened with desire. "I like it this way, too. I can now feel your soft skin caressing mine."

Heat climbed up her face, and she feared she'd combust soon. Trying to dismiss this awkward embarrassment, she pulled her hand away and allowed him to enter. "I'm very happy you came to see me. We have much to talk about."

"I agree." He glanced up and down the hallway. "Do you think your aunt will allow me to have some private moments with you?"

She shrugged. "She doesn't know about your switch with Frederick, so maybe she won't."

"Shall we see?" He slid his arm around her back, pulling her closer to his side as he led them down the hallway toward the sitting room.

"Whatever happened with Frederick," she asked. "I recall losing consciousness for a little while, and when I came to, you and your cousin were arguing about something."

He rolled his eyes. "He'd been missing all night and most of yesterday. I was ready to wring that man's neck…until he told me where he'd been. Apparently," Nic leaned closer as he lowered his voice, "Frederick has found a love interest after all of these years. The reason he was gone so much was because he was getting to know the woman a little better."

"Truly? Does she live in this township?"

"No. Frederick mentioned it was a good thirty minutes traveling to her house."

"Well, I'm very happy for him."

"As am I. And of course, because he found love again, it kept me from strangling him."

She chuckled. "You're incorrigible."

"Thank you. I take that as a compliment."

Once they entered, he released her and closed the door. Tabitha waited for Mrs. Stiles to come run screaming down the hallway, trying to keep this strange man from being alone with her, but so far the house was quiet.

"Would you like to sit?" she asked.

"Not really. What I would like to do is this—"

In two large steps he was right in front of her, taking her in his strong embrace as his mouth lowered toward hers. The beating of her heart quickened with anticipation. Just before his lips touched hers, she closed her eyes and leaned in.

As his mouth moved seductively with hers, she couldn't stop the heavy sigh from escaping her throat. Clinging to his broad shoulders, she pressed herself against him closer—scandalously close. His hands moving over her back only served to keep her in place. But then why would she want to leave? Kissing Nic was the most perfect thing she'd ever done.

He groaned and turned his head, breaking the kiss, but keeping her in his arms. "As much as I don't want to stop, I fear that if I continue kissing you, your aunt might walk in on us wrapped up in a *very* intimate situation."

Tabitha chuckled and stroked her fingers down the side of his face, loving the feel of his soft cheek—free of whiskers. "There's nothing more I want to do but kiss you endlessly, but we do need to talk."

Nodding, he grasped her hand and walked with her to the couch where they sat by each other. Her hand was still cradled in his large fingers, and she loved the protection she felt whenever she was by his side.

"Nic, there's something I've needed to tell you for a while

now, but it might come as a shock." She took a deep breath.

"Actually, my lovely, I think I know—"

She put her fingers to his lips. "Shh… Don't stop me. Let me say this."

He nodded, but kept quiet.

"Since the first time we met, you have told me how I look familiar, and you always wondered why. Well…" she licked her suddenly dry lips, "there's a reason I look familiar."

His smile broadened. "Go on."

"You see, I've known for several years that I'm the illegitimate child of the Duke of Kenbridge—the father of your friends." She held her breath, waiting for him to say something. But he didn't. He continued staring at her with his beautiful, enchanting eyes. Perhaps he didn't hear her correctly. "Nic, do you know what this means? I'm Trevor, Tristan, and Trey's sister. We share the same father."

"Yes, I see the connection." He shrugged. "Do you think it matters to me who your parents were?"

Happy tears spiked her eyes and her heart jumped to her throat. "It doesn't matter that I'm a bastard child?"

"No."

"Why not?"

"Because it's all part of life. Good heavens, have you not heard the rumors about the Duke and Duchess of Devonshire? He sired children that were not from his wife, and she bore a child that was not his, as well. King Henry VIII had a bastard child—probably more than one, in fact. Then there was the Duke of Monmouth who was the bastard son of Charles II…just to name a few off the top of my head."

Relief swept over her, making more tears spill down her cheeks. "You don't think I'll be an embarrassment to you? After all, you are a marquess."

"I shall be proud to introduce you as the Marchioness of Hawthorne."

Her heart skipped a beat as excitement filled her soul. She

tilted her head, narrowing her gaze on him. "How very bold of you to presume such a thing, my lord. You haven't even proposed."

He laughed and took her back in his arms, kissing her forehead. "Forgive me, my lovely. What could I have possibly been thinking?" He shifted off the couch and sank to the floor on one knee. He reached inside his jacket and pulled out a ring. The diamonds and rubies sparkled from the sun's rays streaming through the open window. "My dearest Tabitha, love of my life, and keeper of my heart, I wish for you to share your world with me by my side until we are old and gray, from now until forever."

The tears kept coming and her voice refused to speak. He took her hand and kissed her fingers before slipping on the ring. "Will you marry me and make me exceedingly happy?"

A bubble of laughter sprang forth as she nodded. She cleared her throat, hoping her emotional state would allow her to talk now. "I will marry you, my beautiful Marquess of Hawthorne. But make no mistake; I'll be the one exceedingly happy."

He cupped her face and leaned forward. Eagerly, she met him halfway and pressed her mouth against his, sealing the proposal. Her heart sang as she held him tight. Against all odds, she knew their lives would be happy because it was something they were both willing to work at.

She broke the kiss this time, because she had to wipe the moisture out of her eyes. He sat back on the couch and took her in his arms once more. Resting her head against his shoulder, she snuggled against him. Although everything seemed blissfully happy, there was still one last question that plagued her.

"Nic?"

"Yes, my lovely?"

"What are my brothers doing here?"

His chest shook with silent laughter. "Right after I had seen you at your aunt's birthday party, I sent off a letter to Trey, asking him questions about you. I knew something in your life had changed because you weren't a maid any longer. Apparently, whatever I said in my letter bothered your brothers."

She rolled her head to look up at him. "Why were they bothered?"

"Trey knows me well, and could read from my words that I was infatuated with his sister." He kissed her forehead. "None of your brothers liked that."

"And why not?"

"They didn't want me to break your heart."

She relaxed as she gazed into his eyes. "But it was I who broke your heart, if you remember correctly."

"Indeed, you did."

"So what do you think they will say now that we are engaged?"

"I believe they have already accepted my feelings for you. You were not awake when Trevor made a comment yesterday."

"What had he said?"

He stroked her cheek softly. "He wasn't certain he'd enjoy having me for a brother-in-law."

She laughed.

He touched his finger to the tip of her nose. "But I think it is I who will not enjoy having them for my in-laws."

"And why not? They are good, kind and loving men."

"Yes, they are, but from what I've seen so far, they'll do anything to protect their sister, which means they'll be sticking their noses into our lives all the time."

"Not if we live here," she said softly.

His eyes widened. "Live here? In North Devon?"

"Yes, for most of the time, anyway. I'm sure you have duties as the marquess, but can we not live here as well?"

His expression relaxed and he nodded. "That's an excellent idea. That way we can live our lives the way we want, and the terrible *T's*—your brothers—will not be interfering."

A loud laugh escaped her. "Oh, Nic. Don't ever tell them you think of them as the terrible *T's*."

"Believe me, I won't."

"Nic, you are so very humorous. I love how you can make me laugh. Promise me one thing."

"Anything, my lovely. What is it you wish?"

"I want you to make me laugh all the time, starting today and lasting until we are old and gray."

He kissed her briefly on the lips, and then smiled. "From now until forever."

The End

Join my newsletter
authormariehiggins.com/newsletter

Find more stories by Marie Higgins
authormariehiggins.com/books

About the Author

Marie Higgins, a multi-award-winning, best-selling author, crafts clean romance novels that melt hearts and keep readers falling in love. Since 2010, she's published over 100 captivating stories, spanning mystery, suspense, humor, time travel, and paranormal genres, all while excelling in historical romance. Dubbed the "Queen of Tease" by her fans, Marie is known for her twists and unexpected endings.

Website – www.authormariehiggins.com
Bookstore – mariehigginsbooks.com
Facebook – facebook.com/authormariehigginsbooks
Instagram – instagram.com/author.mariehiggins
Bluesky – bsky.app/profile/authormariehiggins.bsky.social
Bookbub – bookbub.com/authors/marie-higgins
Pinterest – pinterest.com/authormariehiggins